THE THIRD BOOK OF
THE ADVENTURES OF DUAN SURK

BLACK KNIGHTS OF THE SILVER-
GRAY CASTLE

MISHIO FUKAZAWA

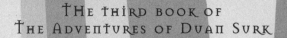

POP
FICTION

STORY   Mishio Fukazawa
ILLUSTRATIONS   Takao Otokita

TRANSLATION   Catherine Barraclough
ENGLISH ADAPTATION   Paul Witcover

LAYOUT ARTIST   Courtney H. Geter
COVER ILLUSTRATOR   Yoseph Middleton
COVER DESIGN   Anne Marie Horne
CREATIVE DIRECTOR   Anne Marie Horne
SENIOR EDITOR   Jenna Winterberg

EDITOR   Kara Allison Stambach
DIGITAL IMAGING MANAGER   Chris Buford
PRODUCTION MANAGER   Elisabeth Brizzi
MANAGING EDITOR   Vy Nguyen
EDITOR-IN-CHIEF   Rob Tokar
PUBLISHER   Mike Kiley
PRESIDENT AND C.O.O.   John Parker
C.E.O. & CHIEF CREATIVE OFFICER   Stuart Levy

First TOKYOPOP printing: October 2007

10 9 8 7 6 5 4 3 2 1

Printed in the USA

Library of Congress Cataloging-in-Publication Data
Fukazawa, Mishio.
  [Ginnezujo no Kurokishidan. English]
  Black Knights of the Silver-Gray Castle / by Mishio Fukazawa ; [illustrations, Takao Otokita; translation, Catherine Barraclough].

    p. cm -- (Adventures of Duan Surk ; 3-)
  "First published in 1997 by Media Works, Inc., Tokyo, Japan" -- Vol. 3,
t.p. verso.
  Audience: 13-17.
  ISBN 978-1-59532-872-4
  I. Otokita, Takao. II. Barraclough, Catherine. III. Title. IV. Series:
Fukazawa, Mishio. Duan Surk. English ; 3, etc.
  PZ49.31.F27913 2007   2006010393
  [Fic]--dc22

In a time not now. . .
In a place not here . . .
In a parallel world
of myths and magic
Where heroes battle
monsters To create
legends that endure
forever. . .
One boy is destined
to become the greatest
hero of all . . .
If only he can manage
to stay alive!

CHAPTER I:

A RUDE AWAKENING

He was standing on a bridge overlooking the frozen canal. The wind was cold as it whistled through his long hair—but with the sun beating down on his shoulders, he hardly noticed. The cries of sea birds could be heard from near and far.

"Duan!"

At the sound of his name, he turned and saw a young girl approaching, her red hair blowing carelessly in the wind.

"Hey, Agnis," he said.

"Don't you 'hey, Agnis' me," she replied testily. "What's the matter? Why are you standing out here? You'll catch cold."

"I'm just on my way back from shopping," he told her. "We have this and that to get ready for, right?"

At once, Agnis' mood lightened. "That's true, Duan. You think of everything! That reminds me . . ." She broke off, seemingly at a loss for words.

"What is it, Agnis?" Was it his imagination, or was she blushing faintly?

Agnis swallowed. "There's something I've been meaning to tell you—but, well, it's kind of difficult."

Duan waited anxiously for her to go on. He couldn't imagine what she wanted to say to him.

After fidgeting for a while, Agnis blurted out: "Thank you for that time, Duan!"

"Er, what time would that be?"

"You know, inside the Red Dragon's dungeon. I definitely wouldn't have come out alive if not for you. It's thanks to you that I'm here right now. So, um, thanks!"

Duan was stunned. Most of the time, the fiery-tempered sorceress was either criticizing or teasing him. He didn't know quite how to react now. "Y-you're exaggerating, Agnis."

"No, I'm not!" she insisted, suddenly grabbing Duan by the hand. Even though her fingers were slim, her grip was powerful.

Before he could say another word, someone else grabbed hold of his shoulder.

"It's not an exaggeration," came another, deeper voice. "I'm really grateful, too. If it weren't for you, Duan, I'm not sure I'd be here, either. Thanks!"

The speaker was a large man with an admirable build and long, dark hair, tied back with a scarlet string. It was the veteran fighter, Olba October. Tightening his grip on Duan's shoulder, he started to shake him to and fro.

"Augh! Okay, Olba, I get the picture. You're welcome, already. Now l-let me go!"

But the big fighter kept right on shaking him. "In fact, Duan," he said, "I think that you—"

"Let him go, you weirdo!" interrupted Agnis. "What are you trying to do, shake him to pieces?"

Olba glared at her. "Weirdo? Why, you exploding-bomb girl!"

"W-what did you say!?" Agnis had that look in her eye— the one that came right before she started chanting a Fire Spell.

Duan screamed in frustration. "Argh! Stop it, you two!"

"Idiot, don't raise your voice."

Olba's voice, so loud a moment ago, now was strangely soft, as though he had just whispered into Duan's ear.

"Olba," Duan began nervously, "please don't tell me you're—"

Duan opened his eyes with a start. He could make out the top half of the fighter's sturdy, muscular body in the faint light streaming in through the window. Olba was shirtless, his skin glistening with sweat.

Ugh, he reeks of alcohol!

Olba was kneeling beside the bed, one hand held firmly over Duan's mouth. He seemed to be listening very carefully to something.

I remember! We ate dinner and started drinking early—but I can't remember when I got to bed, or getting into bed. What time is it now? It doesn't seem like it's that late. Wait! That means it was all a dream!

Duan felt a mixture of relief and disappointment. It had felt good to be thanked by Olba and Agnis, even if it was just a dream.

But now, as he became more fully awake and realized that something was brewing, he began to listen carefully, straining his ears.

At first, he heard nothing, just the thudding of his heart in his chest and Olba's steady breathing. Then, softly, a voice became audible, growing louder as it approached.

"Where are these adventurers staying?" the voice demanded gruffly.

A small voice answered, "Come this way."

Duan recognized that voice. It belonged to the landlord of the inn.

He heard heavy footsteps. It seemed like there were at least four or five of them, whoever they were.

He glanced at Olba, and the big fighter raised one finger to his lips to indicate the need for quiet before unclamping his hand from around Duan's mouth.

"What's happening?" Duan mouthed silently.

Olba shrugged.

Just then, the footsteps stopped outside their room, and the door was kicked open violently.

CHAPTER 2:

THE BLACK KNIGHTS' ARMY

Four knights came bursting into the room. They were huge, dressed in black armor and black helmets with cloaks that were blacker than the dead of night.

Duan's eyes widened. *It's the Black Knights!*

The Black Knights were famous. Even small children knew about them.

W-what are they doing here?

Duan and Olba had traveled to a country called Orland. Orland wasn't a very big country, but it was blessed with rich earth and always had been prosperous. The king was named Evesrin, and his private army—which was loyal to him and him alone, as it had been to his father and his father's father, going back generations—was the Black Knights' Army.

They had received this name because they literally were covered in black, from head to toe. Even the horses they rode were black—and their weapons were black, too. The knights all were masters of sword and spear—and they were handsome, as well, with tall, strong builds. Not only that, but they came from good backgrounds and were highly intelligent. Only men who met each of these stringent requirements could apply to join the Black Knights' Army, and only the cream of the crop were accepted.

The Black Knights' Army had grown so famous over the years that Black Knight souvenirs were sold throughout Orland and beyond. In fact, Duan had seen a small Black Knight figurine for sale in the inn's gift shop. The statuette had been cute and funny; however, the real, live Black Knight standing before him now was neither cute nor funny: It was terrifying. It looked more like a demon than a human being.

Olba seemed just as stunned as Duan. The two of them stood together with mouths agape, looking up at the men in black.

Without a word, without even pausing to remove their helmets, two of the Black Knights started searching the room while the other two, with swords drawn, kept watch over Duan and Olba.

Olba had seen enough. "Hey, you guys," he said angrily. "What the heck do you think you're doing, barging into our room while we're asleep? Huh?!"

One of the knights, most likely the leader, jerked his chin and said with an arrogant attitude, "What bravado from a thief—a half-naked thief at that."

"You callin' me a thief? I'll make you eat those words!" Olba looked as if he were about to attack the man.

"Better get dressed first," sneered the knight.

"Why you—"

Olba was interrupted as one of the Black Knights inspecting the room yelled out, "Company Commander, we've found it! It was stashed under the bed."

9

Duan blinked in surprise.

Huh? Found it? Found what?!

Olba and Duan looked at each other and strained their bodies to see what, exactly, had been found.

The Black Knight who had spoken was on his hands and knees, reaching under the bed. The innkeeper, along with a number of guests roused by the commotion, crowded around the door, peering in with lively curiosity.

At last, the Black Knight stood. He was holding something covered in a black cloth. When he snatched the cloth away, he revealed a golden goblet with two handles. Gems of all colors surrounded the crest of a flower.

A collective gasp went up from the onlookers.

Whatever it is, thought Duan, *it sure looks expensive!*

With a throaty voice, one of the Black Knights exclaimed, "A couple of common thieves couldn't have stolen the royal treasure, Garcia's Goblet, by themselves!"

The man who'd been referred to as company commander nodded very deliberately. "Hm. What are you saying?"

"Isn't it obvious? The theft was an inside job, set up by Schneider!"

"Schneider, eh? But what was he intending to do with the goblet once he had it?"

"Why, give it to the Kingdom of Ganau, of course—to cement a treacherous alliance!"

The commander nodded again. "That makes sense."

As Duan listened to this conversation, a bad feeling started to torment him. It was as if he were in the audience of a bad play, listening to the actors woodenly speak their lines, or watching a puppet show in which everyone was dancing to invisible strings. But who was pulling those strings? And how the heck had he and Olba gotten tangled up in them?

He hadn't seen Garcia's Goblet before—or ever heard of it, for that matter. It was obvious that someone had planted the thing under their bed, intending to frame them. But who? And why?

"This is unbearable," whispered Olba as the knights conferred among themselves.

"What are we going to do?" asked Duan.

"How the heck should I know?"

"I guess—"

Duan broke off as the knights suddenly turned toward them again. They were carrying ropes, and their intent was plain.

"W-wait, please wait," he said quickly. "What's going on? I swear to you, we've never seen that golden goblet before!"

The commander's laugh rang hollowly within his closed helmet, as if there was no one inside the armor. "Well, of course not! A thief wouldn't admit to his crime, now would he? Don't worry. No doubt, you and your friend here had no idea what you were getting into—just a pair of ex-soldiers down on your luck, looking for a little extra cash, eh? That's understandable. It's the man who hired you that we want: Schneider. Just come back to the castle with us, tell us everything you know, and we'll let you go free."

Olba bristled at this. "I don't understand what the heck is going on, but there ain't no way I'm going to any castle!"

Seeing Olba strike at the hands of the Black Knights who were reaching for him, Duan restrained his partner. "Olba, let's do as they say. What choice do we have? We're outnumbered four to two, and there's probably more of them outside. Besides, they're all armored, and we're barely dressed. Let's stay alive."

The commander nodded. "You understand the situation well, boy. You look like you're at least a bit smarter than your giant friend."

"Can we at least put on some clothes first?" asked Duan.

"Okay, but make it snappy."

Grumbling, Olba pulled on a pair of pants, a shirt, and his boots; Duan did likewise. When they were dressed, the leader made a sign, and the other Black Knights swiftly bound the adventurers' hands before they gagged, blindfolded, and marched their captives outside. The knights' efficiency was spectacular—not a single move was wasted. Despite everything, Duan found himself admiring their cool professionalism.

Wow, these Black Knights are pretty good!

Two more Black Knights were waiting outside the room, for a total of six. They marched their prisoners out of the inn, past the curious and angry eyes of the onlookers, some of whom made comments that were nasty enough to cause a few anxious moments for the helpless and blindfolded pair. But the Black Knights kept the crowd back. Outside, six black horses stood ready. The knights placed Duan and Olba on two of them and escorted them to Orland Castle.

CHAPTER 3:

A BRASHLY IMPROVISED SCHEME

t was easy to see why Orland Castle popularly was known as "the Silver-Gray Castle." Surrounded by high walls that sparkled like silver, the castle perched atop a small hill like a gigantic crown. The local people were proud of the castle and had composed many songs to celebrate its beauty and illustrious history.

The master of that castle, King Evesrin, was staring out the living room window at the forest outside, which had a ghostly gray color in the moonlight. The king's wavy blond hair hung loose under his crown, reaching below his shoulders. His silken cloak perfectly matched his blue eyes. Somewhere in the distance, the sad hoots of an owl could be heard.

"Will such a brashly improvised scheme really work?"

Standing behind the king was Evesrin's close advisor and old friend, Lord Shimul. He had an unhealthy complexion and wore dark brown, expensive-looking clothes. A receding hairline accentuated his high forehead and bushy eyebrows, which were the same brown color as his hair—or what was left of it, at least.

"Well, let's wait a while," the lord answered in a reasonable tone of voice. "If the plan doesn't work for some reason, how would it affect you, Your Majesty? We can just say we received some false intelligence."

"Yes, but . . ." King Evesrin trailed off and sighed deeply, his forehead creasing with worry.

What infuriating behavior, he thought to himself. *That Schneider, his servants are superior to mine, and he's more popular than me! Does he think he's better suited to be king?*

"Ugh, my stomach hurts again." Clutching his belly with one hand, the king sank down into a chair.

Lord Shimul sympathetically massaged his shoulders. "Try to calm yourself," he said soothingly. "That's the main thing. There's no reason to get upset every time the man says something. Only a weak man clamors so energetically. Come, why don't you retire to bed now?"

The king shook his head wearily. "What's the use? I haven't had a good night's sleep in months. No, I'll wait until the Black Knights return."

"Ah. Then I shall wait with you, Your Majesty."

"Shimul, thank you."

"No, no. It is both my duty and my pleasure to keep you company." As he spoke, however, Lord Shimul's eyes rolled up toward the ceiling as though his true feelings were quite the opposite.

What King Evresin had referred to as a "brashly improvised scheme" was, in Lord Shimul's opinion, anything but. On the contrary, he considered it a brilliant plan. It ran as follows:

The Black Knights' Army would be sent to an inn near the border of the kingdom, where they would identify some

likely looking adventurers. These unfortunates would be framed for stealing Garcia's Goblet. Arrested and brought back to Orland Castle, they would confess (after a bit of torture) that they had been employed by Schneider, who had planned to use the goblet to purchase the aid of the neighboring country, Ganau, in a scheme to overthrow King Evresin.

Once their purpose was fulfilled, the adventurers would be . . . terminated. After all, dead men told no tales.

As for Schneider, he would be found guilty of treason and severely punished, if not executed outright.

That was how the drama was to run.

Lord Shimul had thought up the plan and—with the aid of a bit of alcohol—had gotten the king to agree to it. Although at first the king had expressed some doubts as to whether it could be executed as quickly as Shimul maintained, all King Evesrin's doubts were washed away after a few glasses of wine: He had clapped his hands in excitement and summoned the leader of the Black Knights' Army, Edward Zamut.

Edward had opposed the idea. He didn't believe that such a blatantly false setup would fool anyone. But the king wouldn't listen. And so, with reluctance, Zamut had chosen some soldiers and sent them about their work.

It was all to come to fruition tonight.

As time went by without word of success, however, King Evesrin was getting increasingly irritated. His stomach pained him more and more. He wondered why he had agreed to such a foolhardy scheme.

In his head, an image of Schneider rose, the handsome face looking down at him with a patronizing expression. The man exuded confidence and competence—making him the complete opposite of King Evesrin.

Shoot. That darn Schneider thinks he's so smart. I'll show him! Once Schneider is out of the way, Father will have peace of mind at last, leaving the country entirely to my rule. Otherwise, Father will continue poking his nose into my business and, sooner or later, he'll end up wanting real power again. That would be awful! What would the queen say?

At the thought of his wife, Queen Milhene, the king's face assumed a fearful expression.

Ugh. I don't even want to think about that!

CHAPTER 4:

THE DREAMS OF KINGS

o better understand why King Evesrin was finding it so difficult to sleep, and why his stomach was constantly aching, and why he had approved Lord Shimrul's plan, a more detailed explanation of the kingdom of Orland is in order.

Orland is a relatively small country located in the northeast of the Seraphim continent. Although of modest size, it boasts a long and eventful history, and its culture is highly advanced. Right next to Orland lies the country of Ganau, which possesses similar characteristics—in fact, the border between them lies in the middle of the thick forest that King Evesrin was staring at from the living room of his castle.

In many ways, the histories of the two countries could be seen as a history of the wars they had fought against each other. Due to their similarity and proximity, the two kingdoms were hyper-conscious of each other's existence and were rivals in every way. Each watched vigilantly for a chance to prey on the other and

take it over. This had led to a number of wars—or perhaps it would be more accurate to say that the war between them had carried on endlessly: sometimes on battlefields, accompanied by the clash of arms, sometimes in subtler (but equally deadly) ways.

King Evesrin's father, King Liesbeck, who was now retired, had kept Orland at peace. But ever since his abdication of the throne in favor of his son, a heavy feeling of unrest had come to permeate the kingdom.

The root of this problem was King Evesrin himself. His weakmindedness, combined with a sensitivity to imagined slights, had helped to divide Orland into three opposing factions.

The first, of course, was the faction of King Evesrin. This was the largest faction. And the king also had the legendary Black Knights Army on his side. In fact, if not for them, his rule over the country wouldn't have lasted as long as it had.

The second faction belonged to Schneider Deks. He was popular with the people; and although he had fewer followers at court and in the army, they were generally of a higher caliber.

Last, there was a small faction headed by the ex-king, Liesbeck. Although still capable of ruling in mind and body, he had withdrawn for the sake of his son, Evesrin. His followers believed that he had been too hasty in this respect—but Liesbeck kept his own counsel, not wanting to undercut his son's authority.

To make matters worse, as chaos took hold in Orland's internal affairs, Ganau had started to scheme. Thus, Liesbeck could not sit still. Although he had retired, he gathered all his old loyal followers and decided to watch Schneider and Evesrin very carefully.

Of the two, Liesbeck was more sympathetic to King Evesrin. This was partly because the king was his own son, but it also had to do with Schneider's popularity, which Liesbeck mistrusted. Schneider was well aware of this and and often directed a scornful attitude toward the ex-king as a result.

This was ironic, because Schneider had gotten his start serving under King Liesbeck. Back then, he had been a meek, handsome boy.

Now, though still handsome, he was no longer meek. And at just under forty years old, he was the same age as King Evesrin. That was where the similarities ended, however.

Schneider had glossy, wavy hair and a moderately tanned, masculine profile. He also had a good build and a thorough mastery of the martial arts. The ladies of the court found him irresistible, and gossiping about his rumored liaisons was a favorite pastime for many of them.

Yes, he was the complete opposite of King Evesrin. Evesrin had weak, thin arms and a pasty complexion, with wavy, golden hair; blue eyes; and a sharp, hooked nose. He was a long way from manliness.

This state of affairs was altogether displeasing for King Evesrin. Even his beloved wife, Queen Milhene, would gossip incessantly about Schneider. In truth, that was what Evesrin disliked the most.

They had been good friends once, when they were children. They were the same age, so they often had gotten up to mischief together, resulting in scoldings by King Liesbeck's butlers. However, all that seemed like a lie now that they couldn't bear the sight of each other. The king tried various different plans to undermine Schneider, giving him the most boring and thankless tasks. But nothing had gone according to plan. In fact, people were starting to feel sorry for Schneider.

For his part, Schneider was equally resentful of King Evesrin. He wondered why he was forced to do the most meaningless and tiring work, even though he was clearly superior. He found it most dissatisfying.

The discontent between the two powerful men was now so great that it could not be disguised. Indeed, it was common knowledge throughout the land. Matters had reached a critical point. Some people even thought that Schneider was on the verge of launching a coup d'etat. And despite the unquestioned prowess and loyalty of the Black Knights' Army, it was far from certain that any such coup attempt could be put down successfully by King Evesrin's forces.

Meanwhile, the king of Ganau, Tylus IV, was licking his chops, thoughts bent on taking advantage of this domestic conflict and weakening the power of Orland. It was even possible that, if all went well, he might be able to take control of Orland in one fell swoop, adding the country to his kingdom as his ancestors had dreamed of doing for centuries.

Such were the dreams of kings, ex-kings, and would-be kings.

For the common people of Ganau and Orland, though, these dreams were more likely to become nightmares.

CHAPTER 5:

THE STAR OF THE WHITE HORSE

Beneath a field of stars that sparkled like diamonds in the velvety night sky, a slim warrior galloped upon a white horse. Despite the lightweight armor and billowing dark cape that streamed behind the riding warrior, a closer look revealed an elegantly contoured profile; a graceful chin line; calm, violet eyes; and sharp, rose-tinted lips. Yes, the rugged, hard-riding warrior was a woman!

This heroic angel of justice—who protected unfortunate people and children everywhere, despite putting herself in danger—was the famous "Star of the White Horse," a name that had taken on the glow of legend.

The warrior-woman's real name was Lulu Chatelaine. Born a wealthy nobleman's daughter, she hid her flaming red hair inside her helmet and pretended to be a man as she fought for justice and honor. Just now, however, what she held inside her heart was not politics or war.

"Oh, Andre," she breathed. "Until I see that you are safe, I won't feel alive!"

She yearned for Andre Ruben with every fiber of her heart. She had only just found out about his being in danger. And on top of that, her *surprise was great when she learned that she herself might have been the cause of it. She felt real pain, as if a stake had been pounded through her heart. They said that she had placed a secret letter to the king in his cape . . . and furthermore, they said this document was a forgery. If this became public, Andre would not be allowed to live.*

Lulu had once again become involved in a conspiracy of darkness. And even now, as she rode pell-mell across the plains to Andre's rescue, a pair of eyes was watching her. Beneath those eyes, the watcher was sporting a devilish grin.

Agnis sighed deeply. Overwhelmed with emotion, she clutched the old, leather-bound book to her chest. She turned to her attendant, Manuela, who was helping her pack, saying, "Don't you think this bit is really good? 'She felt real pain, as if a stake had been pounded through her heart.' I understand that. I mean, at such moments, it really does feel painful. That's what real pain is—real suffering!"

With that, still clutching the book, Agnis flung herself back onto her canopied bed in her room at the summer palace in Fiana. It was the fine-textured bed that her considerate mother, Rubis, had ordered so that her daughter, whenever she returned from adventuring, would be able to sleep comfortably. Surrounded by the faint aroma of flowers, Agnis sighed again and again.

Manuela laughed. "Yes, isn't that so? I thought you'd enjoy it, Miss Agnis."

"I probably won't be able to sleep tonight until I finish."

"No, I wouldn't recommend that. You should enjoy these things bit by bit. Even I took at least a week to read that book."

"A week? Manuela, I didn't know you were that patient."

"Well, I have work to do; I can't stay up all night reading."

"But I bet you've read it many times already!"

"Yes, in truth, I have. I've read it ten times now."

"I thought so! In that case, though, is it really all right if I borrow the book?"

"Of course! I just worry that your luggage will be heavier because of it."

"A little extra weight is nothing compared to the courage this book will give me!"

Agnis, Princess of Fiana and also a sorceress, had parted temporarily with Duan and Olba to be with her mother. She needed to repack her things, and she also had promised to visit home frequently so that her mother could see she was alive and well. Besides, Fiana was on the way to her next destination: Orland.

Yes, Orland, the same place Olba and Duan had gone. In fact, it was because of Agnis that the two adventurers had traveled there.

Agnis had received an unhappy letter from her close childhood pen pal, Charles, the Prince of Orland. She'd been hearing for some time that there was some domestic conflict in the country; recently, tensions seemed to have gotten worse. In his letter, Charles had inquired politely whether she could discuss this problem with her father, Palea IV, the King of Fiana. Indeed, if—as Charles hinted in the letter—a coup took place, and there was a change in political power, the prince would be in grave danger. Although it was unlikely that thirteen-year-old Charles would be put to death, he still could be exiled or imprisoned somewhere.

Agnis had gone to her father without delay, pleading for him to help Charles. But the king had responded with a powerful argument:

"Agnis, interfering in the internal politics of another country is serious business. If it becomes known that Prince Charles had tried to discuss this with me, there would be problems on a national level. There would be speculation that Fiana was plotting to join forces with Orland, as well as other rumors. I am sure you know this already: My policy as king has been to protect the peace of our nation by maintaining a policy of neutrality to all other countries. I would like to help your friend, but I cannot endanger our entire nation to do so. I hope you can understand that."

After that, Agnis didn't feel she could trouble her father anymore. She had written Charles a letter of encouragement to cheer him up. However, that was months ago, and he hadn't written back. She became so worried she couldn't bear the suspense any longer. After receiving her mother's blessing, Agnis had decided to set out once again as an adventurer, determined to come to the assistance of her friend.

Although she would be accompanied by her faithful snow leopard K'nock, who had been like a knight to her since she was a little girl, she couldn't help feeling a little nervous about traveling alone to a troubled country like Orland. *What could one low-level sorceress do?* she wondered. It felt so futile.

That's when she thought of the two fighters she had met and fought side by side with in the Witches' Forest— Olba and Duan.

Thinking that the two adventurers could help her again, she had pursued them to Luca Island, where they had undertaken the quest of the Red Dragon, finally meeting up with them in the dark and dangerous dungeons below the dragon's lair.

After the quest, when they all had returned to Kovenia, Agnis told Olba and Duan about Prince Charles and asked them to come with her. Actually, she pretty much forced them into coming—though, to be fair, they hadn't really decided anything about their next quest, anyway.

It never entered Agnis' mind that they would be dragged away from their inn by the Black Knights' Army almost as soon as they arrived in Orland. She had promised to meet them at the inn after a couple of days spent visiting her mother. In fact, she was due to rendezvous with them tomorrow.

For now, while Manuela packed her things, she was savoring the romance and adventure *The Star of the White Horse,* a novel that was tremendously popular with noblewomen.

In the book, Lulu Chatelaine, herself a noblewoman, possessed two identities. The first was a quiet and calm young woman prone to gloom and melancholy. The other—with her magnificent red hair tucked up under her helmet and her slim, feminine body hidden beneath fine armor—was a mysterious fighter for justice known as the Star of the White Horse. These were her two personas: one public, the other secret. Who was to say which was the more real?

The Star of the White Horse came to the aid of nobles and commoners alike whenever evil schemes were afoot. Along the way, there were various dramatic moments.

Agnis had just finished reading one such scene. In it, Lulu discovered that her lover, Andre, has been exposed to terrible danger all because of her. Dashing to his rescue, she rushed right into the jaws of a deadly trap!

It was a typical story, with a lot of ups and downs, but the belle masquerading as a man was particularly popular.

"Don't you think it's good when she takes off her helmet?"

"Yes, yes—when her soft, shining hair flows out. Why, it's just like you, Miss Agnis!"

"W-what!? Stop it, Manuela!"

"No, it truly is. We've all been gossiping about it."

Agnis blushed, secretly pleased by Manuela's flattery. She herself had immediately picked up on the similarity between Lulu's fiery red hair and her own. It made her feel that there was a special bond joining her to the Star of the White Horse, even though Lulu was only a fictional character, of course.

"Maybe on this adventure, I should dress as a man, too," she said now, only half-joking. "It's so difficult to move in a long skirt!"

"That's a good idea! In that case, you should ride a white horse to get the full effect. I mean, nothing against K'nock, but he doesn't exactly produce the same image."

"Hm. That's true. I've been thinking it would be easier to ride a horse than K'nock on long journeys. Sometimes, I nearly get flung off, and it's actually quite tiring hanging onto him."

The subject of the chatter, the snow leopard K'nock, was drowsing in the corner of the room. He slightly opened his eyes when he heard Agnis say his name—but as soon as he realized that she wasn't calling him, he shut his eyes again.

"Maybe I should ask Mother," Agnis mused meanwhile.

"I'm sure she'd give you a splendid horse."

"Well, it wouldn't have to be that fine. You see, I might have to sell it quite soon."

"Really, Miss Agnis?"

"Yeah, that's what adventures are like," she replied casually. "And I'm sure there will be times that I just won't be able to take it with me."

"I see."

Gazing appraisingly at her mistress, Manuela felt that the young girl really had matured a lot in a short space of time. It occurred to her that adventures forced people to grow up more quickly than they otherwise might.

"I suppose I should be getting to bed soon," Agnis said with a yawn.

"Yes, indeed. It's already so late. I'll do the rest of the packing myself. You'll be leaving early tomorrow?"

"Yeah . . . I really want to know what happens next in the book, though!"

"No, Miss Agnis. I'll hold onto that book until tomorrow."

"Hm," grumbled Agnis, trying to hide the book beneath the covers of her bed.

Manuela was not so easily put off. Suddenly, it seemed to her that Agnis was once again the mischievous girl she knew and loved, her darling princess, adorable as ever, always up to her tricks. "Now, you just stop this foolishness and give me the book," Manuela said sternly, reaching out and wresting it away from the protesting princess.

"Don't worry, I'll make sure you get it back before you leave," she added.

This seemed to mollify Agnis. With another yawn, she lay back and pulled the blanket up to her chin. "Good night, Manuela."

"Good night, Miss Agnis." Manuela smiled as she blew out the candle. "Sweet dreams."

CHAPTER 6:

QUITE A LITTLE BOOZER

n the end, Agnis gave up hope of traveling by horse.

This was because riding a horse turned out to be a lot harder than she'd imagined. As a princess, she'd enjoyed plenty of opportunities to become an expert rider; for some reason, though, Agnis hadn't been interested in horses until now. She'd thought that she'd be able to ride one quite easily if the occasion ever arose. Now, when it finally did, she was surprised by how difficult it was.

First of all, there was the height problem. Horses were taller than she'd realized. When, after a lot of struggle and quite a few tumbles, she managed to get on top at last, she thought she might faint when she realized how high above the ground she was. Furthermore, the horse she'd chosen wasn't very agreeable to being ridden. Not that the animal tried to buck her off or anything. When Agnis had come down to the royal stables and expressed her desire to ride, the stable boy had given her the most docile horse in the place—too docile, as it turned out. The horse would walk only a few grudging steps if the stable boy was tugging on the reins. When Agnis shooed him away and tried to get the horse moving on her own, the beast refused to budge.

When a less sedentary mount had been located and Agnis was once again in the saddle, she nearly was thrown from her precarious perch the first time the horse began to canter. As for trotting or galloping, forget it. She didn't even bother to try.

"I never would have thought horseback riding was so scary," said Agnis later, as she rode along her snow leopard's back. "With only one attempt, my butt is sore already! I'm glad you're so furry and soft, K'nock!"

They traveled all day without stopping. Finally, just when the sun was beginning to set, Agnis arrived at the inn where she'd arranged to meet Duan and Olba. But there was no sign of her friends. When Agnis asked the landlord if he'd seen them, the man opened his eyes wide in shock.

"Child, are you friends with those thieves? No, I can't believe it! Not a pretty thing like you!"

Agnis was a bit taken aback. "Er, thieves?"

The man nodded. "Yes, indeed—brutal cut-throats, by the look of 'em! I shudder to think what they might've gotten up to if the Black Knights hadn't arrested them."

Once Agnis had listened to the details of the arrest, she asked to be shown the room in which the "thieves" had been staying.

There may be something there, she anxiously thought to herself, *some clue as to what happened to Olba and Duan . . .*

Unfortunately, the room had been cleaned thoroughly. There was nothing left of Duan's and Olba's gear. And when Agnis asked the landlord if he'd retained any of their possessions, he replied that the Black Knights had taken everything back to Orland Castle with them. Then, he returned to the front desk, where some new arrival was clamoring for service.

Agnis remained behind in the room, thinking. *The Black Knights!* She had heard of the famous army but couldn't for the life of her understand why they would've arrested Duan and Olba. Well, Olba could on occasion drink too much and become a bit rowdy—still, to call in the Black Knights' Army over one inebriated adventurer seemed a bit much. She realized there was only one way to get the answers she required: She'd have to enter Orland Castle herself.

It probably would be quickest and simplest to go not as a common adventurer but as the Princess of Fiana, the long-time pen pal of Prince Charles. She'd say that she happened to be in the neighborhood and had decided to pay a friendly visit. *That wouldn't be so strange, would it?* It wasn't as if her father, the King of Fiana, was paying an official state visit or anything. *No,* she decided, *there'd be nothing strange about my showing up at all.*

Convinced by her own logic, Agnis had just turned to leave the empty room when suddenly, K'nock made a soft growling sound. The snow leopard began to scratch vigorously under the bed with one paw.

"What is it, K'nock? What have you found?"

She knelt down and peered under the bed, but it was too dark to see anything.

"What can it possibly be?"

Lying flat on the floor, Agnis extended her hand under the bed. She touched something, something soft and fluffy. With determination, she grabbed the mysterious object, pulling it out from under the bed.

Her eyes almost popped out of her head.

It was Check.

Check was a baby grinia, a small winged lizard who'd been with Duan ever since he'd hatched from his egg. He could speak a few human words and could use his wings to fly. He also could use some low-level healing magic. He was a strange monster.

"Check! Are you okay? Check?"

There was no response, no movement. Regarding the limp body in her hand, Agnis thought at first that the grinia must be dead, that he had perished defending Duan from the Black Knights.

Cupping his body in both her hands, she placed her ear to his tiny chest and heard a strange gurgling sound. And then, before she could move, he burped loudly, right in her face!

She drew back in disgust. "Ugh! Th-that awful smell! He's been drinking again!" She gently shook the grinia. "Wake up, Check! Wake up!"

At last, Check blearily opened his eyes. If he was surprised to see Agnis, he gave no sign of it. "Head hurts," he said. "Go 'way, cha!"

And then, he burped again, louder than before.

You wouldn't guess by the look of him, but Check was quite a little boozer. Despite his size, he was more of a heavyweight drinker than Duan was! He'd always accompany Olba when the big fighter went out drinking, and he'd try to match him glass for glass. This never turned out well. For one thing, Check turned into an obnoxious drunk, picking fights with everyone around him. And then, after stirring up so much trouble, he would keel over suddenly, passing out and sinking into a sleep so profound that it was as if he had died.

Duan had been trying to get Check on the wagon—but judging by the snoring grinia in her hand, not successfully. She sighed in frustration. "Listen, Check," she said loudly. "Do you happen to remember seeing the Black Knights' Army burst in here and arrest Duan and Olba?"

Another burp was the only reply.

Agnis realized she wasn't going to get any answers from Check in his present condition. Nor could she be bothered to wait for him to sober up. Slipping the grinia into her cape's pocket, she turned to K'nock.

"I'm glad you don't drink," she said.

"Grrow," affirmed the snow leopard, eyes shining.

"Come on, let's go see Charles and find out what's become of our friends."

CHAPTER 7:

SOME GOOD ADVICE

eanwhile, Duan and Olba were sitting in a dirty jail in the Silver-Gray Castle. As far as jails went, it wasn't so bad. At least straw had been laid down over the floor. If the straw hadn't been there, the two fighters would've had to rest on the smelly, bumpy rocks, which would've made them ache all over. On the other hand, the straw wasn't without faults: It was damp and slimy to the touch, as if beginning to rot. And it smelled like it was rotting, too.

Duan strained his neck and looked around nervously for what must have been the hundredth time. No matter how often he looked, the surroundings didn't improve. Lacking Olba's vast experience with jail cells, Duan found the present example more savage and terrifying than he could have imagined. Located in the basement of the castle, it had no windows, which made it impossible for Duan to tell whether it was night or day. The only illumination was flickering red torchlight. The sounds of groaning and weeping rose from other cells. From time to time, prison guards passed in front of the cell door, but they were far different from the handsome figures of the Black Knights' Army. With their rough faces and rougher manners, they seemed more like criminals than guards.

"Here ya go," said one as he slid a dirty plate under the cell door.

On the plate was an unappetizing stew that looked like it had been made from whatever was left in the garbage after the rats were through. There was also a piece of black bread that looked as if it would be as hard as a rock. Duan turned to Olba with an expression of utter desolation, ready to cry.

Olba, on the other hand, took his plate as though it had been served to him at a restaurant. He picked up the bread and gazed at it suspiciously. "How the heck do they make bread so black?"

Duan regarded Olba with disbelief.

Spooning the stew into his mouth, Olba glanced over and said, "C'mon, Duan, quit looking at me like that and eat up. You never know when you might need the energy."

"B–but if we eat this swill, we might get food poisoning, in which case we'd lose more energy."

Olba just shrugged. "You can't live an adventurer's life with a delicate stomach, kid. Now dig in."

"Shoot."

"Even if it does make you sick, next time your stomach will be tougher and you'll be able to eat whatever they give you. Besides, this stuff ain't so bad. Believe me, I've had plenty worse."

"Does that mean you've been in jail before?"

"Oh yeah, I've lost count of how many times. Why, I remember once . . ." Olba trailed off, feeling slightly ashamed of himself.

Duan, however, was fascinated. He leaned forward on his knees. "Tell me, Olba! Come on, you never tell me any of your old stories!"

"Hmph. Stop trying to change the subject. Eat your stew, and then we'll get a little shut-eye." So saying, Olba slurped up the rest of his stew, carelessly tossed the plate to one side, and leaned back, closing his eyes.

"Sh-shouldn't we be thinking about what to do next?" stammered Duan.

Olba cracked open an eyelid. "Like what?"

"Like a"—and here, Duan glanced around furtively, lowering his voice to a whisper—"prison break?"

"What's that?" asked Olba in an exaggerated, loud voice. "A prison break?"

Duan panicked. "I-idiot! Why are you shouting? The guards will hear!" He tried to shut Olba's mouth.

"Hey, get your paws off me!"

The two of them fell to the straw as they struggled.

Suddenly, a voice rang out: "Sounds like you two are havin' fun over there."

The voice came from the cell next to theirs. They couldn't see who had spoken because of the intervening wall, but it seemed likely that the voice belonged to another prisoner.

"Fun? Not really," said Olba, pushing Duan off him.

The voice sounded disappointed. "Really? Oh, what a shame. I've been on me own down here for so long. And I've been so, so bored. I was hopin' for a little entertainment."

"Oh, right," Duan said awkwardly.

"But I wouldn't be thinkin' about escapin' if I was you," the voice went on.

"Oh, um, right," repeated Duan.

The voice cackled. "There was one man who tried to escape, he was me partner. He got caught straightaways, and then he was executed the very next day, poor fella. This country is quite strict when it comes to prison breaks."

"I suppose any country would be quite strict," Duan observed.

"Yes, yes. Look, would you like some good advice?"

Olba rolled his eyes, but Duan answered, "Yes?"

"That meal you just had . . . It wasn't very good, was it?"

"N-no."

"It don't have enough salt, that's why. So when you're eatin', what you want to do is just give yer arm or yer leg a good lick every once in a while. It ain't half bad once you get used to it. Sweat's quite salty, see. And people need their salt. You'll also need protein. You've seen those bugs crawlin' around? Just pick 'em up and eat 'em. The wings are a bit hard at first, but they're not too bad when you get used to 'em. And then, for dessert, there's—"

Duan had heard enough. "O-oh, okay. Thanks a lot, really." He was feeling ready to vomit.

The voice had worse information to impart. "Let me tell you one more thing. There's a torture chamber at the end of the hall here, and it's quite famous. Apparently, the collection of tools in there is amazing. I'd kind of like to see 'em for myself. Then again, I ain't all that eager to end up in there, if you know what I mean! Heh heh."

Now it was Olba who'd had enough. "Hey, Duan," he shouted. "Shut that guy up, will ya?"

Duan started to object that there was nothing he could do about their loquacious neighbor but gave up when he saw the expression on Olba's face. Instead, he said nothing, as did the voice from next door.

All the while this was going on, Duan could hear spine-chilling groans and screams, something being dragged across the floor, the rattling of chains, and the sharp cracks of a whip.

This is awful, just awful . . .

Duan rubbed his eyes when Olba wasn't looking.

Shoot. This is no time to cry.

Even as he surreptitiously tried to brush away his tears, he was thinking of Agnis. She was their only hope.

She's a princess. She'll be able to do something!

And where the heck is Check? In all the commotion, I ended up leaving him behind at the inn. Shoot, I hope Agnis found him safely! What if he wandered off before she got there, though? I might never see him again!

Duan couldn't imagine life without the brave—if sometimes annoying—grinia by his side.

No, I'll definitely see him again. Check always comes back to me. . . .

CHAPTER 8:

A STRANGE BOY

He spread his pale green wings and flew. His head still hurt a little, but he felt a lot better. Besides, his curiosity was driving him to check out all the interesting-looking objects in the room.

"Check, don't break anything, okay?"

Agnis was dressed in her best clothes. She'd even changed her trademark hat decoration to a lily, her birth flower. So, while she hadn't come to Orland Castle on an official state visit, she still was wearing rather formal clothes. She'd hoped that doing so would help her get an interview with Prince Charles right away. Instead, the majordomo of the palace had shown her to a guest room. That was an hour ago. The tea and biscuits that were brought out were already finished, mostly due to Check.

Now, fueled by all the tea, Check was flying here and there about the room, investigating everything.

Agnis sighed and spoke to K'nock, who lay at her side. "This wait is so typical of Charles. What a strange boy he is! A bit dopey and slow—and when it comes to getting dressed, he takes a hundred times longer than any girl I know. But one can't help liking him!"

Just as Agnis finished speaking, the door opened, and a young boy came in.

"Charles!" called Agnis.

The boy happily ran over. "Agnis! You came!"

"Of course I did! I'm sorry I'm so late. It'll take too long to explain, but I've been super busy."

"No, it's okay," said Charles. "I'm just so happy to see you, I could cry."

The young prince's skin was so white that it was almost transparent. He had pale blue eyes and soft, blond, wavy hair, which was arranged into a bob. He was the sort of boy who seemed too fragile and beautiful to exist outside of a dream, like a rare flower that enraptured everyone who saw or smelled it yet would wither if it were removed from the sheltered confines of the greenhouse.

For that very reason, Charles found it difficult to make true friends. People—girls, especially—were too timid to talk to him, either awed by his beauty or afraid of somehow damaging him by inadvertently saying the wrong thing. Agnis was different, however, not only because she'd known him for so long, but—or so she told herself—because she wasn't attracted to the sort of "pretty boy" type Charles exemplified. She preferred someone a little more mature and masculine.

Charles was wearing a light navy velvet suit with lapels bordered in luxurious white lace. He looked so perfectly dressed that Agnis had to smile.

"Charles, you haven't changed one bit. You're still the same hothouse flower as ever," she said.

Charles blushed immediately. "Stop teasing. I'm already worried enough about it as it is."

Agnis couldn't help bursting into laughter. "What, you're worried about being so beautiful?"

"Of course I am," he said. "I'm not a girl! Anyway, you really came at a good time. It's a little complicated, but . . ." He trailed off as if unsure how to continue.

"Hm, it's what you wrote about, isn't it?" asked Agnis in a lowered voice.

Before Charles could reply, the door opened again. A middle-aged gentleman appeared: Loren Bator, Charles' minder.

Charles made a frosty frown with his beautiful eyebrows. "Oh, Loren. What is it now? I'm trying to have an important conversation."

Loren lowered his gray-haired head and said apologetically, "I'm sorry to disturb you. Her Majesty heard that Princess Agnis is visiting and wishes to see her."

"Mother wants to see her?" echoed Charles. He sighed dramatically and pursed his lips into a pout. There was nothing to be done. The queen had spoken. "I'm sorry, Agnis," he said. "Would you mind terribly paying Mother a visit? I can talk to you about all this later."

"Of course. I was meaning to say 'hello' to your mother, anyway. After all, it's been a long time since I've seen her. Besides, I have some letters from my mother to give her. There's no rush, is there? We have plenty of time. Er, that is, I was hoping I could stay for a few days."

"You can stay as long as you like," said Charles. "Only . . ."

"What?" asked Agnis.

Charles leaned close and whispered nervously, "I just hope we really do have plenty of time."

CHAPTER 9:

An Interview With The Queen

One look at Queen Milhene was enough to settle the question of where Prince Charles got his extraordinary beauty.

Her clear blue dress liberally exposed a dazzlingly snow-white chest. Her luxurious hair was piled up high, and her face was made entirely of elegant features.

Unfortunately, the only thing that interested Queen Milhene was how things compared with her own beauty.

And just now, she was filled with discontent because she found Lord Schneider attractive, even more attractive than the king, her husband. Schneider was married, but his wife was not especially beautiful. The Queen found this state of affairs extremely vexing.

It wasn't that she disliked the king; it was just that he wasn't a particularly good match for her in the looks department. When she was with him, she felt like a gorgeous, sparkling diamond set in a cheap plastic frame.

Why can't life be the way I want it? If only the king could be as manly and beautiful and good-looking as Schneider—why, then I'd have no problems at all!

These were the thoughts running through the mind of Queen Milhene as she greeted the princess of Fiana.

"Agnis, thank you for coming. We have not had the pleasure of visitors recently, and we were becoming quite bored. I hope you can stay a while."

The queen's smile was sweet and generous, but there was something a little off about it. Agnis realized that it was the woman's beauty: Her features were so perfect that her expressions didn't seem quite real, taking on a masklike quality. A thought suddenly occurred to Agnis: *When you're this perfect, beauty is comedic.*

Of course, she showed none of this in her own features. Instead, she curtsied graciously. "Queen Milhene, I brought a gift from my mother."

As Agnis spoke, Loren brought out a box that Agnis had given to him earlier, presenting it reverently to the queen, who accepted it with delight.

The queen's cheeks reddened prettily, and her eyes sparkled as she opened the box. Inside was a jeweled brooch in the shape of a bouquet of blue flowers—which were made of sapphires, of course. And on one of those sapphire flowers was a small, lifelike bee, exquisitely fashioned from ebony and gold.

"Oh my! How lovely. Look, it's perfect for this dress." Queen Milhene brought the light, white veil she wore to her bosom and pinned the brooch there, beaming with pleasure and pride.

"It suits you," Agnis said, unable to repress a smile at the queen's girlish excitement. "My mother will be so pleased that you like it."

"Oh yes, poor Rubis. I heard of her misfortune. No details, though. What happened? Something about a witch's curse? How terribly frightening!"

"Um, well . . ."

Agnis didn't really want to talk about it. It wasn't easy to explain that her mother had been turned into a bird; even when she'd made the effort, most people just didn't understand. She'd come to the conclusion that it was best to leave the subject alone.

Queen Milhene pressed on with her questions, oblivious to Agnis' increasing discomfort. "I hear that your mother is living separately now. Why is that? I suppose that Rubis, being the king's, er, *second wife,* has no other options. She is certainly better suited to the throne than Queen Ramua, if I may say so! Why, no one could dispute that. And His Majesty, King Palea, clearly adores her. I heard that it was quite romantic when they first met—a real case of love at first sight!"

Agnis was stupefied by the ceaseless flow of questions coming from the queen. She was too taken aback to be offended. *Where on Earth did she hear all these details?*

Charles, grasping the situation, was quick to intercede.

"Mother, you must not pry into private matters. Look how Agnis is troubled."

Queen Milhene's expression soured immediately. "How rude! Charles, you know it is impolite to interrupt a conversation."

Charles wished he could respond sarcastically and say "What conversation? You were doing all the talking, as usual!" How good that would feel. Of course, he didn't speak these thoughts aloud. He loved his mother, despite her faults. No matter how vain or thoughtless she acted, he still hated to upset her.

The queen nodded in satisfaction at her son's silence. "Poor boy, you are still such a child."

Treating Charles like a child and watching him accept it downheartedly was a great stress-reliever for the queen; it never failed to cheer her up. She turned back to Agnis with a smile.

"Agnis, dear. Would you like to join me for a walk in my garden? I recently redesigned it. Gardening is such fun! And the bathokiss is in bloom, too."

"Um, well . . ." said Agnis again. What she really wanted was to hear Charles' story. She glanced at him sideways, hoping he would make some excuse, allowing the two of them to go off together.

Instead, the prince looked up suddenly, as if he'd just thought of something, and his downcast features brightened. "What a splendid idea, Mother. I believe I shall join you!"

CHAPTER 10:

THE LEGEND OF BATHOKISS AND SAPHORIA

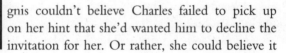gnis couldn't believe Charles failed to pick up on her hint that she'd wanted him to decline the invitation for her. Or rather, she could believe it only too well.

Typical! Charles really needs to become more assertive!

He would act the same way even if he were talking to someone other than his mother. The only person he ever allowed himself to speak to without bottling up his real feelings and desires was Agnis. Otherwise, even if he was burning to say something, he held his tongue. Perhaps because Agnis was not known to possess this quality, she found that aspect of the prince's character especially irritating, though she could never stay annoyed with him for long.

Now, Charles took Agnis' hand and began to escort her from the room.

K'nock and Check followed them, while Queen Milhene looked on with an amused smile.

"You two are quite well suited—you look like a pair of beautiful dolls. Maybe Charles needs someone reliable like you, Agnis. I have no objections about your background; in my eyes, you are practically a true, legal princess, even if your mother is only a, er, *second wife*. It would be nonsense to fuss over something as trivial as that."

Agnis' blood was boiling as she listened.

Hmph. If you really didn't care, you wouldn't keep saying "second wife" or "legal princess"!

However, even Agnis, who was known for her short temper, knew better than to argue with a queen in her own castle. She tried to remain calm, distracting herself by looking out into the large inner garden.

In the garden, there was an open lawn, well lit by the sun and adorned with white benches, which were surrounded by different kinds of trees.

As they entered the garden, a number of odors reached Agnis' nostrils, but the strongest—so potent it nearly sent her reeling backward—was the smell of the bathokiss flower the queen had mentioned earlier. The flower was named after Bathokiss, a man who had loved the Goddess Saphoria.

When they reached the bathokiss tree, at the back of the garden, Charles suddenly halted.

"Mother, remember what we were talking about before, the statue that used to be here . . ."

"You mean that strange statue of a dog with the face of a human?"

"Yes, that one. You really have no knowledge of where it is?"

The queen frowned. "You really are pigheaded, Charles. How many times are you going to ask me that question? I do not know."

Sighing dramatically, the queen turned to Agnis. "My dear, when I saw that statue for the first time, I was shocked. Shocked! I could not understand why something so ugly and disturbing would be placed here in the royal garden."

Then, she turned back to her son. "That is the real mystery, as far as I am concerned." A sudden look of suspicion flashed in her eyes. "Charles, is there something you have not told me?"

Charles, now on the receiving end of the questions, hastily waved his hand. "N-no, Mother. I just wondered whether it was all right to move something like that without the king's permission."

Queen Milhene's eyebrows shot up. "What did you say? The king's permission? Who do you think you are addressing?"

"Oh, um . . . no matter. Everything is okay." Charles, looking paler than ever, gave a pathetic little laugh, as though making fun of his inability to stand up to his mother.

Oh dear, thought Agnis. *How annoying! There's no need to hold back. If it were me, I'd be saying whatever I liked, even to my own mother.*

But this is Charles' business. I don't really know any of the details, so it wouldn't be right of me to butt in.

Agnis felt quite proud of herself for this decision. She knew very well that not too long ago, she would have responded without thinking, very probably making matters worse between Charles and his mother.

Still, it wasn't easy controlling herself. She bit her tongue and walked away a few steps, pretending to look at the bathokiss tree.

The Bathokiss

The bathokiss is a short tree that blooms from late fall to mid-winter with a profusion of white flowers. It is famous for its strong, sweet smell. The tree and flower are both named after Bathokiss, a young man who fell in love with a goddess.

Bathokiss prayed to the goddess Saphoria night after night, always with the same prayer: "If only I could spend one night with you, glorious Sophoria, I would die happily in the morning!"

When they heard this, Saphoria and the other goddesses laughed at the young man's ardor. If his wish were granted, they said, he would be begging for mercy in the morning. That's how it was with mortals and their prayers, always making promises they wouldn't keep, swearing this, vowing that, and then trying to weasel out of it when the time came to pay the price.

Saphoria decided to teach Bathokiss a lesson. She fashioned a replica of herself out of white flowers, breathed life into it, and sent it to Bathokiss as he knelt in prayer on the floor of his room. The young man was overjoyed that his prayers had been answered. The night was all that he had imagined and more. The next day, giving thanks to the goddess, he threw himself into the ocean.

Saphoria, watching from above, was touched deeply by his sincerity and moved to tears by the tragic turn her joke had taken. As her tears fell over the ocean, they turned to white petals.

From that time on, everyone called those white blossoms and the tree from which they came the bathokiss.

"Gi—is. Flower stinks, cha!"

Check, who had been investigating the garden, wrinkled his little face and came flapping toward Agnis. "When eat, girl? When eat?"

Agnis looked at him in surprise. "What?"

"Check hungry, cha!"

"Hungry? You just had loads of cake and tea!"

Check made a rude noise to show his opinion of cake and tea.

Agnis blushed. "Be quiet, will you?"

Charles, who had noticed the exchange, called out to her. "Agnis, is everything all right?"

"Yes," she said. "We were just admiring your bathokiss."

"Flower stink!" said Check, using a low voice so that only Agnis could hear. But he flew off when Agnis made shushing motions with her hands.

"Listen," Charles continued, "do you think you can come to my room now? I have something I want to show you."

"Yeah, sure!" answered Agnis without thinking. But she quickly clapped both hands to her mouth as she caught sight of the queen's disapproving expression. Queen Milhene was a stickler for the kind of elevated speech that—in her own mind, at least— set the aristocracy apart from the common herd. Now, blushing more than she had been already, Agnis hurriedly amended, "Er, that is, yes, of course, Charles. I would be delighted."

The queen smiled approvingly at Agnis' gracious speech.

Agnis sighed, shooting Charles the kind of look that children have been giving each other behind their elders' backs since the dawn of time.

It's not easy being a normal princess. It really isn't. . . .

CHAPTER II:

THE DEVIL AND THE HOLY DOG

hat!? The devil Senzeblurb-something has been resurrected?" Agnis cried without thinking.

Charles frantically shushed her. "Quiet, Agnis! Don't be so loud!" He cast fearful glances about his bedroom. "Who knows who might be listening?"

"Listening? Who?"

"It doesn't matter who. Anyone. It'd be bad if anybody heard us talking about this."

"Right, I get it. They might worry you've gone off your rocker!"

At this, Charles gave a bitter smile, as though he had expected no other response. "Yes, I suppose that would be the normal reaction," he admitted glumly.

"Well, but come on! You're talking about devils here! You have to admit that's a bit crazy."

Then, at the sight of Charles' disheartened face, Agnis repented her words.

Hm . . . at this rate, he'll end up bottling up everything again.

"On the other hand," she added quickly, "I've seen some strange things myself. Not only have I met a dragon, I've actually spoken to one! So maybe what you're saying isn't so crazy, after all. A devil? Sure, why not? Bring it on!" And she struck herself in the chest for emphasis.

Charles, who'd been listening open-mouthed, burst into laughter. He laughed so hard that his whole body shook.

"Er, Charles, I don't think there's any need to laugh quite that much."

"Ha ha ha! Sorry, sorry," Charles gasped out, wiping his eyes. "Oh my. Ha ha. You're so funny Agnis. You're definitely going to make it big time!"

"What? Make it big time? I'm an adventurer, not a comedian!"

"Ha ha ha. Sorry. Anyway, is it true? Did you really meet and speak with a dragon?"

"Yup, it's true . . . never mind about that, though! Tell me about the devil Whatchamacallit."

"You can't take it seriously, can you?"

"Go on, I'm listening."

"Okay, I'll tell you. But you have to promise you won't breathe a word of this to anyone else," said Charles, peering deeply into Agnis' eyes.

She nodded with a sincere expression. "I understand. I promise."

PRINCE CHARLES' STORY

I don't have many friends, and I can't sword fight. I can't ride, either. What? Really, Agnis, you can't ride? That's surprising.

Recently, I've spent at least half a day every day in the archives, and I've been reading through all the books in every genre. Thanks to this, I can understand the languages of different countries now. However much time I spend reading, though, I still don't make a dent in all the books—that's how large our archives are. So I made a resolution to myself.

Our archives are largely divided into seven bookshelves. I've assigned a number to each shelf, and I've promised myself that every day, I'll read one book from all the shelves, from one to seven. Basically, I have an obligation to read seven books a day.

I suppose it sounds like hard work. Some of the books are filled with nothing but maps or other illustrations, though, and some are ancient texts whose languages no one alive remembers how to decipher. I skip over those. It's been tough going but doable. Not that this matters at all.

Anyway, seven days after I made this resolution, I found a strange book. This is it, Agnis—this book here. Yes, if you open the front cover, it's just a box. There's an empty space inside. Empty now, that is. But when I found it and pulled it off the shelf for the first time, there was a rattling sound inside.

Ha ha ha, there's no point shaking it now—it won't make any noise. That's what I'm trying to tell you. It's over here, what I found inside. Yes, there was a piece of paper inside. Go on, take a look.

Ha ha. Sorry, sorry. Yeah, I know you can't read it. It's a very unique script from ages ago. But I was really determined to read the paper because of how I'd found it, so I turned all the bookshelves upside down and checked every single book we had, looking for anything that could tell me more about this strange writing.

And then, I finally found it. This is it, it seems. It's a book of black magic. See the pictures of frogs and snakes? This book consists of ingredients used in black magic spells. I tried to find the same writing as I found on the mysterious hidden note.

I did find it . . . but only a little.

See this word? I think it means something like "can see" or "to see." At least, that's the best I can figure from how it's used in this black-magic book.

This word means something like "to lock" or "to seal." So I tried to decipher the note using these clues, but it was still too hard. I wasn't getting anywhere. Then, just when I was about to forget the whole thing, I decided to check the first book again, the one that had been holding the note. I don't know why, but the idea just came to me.

What do you know? I found a small piece of paper pasted on the inside of the book! With difficulty, I managed to peel it off. This is it.

In the southwest of the castle, behind the stone wall that can be seen from the third floor of the Silver-Gray Tower, the devil Senzrabur has been sealed by the Holy Dog. However, when the Dog leaves, the power of darkness will return . . . and the world will fall

Corny, huh? I wasn't going to believe something as childish as this, either. I figured that one of my ancestors was quite mischievous and had decided to fool one of his grandchildren one day by creating some elaborate hoax.

Yeah, that's what I figured . . . at first.

Just for fun, I decided to follow the hoax through to the end, so I went up to the third floor of the Silver-Gray Tower. Believe it or not, although I've lived here my entire life, I'd never entered that lonely and eerie tower. I'd always heard the top floor was a jail where they kept important people.

But now, I screwed up my courage and went in. What? No, not by myself! I asked Loren to come with me. Oh no, I didn't tell him anything. No need. If I say I want to

go somewhere, Loren will come along without asking any questions. He's just that type of person.

Anyway, on the third floor of the Silver-Gray Tower, there was a small window. I poked out my head to have a look, but I couldn't believe my eyes. There was absolutely nothing there like a stone wall. Instead, I was looking at the inner garden. Yes, the same garden we just visited—my mother's pride and joy.

I hurried down and ran to the garden. I looked around, but I saw no sign of a stone wall or a Holy Dog or any kind of dog at all! Then, the gardener started to talk to me.

"Your Highness, what are you looking for?"

I came right out and asked him if there was a statue there that looked like a dog.

A creeped-out expression came over his features. "Ugh, you mean that hideous statue of a dog with a face that was half man, half woman?"

"Er, yes, that one. Where did it go?"

"I had no idea it belonged to you, Your Highness. In fact, you couldn't tell how old it was—all overgrown with moss and covered in dirt and dust. I showed it to Her Majesty, and she told me to throw away the disgusting thing."

"Do you know where it was thrown away?"

"Not really—probably on the hill to the back, that's where we threw the remains of the stone wall that was here originally."

"I see. Can you find it for me? And when you do, could you inform me discreetly, without telling Mother? I shall reward you."

The man agreed; unfortunately, the statue hasn't been found yet. However, I did find out where it used to stand. It's the place I stopped today.

After he finished his long explanation, Charles heaved a sigh and sank into a luxurious chair that was upholstered in rich, red velvet.

Agnis chose a chair for herself and curled into it, resting her chin on her knees. Silence spread in the luxurious room. The golden light of a sunny afternoon streamed in through a high window.

K'nock was sprawled out by Agnis' feet, sleeping quietly. Check slept there, too; having stuffed his belly full of desserts again, the little grinia was using the big cat's soft tail as a pillow.

At last, Agnis spoke. "But—"

"But," began Charles at the same instant.

They broke off, laughing nervously, flustered at having interrupted each other with the same word.

"Oh, sorry," said the prince. "You go first, Agnis."

"No, no. Charles, you first."

In the end, it was Agnis who finally started to speak. "You said that maybe it was all an elaborate hoax contrived by some mischievous ancestor of yours. That theory hasn't been disproved yet, has it?"

"That's exactly what I was about to say," exclaimed Prince Charles. "No, it hasn't been disproved. And it isn't as if anything else unusual has happened. But I don't feel I can ignore it, either. I mean, what if it's true? It's better to be safe than sorry in matters like this. I don't want to put my countrymen at risk."

"Yes, that makes sense . . . and does you credit. But let's face it, Charles, we don't really have a lot to work with. I think it would be best if you found the dog statue and put it back where it used to be. Hm . . . would that even make a difference at this point? I mean, if—and I mean *if*—the devil that was imprisoned has been released, then it means it's no longer there, right? So, what was its name again?"

"Senzrabur."

"What a tongue-twister! So, okay, if the devil Senzrabur isn't there anymore, then there's no point replacing the statue, is there?"

"Exactly!" Charles held his head in his hands. "It's so complicated!"

"When was the statue moved?"

"The garden was remodeled about a month ago. It must have happened then."

"A month, eh? That's a relatively long time. If Senzrabur were free, wouldn't he have gotten up to some mischief by now?"

"You'd think so."

"And you said yourself there hasn't been anything unusual going on. This is probably all just nonsense, Charles—like you said, a hoax."

"I hope you're right."

Agnis sighed when she saw how depressed Charles looked. Regardless of what she'd just told him, if the devil Senzrabur had been resurrected, who knows how long it would take for him to revitalize and start to wreak havoc? She was no expert in demonology, but she'd heard that a full resurrection could take quite a bit of time; it seemed possible that the devil was just biding his time, slowly regaining strength.

"Hm . . ."

But Agnis couldn't think of anything else. She was stumped.

If only Duan were here! He's good at figuring out stuff.

Agnis suddenly shot to her feet with a scream.

Charles, K'nock, and Check all leaped up in surprise.

"Oh no," Agnis whispered. "I totally forgot about Duan and Olba!"

CHAPTER 12:

MEANWHILE, BACK IN THE DUNGEON...

choo!"

Duan woke up with a start to his own sneeze. His eyes sprang open to the sight of a sticky black wall, poorly lit by a flickering torch. There was a sour smell. Where was he? His head was spinning. It was as if his memory had shattered to pieces, and now those pieces were whirling around inside his head. He stretched out his hands and struggled to reach them, as if he could put them back together like a puzzle. Soon enough, they fell back into place of their own accord, and he remembered where he was.

"Oh yeah," he groaned. "I'm in the dungeon."

He accidentally spoke aloud. At this, the voice from the neighboring cell began talking again, as though its owner had been waiting for just this opportunity.

"Awake, are you? That's what everyone's like at the beginning! However many times you wake up, you can't remember where you are. The good news is that you get used to it. The bad news is that things only get lonelier the more you get used to it."

Duan didn't reply. He got to his feet and looked around. Olba was sound asleep, resting his head on his knees like a pillow.

"How can he sleep?" Duan whispered to himself.

Olba promptly opened one eye. "I ain't sleeping."

"N-no, of course not," said Duan, startled. "Hey, what time do you think it is, Olba?"

The big fighter shrugged, but the voice from next door piped right up.

"Now? It's probably afternoon. That meal just gone was supposed to be lunch. Who knows if they really serve lunch at lunchtime here, though. Maybe they serve lunch at dinnertime. It's all part of their plan to mess with yer head. You know, drive you crazy!"

Olba's face turned sour as he replied with his scariest voice, a voice even Duan had heard only a handful of times: "That must've been a short drive for you! Now shut up!"

Quite sensibly, in Duan's opinion, the nosy neighbor said nothing to this.

After a moment of silence, Olba nodded in satisfaction and said to Duan, "We haven't even been here a whole day yet, Duan, and here you are, acting like we've been locked up for weeks. Kid, this is nothing! You gotta toughen up, mentally and physically."

"What's the longest you've been in jail, Olba?"

"Hm . . . The longest stretch was a little more than a month."

"A month! What happened? Were you falsely accused?"

The big fighter barked out a laugh. "Heck, no. I deserved every day, maybe even more." He sounded proud.

"What did you do?"

"You really want to know? What the heck—it ain't like we've got anything else to do in this dump. I'll tell you the story just to kill some time."

"Yes, please! I'm really interested in your life, Olba. I have a ton of questions—for instance, how did you get to be so strong? What kind of adventures have you been on? Where were you born? Do you have any siblings? What were your parents like? What did they do?"

Duan continued to babble out question after question after question.

Olba rolled his eyes with disdain. "Hey, I said I would tell you the story of this one time I was in jail. I don't want an investigation into my personal history. What do you think this is, a game of twenty questions?"

Duan blushed. "S-sorry, Olba. Go on, tell me whatever you want."

"Hmph. Then listen carefully."

Olba stretched, cracked his neck, and began.

OLBA'S STORY

This happened when I was about your age. Okay, Suche— What? Who's Suche? A girl, of course. What, do I have to spell out every little detail? Now shut the heck up and listen!

Anyway, the girlfriend I had around that time was unusually. . . well, let's just say she was from a good background. Where did we meet? That doesn't matter. I liked her and she liked me. That should be enough, right? Wrong. See, her parents weren't too happy about our association. They kept trying to get her to dump me, but she wouldn't listen. It made their blood boil. Finally, they decided to get rid of me at any cost.

One day, they pulled me aside and told me their daughter was suffering from a fatal illness and had only a short time to live. They told me that she had kept her illness a secret from me because she was afraid I would leave her if I knew. They mentioned a cure—a rare plant known as Lumpaway that could be found in the treasury of such-and-such country. Never mind which one—the point is, because the plant was so rare and valuable, they didn't think the country's rulers would give it up just to save the life of some foreign girl. They were trying to tell me there was no hope. "If you pity our daughter, please let her be," they begged me. Those stinkin' liars!

But what did I know? I was young and easily fooled. Of course, I went to fetch the Lumpaway myself. What? What's that face? I was earnest back then, okay? Sheesh! So, what happened? What do you think?

Like I told you, I got caught busting into the treasury. They tossed me into a cell a lot worse than this one. I was in there for a month or so. And yes, I got tortured during that time. Why? Well, because there was no such plant as Lumpaway. When I told my story about only wanting the plant for my sick girlfriend, they just laughed. They thought I was really a spy.

Finally, they decided to execute me. What's that? Harsh? Nah—that's just the way of the world, kid. So, I escaped.

How? Well, it was like this. The prison guard came to me one day. "You're going to be executed tomorrow," he informed me. "I feel sorry for you, so I'm going to help you escape . . . for ten thousand Gs. You're a thief—I'm sure you have that much."

Naturally, I replied that I did have that much and more, stashed away in a certain dungeon somewhere. It wasn't exactly a lie. I just didn't mention the fact that the money didn't belong

to me yet, that it was part of a quest I'd been planning to go on before they arrested me. The guard didn't believe a word, of course. He said that he wasn't making a deal unless I paid him up front. So, I said that he should come with me, instead. He'd earn a heck of a lot more than ten Gs that way.

Well, it turns out this guy was bored with being a prison guard. He didn't like all the torturing. He wanted to get out into the sunlight and open air. So, he agreed, and the two of us escaped together. There—that's my story.

What happened next? It doesn't matter. Maybe I'll tell you later . . . if I feel like it. Okay, don't make that sad puppy-dog face!

To make a long story short, I teamed up with that prison guard for a while. We did two or three quests together. I have no idea what he's doing now. He's probably a respectable fighter. He got his qualifications as an adventurer right after he started to work with me. It turned out that he had natural talent and was actually more or less a knight from somewhere or other. He had left home under a dark cloud and wandered around for a while before falling into that job as a prison guard. Maybe I'm not one to talk, but he was a pretty strange guy.

His name? Hm, what was it? I can't remember.

☐

Duan pressed on. "What happened to Suche, your girlfriend?"

Olba shrugged. "Like I said, I've forgotten."

"No, you *didn't* say. You just said you'd forgotten the name of the ex-prison guard. You haven't spoken about Suche at all. She must've waited for you, right?"

Olba stared into the distance. There was a nostalgic cast to his gaze, as if he were reminiscing about the past. Then, he blinked suddenly and said in an irritated tone, "It doesn't matter, Duan. The point is to get over yourself. One day in prison is no big deal."

"I guess not. . . ."

Duan sighed softly. Olba's story had distracted him for a while—which, come to think of it, was the only reason Olba had told it in the first place. In fact, how did Duan know the story was even true? It would be just like Olba to make up a story about himself! On the other hand, in just the relatively short time he'd been Olba's partner, he'd already experienced more exciting adventures than he'd imagined one person could have in a lifetime. This was an adventure, too, wasn't it? Maybe that's how he should look at it.

Maybe then this crappy dungeon wouldn't seem so bad. . . .

No, who was he trying to kid? It was still pretty bad!

Agnis, where are you? You must know where we are by now! You've probably gone to that inn where we arranged to meet and heard about what happened yesterday. Next, you probably went to see Prince Charles, then directly appealing to the king for our release.

Hm . . . I suppose all that takes time. But I'm sure we'll be rescued soon. And then it's goodbye to this dank hole. Yeah, goodbye and good riddance!

Once they realize they've made a mistake and arrested the friends of Princess Agnis, they're bound to be really hospitable just to make up for it. Although at this point, I'd settle for some hot soup and fluffy, fresh-baked bread. And a soft, nice-smelling bed . . .

▭

Unfortunately, Duan was completely wrong. Agnis hadn't yet taken the first step toward rescuing them.

Furthermore, Charles didn't know where their jail was. He could say only that it was probably at the bottom of some tower. Of course, he had never been to any of the jail cells, nor would he ever be allowed to visit such terrifying places. He told Agnis that even Loren wouldn't allow him to do something like that.

Agnis, however, wasn't thinking that Charles should try to help Olba and Duan escape directly. "Couldn't you just ask the king?" she pressed him. "You know, inform him that the Black Knights arrested two adventurers yesterday, and the two men were falsely accused? You can tell him that the men are my attendants; so, of course, they must be innocent!"

"Oh, I see," said Charles. "In that case, I'll go speak to him straightaway. There is one thing, though: He's my father, but he also is the king. It isn't that easy to see him, even for me, his son and heir."

Agnis found this shocking. "No way!"

"No, really. That's normal."

"My father is king, too; I can see him whenever I like!"

"That's because you're different. You're the exception."

"What do you mean, 'different'?!"

"Sorry, were you offended? I didn't mean it like that."

"How did you mean it?"

"Agnis, please don't take out your anger on me."

"Hm . . . " Agnis took a deep breath. She realized Charles was right: She was taking out her frustration at having forgotten about Duan and Olba on him.

Charles, seeing that Agnis understood what she'd been doing and felt bad about it, spoke kindly to her. "Don't worry about it, Agnis. You'll always be my friend! And I'm going to help *your* friends. In fact, I'll go to the king right now and insist on an audience!"

"Great! I'll come, too."

"Okay, we'll go together."

"Right."

As Agnis and Charles got up, K'nock also rose to his feet. This displaced Check, who'd been using the snow leopard's tail as a pillow. Flapping his wings, he flew to Agnis' shoulder.

"I see you've made a new friend," Charles said, pointing a finger at Check.

Check, ever curious, grabbed the finger in his small hands and carefully examined it.

"Who, him?" asked Agnis. "That's just Check, a baby grinia. Duan, one of the friends I just mentioned—well, he and Check are like brothers."

"Brothers? You mean this Duan isn't human?"

Agnis put her hands on her hips and glared at Charles. "Are you being willfully obtuse?"

Charles burst into laughter. "Ha ha ha! Just teasing!"

"Really, Charles," Agnis said, rolling her eyes. "You act so normal when you're around me, always joking and teasing—why do you behave so differently in front of other people?"

Charles gave a shrug and frowned. "I wish I knew. It seems weird to me, too." So speaking, he guided her out.

◻

Within ten minutes, they were back in Charles' room, shoulders drooping with disappointment.

"Busy?" said Agnis. "What do they mean, 'busy'?"

Charles laughed bitterly. "Who knows? Judging from what just happened, my father and the others definitely know about your friends."

"You're right—they definitely know. Something smells fishy. There's more going on here than meets the eye."

Here's what had happened: When Charles explained to the king's majordomo that Princess Agnis of Fiana wanted to meet and speak with him, the man said it was impossible. True to his word, Charles had insisted.

"It seems that Agnis' attendants, Duan and Olba, were arrested mistakenly by the Black Knights' Army last night."

As soon as these words passed Charles' lips, the majordomo turned as white as a ghost and signed to one of the guards, who rushed the prince and Agnis out of the room.

Now, back in Charles' room, Agnis was trying to make sense of things. "The story is that Duan and Olba were trying to steal the royal treasure. That's impossible! Well, maybe not impossible for Olba, but Duan would never—"

"Wait," interrupted Charles. "You mean one of your friends is a thief?"

"N-no, never mind," said Agnis hurriedly. "Anyway, they came here to help me, not to steal anything. Besides, they were here such a short while before the arrest, they wouldn't have had time to grab Garcia's Goblet." At this, Agnis clapped her hands. "I know! Charles, where is this goblet usually kept?"

"The treasury, of course. Why?"

"Oh, no reason," said Agnis.

Despite her dismissive words, the prince couldn't help noticing that Agnis looked different all of a sudden. Her green eyes were sparkling like the eyes of a child brewing up some new kind of mischief.

CHAPTER 13:

SCHNEIDER ACCUSED

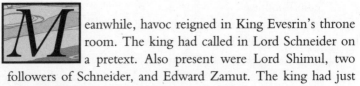eanwhile, havoc reigned in King Evesrin's throne room. The king had called in Lord Schneider on a pretext. Also present were Lord Shimul, two followers of Schneider, and Edward Zamut. The king had just exposed Schneider's "conspiracy."

"What? I have absolutely no idea what Your Majesty is talking about. Please, go through it again."

As he spoke, Schneider's expression seemed inappropriate— at least, it did to the king. Schneider was not agitated, did not rush or make a fuss—even the color of his face remained unchanged. King Evesrin found it infuriating to see that Schneider did not lose his nerve.

Hmph, he's a cold fish, all right. Couldn't he even have the decency to be a little bit surprised?

"What brazen behavior for such a heavy crime!" the king thundered to mask his nervousness. "We've uncovered your dirty deeds, Schneider. Didn't you think we'd find out you hired those men to steal Orland's treasure, Garcia's Golden Goblet, and trade it with our enemy, the Kingdom of Ganau?"

The blood rushed to his head in anger, and King Evesrin was rattling on without much evident reflection. Listening, Edward Zamut felt overwhelmed with a terrible apprehension.

Good Lord—how can His Majesty go on like this, without thinking things through?!

Now, as Schneider replied to the king, he allowed himself a small grin. "These are serious accusations, Your Majesty. I assume you have some definitive witnesses or proof?"

At this, the king grew more flustered. "Er, l-like I said, this goblet here is proof of everything! Edward and the others are witnesses!"

"Please, do not joke," Schneider said calmly. "Garcia's Goblet is the property of the crown and, hence, Your Majesty may produce it whenever he wishes. That it is here now proves nothing. As for Edward and the others, they are all your close aides."

"What?!" The king glared at the impeccably cool Schneider and belatedly realized how persuasive the man's arguments were.

Shoot! What the heck do I do now? Why aren't they helping?

The king glanced sharply at Edward and Lord Shimul. Lord Shimul looked away, avoiding his gaze. Edward, his face still bewildered, stared at the golden goblet he held in his hands.

Schneider observed all this in amusement. Then, he strode toward Edward and began to examine the golden goblet himself.

"What?! What are you doing?" cried the king, as though he had snapped.

Schneider did not answer but continued to examine the goblet while whispering under his breath.

"I'm asking, what are you doing?!" the king yelled, his face bright red.

Schneider did not react brashly, instead responding as coolly as possible. "Why don't we go check the treasury? If I did get thieves to steal the goblet, as you say, surely there'd be some evidence of it there."

CHAPTER 14:

A DECLARATION OF WAR

The treasury had two secure defenses, and it was constructed so that only people who were authorized could approach it. King Evesrin led the party from the throne room past these guard posts; then, he turned the key to the thick doors of the treasury himself. There was a creaking sound as the heavy doors opened.

It was mid-afternoon. The room was always dark, even during the middle of the day, but it was darker than ever now because the weather had turned cloudy. Servants scurried to light the lamps. They flared to life, illuminating countless treasures. On display were the tiara that Queen Milhene had worn during her wedding to King Evesrin, a sword embedded with many glittering jewels, dresses and capes as far as the eye could see, and various other items related to the royal house of Orland.

In the center of it all was a marble pedestal that was worth a considerable sum itself. The king was standing in front of it now as if he'd turned to stone. Really, this should've been the moment when he cried out in triumph, "See, the goblet is gone!"

Unfortunately, the goblet was *not* gone. It stood atop the pedestal.

"Oh, there it . . . is. . . ." King Evesrin looked alternately at the golden goblet, Lord Schneider, and Edward Zamut.

What a horrible feeling . . . my heart is throbbing as though it's about to explode.

Schneider stroked his glossy black hair and addressed the king in a condescending tone. "What's this? Garcia's Golden Goblet is still here?"

"Uh . . . uh . . ." The king could only stammer, looking at Edward and Lord Shimul in confusion.

They, however, did not want to be seen. Edward made an awkward cough, and Lord Shimul continued to avoid the King's gaze as if his life depended on it.

Schneider continued speaking. "What ever do you mean Garcia's Golden Goblet is gone? And to say that I made some *adventurers* steal it as part of a conspiracy—that was what His Majesty said, wasn't it?" Schneider glanced toward his followers for confirmation; they responded silently with heavy nods. Schneider slowly turned back to the king.

"Your Majesty, this is a serious mistake. If Garcia's Golden Goblet is here, right where it's supposed to be, then where did *that* golden goblet come from?"

"W–well, it's p–probably a fake," stammered the king. "Is it not a tactic of thieves to leave behind a fake?"

"Hm. When did Your Majesty learn so much about thieves? And how is it that Edward couldn't tell *that* golden goblet is the fake, not this one?"

"What?"

"I am a novice in such things, but even I can see that goblet is a fake," Schneider responded plainly.

The leader of the Black Knights' Army, Edward Zamut, looked once again at the golden goblet he held. Regarding it now, it didn't seem to be worth much. He hadn't paused once to think about it, but it really did seem like a cheap object. The others in the room felt the same. They brought their heads together to peer at the goblet before looking at one another in distress.

Seeing this, King Evesrin snatched the golden goblet from Edward's hands. When he did so, one of the handles broke clean off. There was no way the real golden goblet would break with so little force. In that moment, it was all too clear that this goblet was the fake.

His face deathly pale, the king wrung his hands. "This is some kind of conspiracy!"

However, Lord Schneider had reached the limit of his patience. Now, he spoke with a voice loud enough to shake the entire treasury. "This is no joke!" As if on cue, at that very instant, there was a blinding flash of lightning outside the dark window. Rain began to pour down. . . .

Lord Shimul and everyone else cowered back and went quiet. The tension kept climbing inside as the sound of the rain intensified outside.

Schneider spoke again. "Conspiracy? That is what *I* should be saying! I was accused of being a thief and trying to overthrow the royals!"

"I don't know anything. It must be some kind of mistake," responded the king in a tiny, meek voice.

"Really?" Schneider said almost mockingly. "I don't suppose you know anything about this, do you, Lord Shimul?"

Finding himself suddenly spoken to, Lord Shimul shuddered and, like a sleepwalker, took a few unsteady steps forward.

"Yes, I do know," he said. "This is the work of King Evesrin. His Majesty was afraid you would spark a rebellion, Lord Schneider, and so he employed this scheme to disgrace you and remove you from power."

At this, Schneider's followers, who had been standing silently by his side, spoke, red-faced.

"What? Do you understand what you're saying?"

"What cowardly tactics!"

"You won't go unpunished, even if you are king!"

Schneider observed them for a while. Then, he pointed at them and asked Lord Shimul once more. "What do you mean, I would spark a rebellion?"

"Well, because you're more refined and popular than the king," answered Lord Shimul, feeling the painful gaze of the king and those around him.

King Evesrin finally understood who had planned this plot. Of course, it wasn't Lord Shimul, his only friend since childhood. No, Shimul obviously had been used; he was slightly timid and—although you couldn't say exactly what his good points were, and he wasn't very popular—he was the one friend that the king could grumble to.

Unbeknownst to the king, however, the truth was that Lord Shimul had switched to Schneider's side a long time ago.

The king had intended to trap Schneider but had gotten himself trapped instead. Suddenly, he felt as if he were falling down an endless hole, and all he could see before him was eternal darkness. Everything in front of his eyes turned black. The charade continued in front of him, and he just stood there, dumbfounded.

"I see," said Schneider. "The king recognized that and didn't like it?"

"Yes," said Shimul as though reading from a script. "The king worried almost on a daily basis that you were after his crown. There are others who can confirm this, too."

"That was all? That was enough reason to trump up a cowardly, dastardly plot to ensnare me? Is that correct?"

"Yes, yes."

"Furthermore, involving the Black Knights' Army . . ."

Edward Zamut stared back calmly when these words were spoken. "We acted in accordance with orders from the king. Protecting the king is our sacred duty."

"Even if your orders are morally wrong?"

"Naturally."

"Hm. How foolish . . . I suppose there is knightly honor in it; still, that means you are our enemy now. Protect your incompetent king well."

The air in the room seemed to tremble. This was a declaration of war. Schneider abandoned his mask of composure; with a face twisted in hate, he declared to the king, "Your Majesty, be prepared."

At that moment, a second flash ripped through the sky and, without a pause, it was followed by a thunderous roar, powerful enough to shake the earth.

Schneider turned, whipping his cape around in front of the speechless king, who stood with mouth agape. Calm and composed again, Lord Schneider led his followers from the treasury. Lord Shimul sidled out behind them.

CHAPTER 15:

AGNIS TAKES CHARGE

W ow, that lightning scared me!" whispered Agnis. "So, that old guy who just walked by . . . was that Lord Schneider?"

"No way," Charles whispered back. "That was a boring nobleman called Lord Shimul. Schneider was the younger guy with the mustache and the cape."

"Oh, the nice-looking guy."

"Shh! Quiet, Agnis, you're too loud."

"Sorry, sorry. I wonder what happened. Why was everyone in the treasury? It doesn't seem like Olba and Duan were there, though."

"Who knows?"

Agnis had come to the treasury with the idea of checking out where the golden goblet was supposed to have been and looking for any clues to its disappearance. She hadn't told Charles, but she'd been thinking to herself that if nothing turned up at the treasury, she would cause a fuss then and there.

When they'd arrived, though, it immediately became clear that something was happening inside. The duo hid behind a nearby curtain so they could observe the entrance of the room. Luckily, they'd left K'nock and Check behind in Charles' room; the little grinia would've given them away for sure.

"I wonder what's happening with Father and the rest of them. They're not coming out."

"Yes, really! What are they talking about in there? But this could be our chance. When His Majesty comes out, I can speak directly to him."

"Y-yes . . . Oh look, here comes Father!"

King Evesrin was accompanied by Edward Zamut and three other Black Knights. The air around them practically crackled with tension. Agnis and Charles felt like they shouldn't even be breathing—they literally held their breath until the grim procession passed.

When it was certain they were gone, the two friends let out a big sigh.

"Oh, they're gone."

"I really wonder what's happening," whispered Charles, his face paler than usual.

The sound of the rain was getting stronger, and this made the feeling of unease worse. Indeed, Agnis had a bad feeling. That caped man called Schneider—the sight of his cold, laughing eyes had sent shivers running down her spine. Charles must have felt it, too; he was hugging himself tightly, shoulders hunched. Seeing this, Agnis gave his shoulders a squeeze. She was older than him and felt responsible. Charles gave her a weak smile as he nervously bit his lip.

They couldn't stay behind the curtain forever, so they decided to return to Charles' room. There, as K'nock and

Check looked on with curiosity, they sat in silence for quite some time. At last, Agnis spoke.

"Anyhow, I should go rescue Duan and Olba myself."

"No! I'll go with you," replied Charles.

"No, I'm fine on my own. If only I knew where they kept prisoners around here. Hey, do you know someone who would know? Like, maybe that Loren guy?"

Charles shrugged. "Maybe . . . I think if he found out you were going on your own, though, he definitely wouldn't tell you."

"Right . . ."

"See, that's why we should go together. Don't forget: I'm the prince. The guards will let me pass by without question in most places."

"Don't you think you have other concerns now, though? Shouldn't you find out what just happened at the treasury?"

"Y-yes . . . but I don't think Father will tell me."

"That's weird. Your family is so reserved!"

Charles' expression darkened. "*Your* family is different."

At this, Agnis decided to concentrate on Charles before doing anything about Olba and Duan. Charles had to be her priority. Anyway, Duan and Olba certainly wouldn't be executed yet. The Adventurer Support Group didn't allow its members to be executed without a trial.

Usually, Agnis was reckless, always leaping without looking; recently, however, she had begun to change and become a bit more reflective. Maybe it was Duan's influence. . . .

"I know," she said now. "The Black Knights were there in the treasury, right? Maybe they'll talk to you! There were four of them—did you recognize any of their faces?"

"It was the leader of the Black Knights, Edward Zamut, and three other commanders."

"Are you friendly with any of them?"

"Well, I know the company commander, Sven Giesen."

"And he was with them?"

"Yeah, Sven was the one who came out last."

"The young one, then."

"Yes. He's also my sword-fighting teacher. Not that I'm a very good student. But he likes to talk, and he often tells me his old adventuring stories."

"Hm. Okay, we'll go speak to him."

"Okay."

Without further ado, they headed toward the barracks of the Black Knights' Army.

"Oh, wait a second."

Agnis returned to the room.

"What is it?" asked Charles from the hall outside.

"Just in case . . ." Agnis reappeared, carrying her magic staff.

"Wow, so that's your staff, huh?" asked Charles, his eyes wide.

"Not that I think I'll use it—at least, I hope not. I have a bad feeling, though."

"Yeah, I know what you mean." Charles nodded his head and frowned. "Hold on a second, I'll bring something, too." At that, Charles ducked back into the room. Seconds later, he reemerged.

"What is it?" asked Agnis. "What did you bring?"

"A sword for protection. I've actually been practicing."

Agnis glanced at the sword that hung at Charles' hip. It was a delicate and useless thing compared to the practical short sword that Duan carried, to say nothing of Olba's blade. Although this one was probably a hundred, no, a thousand times more expensive than both those weapons put together. It seemed to make Charles feel more confident, though, so Agnis didn't mention any of her thoughts aloud. Instead, she gave him an encouraging smile as they set off down the hall.

Meanwhile, back in the room, K'nock lay sprawled out on the carpet. The snow leopard would have accompanied Agnis, but she'd ordered him  to remain behind. She also told Check to stay put and keep out of trouble. But the baby grinia was tired of waiting. Bored to death, he decided to sneak out the window and go outside. Luckily, the roof gave some cover, allowing him to move from place to place without getting soaked in the rain. At last, Check reentered the castle through another window—smashing right into a beautiful vase. The vase toppled but didn't fall. The hallway was empty.

There were some stairs there, and dotted along the stairs were torches that brightly lit the way down.

CHAPTER 16:

THE EX-KING OF ORLAND

he Black Knights' Army barracks were located in a wing of Orland Castle that was some distance from the royal apartments.

The rain was falling more heavily as Agnis and Charles hurried along a small corridor that led to the barracks. The corridor provided some shelter from the storm; but because the wind was gusting so fiercely, they couldn't avoid getting spattered.

"Are you okay, Agnis?"

"Yes, I'm fine. A little rain never hurt anybody—this is par for the course when it comes to adventuring. How about you, Charles—are you okay?"

Despite their solicitous banter, both Agnis and Charles couldn't help feeling that something awful was about to happen. Agnis kept feeling a prickling at the back of her neck, as though someone was following them from behind. Whenever she looked, however, she saw nothing.

The first floor of the barracks was a stable, and the main entrance was nearby.

Two Black Knights stood guard there. They weren't in full armor; like the officers Agnis and Charles had seen leaving the treasury, they were dressed in black, with black chain mail on top of black shirts, black leather pants, and long black boots.

They looked surprised at the sight of Prince Charles but quickly regained their composure and saluted him.

"I'm looking for Sven Giesen," said the prince, trying to sound commanding.

One of the Black Knights again saluted, saying, "Commander Giesen was summoned by Lord Liesbeck."

"By Grandpapa? Oh. When was this?"

"A moment ago. He's probably just getting there now."

"Okay, I see. Thank you."

"Yes, sir."

Charles silently signaled to Agnis, who quietly followed behind him.

"Grandpapa is . . . No, Grandpapa must have some information, too, if he called for Sven," mused the prince as he wiped away the wet fringe of hair that was stuck annoyingly to his forehead by the rain and his own nervous sweat.

"Really?"

"Yes, Sven is one of Grandpapa's favorites. In fact, I think Sven won an annual sword-fighting contest; because Grandpapa liked him so much, he permitted Sven to enter the Black Knights' Army."

"Okay, so let's go see Lord Liesbeck. Does he live far from here?"

"No, he lives right here."

"What, in the castle?"

"He has his own castle, smaller than the main one but still quite impressive, with a full kitchen, guest rooms, and a big reception hall, as well as barracks for his personal guard. He had it built for his retirement. Anyway, you're right that we should go see him, Agnis. Grandpapa will let me in straightaway."

"Hm." Agnis couldn't understand why Charles' father, the king, wouldn't see him, while Charles' grandfather, the ex-king, would. But she knew that if she mentioned it, Charles would reply that it was perfectly normal and that Agnis was the one with the weird family. She decided not to speak up.

"How grand!" Agnis said in appreciation when they reached Lord Liesbeck's castle. "It may not be that big, but it's quite impressive, isn't it?"

The prince nodded proudly. "Of course. And it's very secure. If Father and Schneider combined forces, they still couldn't beat Grandpapa. He could hold out for years in that castle."

"Hm. If this Schneider tried to instigate a coup, your grandfather could stop him?"

"Well, I think so. . . ."

It would soon become apparent that this wasn't the case.

Charles looked nothing like Liesbeck, who had the sharp-nosed face of an eagle. Liesbeck's white hair was long and curly, though he wore it pulled straight back and tied in a ponytail. The ex-king exuded a dominant air as he sat comfortably in a large armchair, his posture denoting dignity and majesty.

Usually, Liesbeck would be grinning to pieces, as though his cheeks would crack, whenever his grandchild Charles came to visit. Today was different today. The creases on his face ran deep as he listened with a frown to Company Commander

Sven Giesen. He glanced up with a distracted frown when Charles entered the room. "Prince Charles . . ."

"Grandpapa, do you remember Agnis?" inquired Charles, knowing he had to introduce Agnis first.

Liesbeck momentarily softened his face and smiled. "Oh, Agnis . . ."

"The Princess of Fiana," Charles reminded him.

"Of course. How beautiful you have grown! I do, indeed, remember you—the smart girl from Fiana. I hope your father, the king, is well?"

"Yes, thank you. I am here by invitation of Prince Charles . . . but I actually have something I would like to discuss with you."

"Hm," said Liesbeck. "I should like nothing better. Unfortunately, Commander Giesen and I have some important business. Can this wait a while? I will have plenty of time to listen to you in two or three days."

Agnis didn't retreat an inch. "No. In fact, I think this regards the same matter, which is why I request that you listen to me now."

Commander Sven Giesen looked at her wide-eyed.

She's speaking up to the ex-king, and she's only a young woman. . . .

Agnis looked straight at Liesbeck and waited for his answer.

Liesbeck wrinkled his brow in plain annoyance; then, he heaved a diplomatic sigh. "Very well—but please, be brief."

"Thank you." Clearing her throat, Agnis told him everything—everything, that is, apart from what she'd learned about the devil Senzrabur.

"So, you see," she concluded, "I thought I would head to the jail on my own to help my friends, but I was worried

about what I saw at the treasury and decided to make my way here first."

Liesbeck nodded several times. "Thank you. Prince, you have a good friend. Look after her well."

"Yes, Grandpapa."

Once again, the prince had turned back into the diffident, shy, silent person he was with everyone except Agnis.

"In truth," continued the ex-king, "I was just talking to Sven about what took place at the treasury—exactly as you assumed, Princess Agnis. However, I did not know the people who were falsely accused of stealing Garcia's Golden Goblet were your travel companions."

Sven nodded. "I was not aware of this, either. Of course, I heard about the arrests, but who would have guessed that those two adventurers were companions of the Princess of Fiana? I will speak to Edward as soon as possible and have them released from jail."

Before Agnis could thank him, Liesbeck raised one hand. "Not so fast, Sven. Let me hear the end of your report. We will decide what happens then."

Sven bowed and resumed his report. Charles and Agnis gasped in surprise when they heard about Schneider's declaration of war.

Liesbeck sighed heavily at this news. Then, in an incredibly angry voice, he said, "What is this! I extinguish one spark of fire and another is already burning!"

CHAPTER 17:

THE SPY AND THE ASSASSIN

Approximately one week earlier, a spy had arrived at Orland Castle from the neighboring kingdom of Ganau. Some time ago, ex-King Liesbeck, acting on his own authority and in secret, dispatched four spies to Ganau, deciding it was necessary to keep a close watch on the movements of the King of Ganau, Tylus IV.

Two of these spies worked as servants in Ganau Castle; the other two posed as clerks for the cabinet minister. It was one of these latter spies, Chris Pikra, who had returned to the castle.

Needless to say, no one doubted there were also spies at work in Orland who had been dispatched by Tylus IV, though their identities had not been discovered by Liesbeck's spies yet. Still, it had been pretty well established that the agents of King Tylus were intent on exacerbating the divisions that were threatening to cast Orland into a three-way civil war between the factions of King Evesrin, Lord Schneider, and ex-King Liesbeck.

Pikra, standing before the king, gave his report in a nervous voice. "'Forget Liesbeck, that old badger. It seems he has taken up regretting his early retirement. He is the one who is the most troublesome; it will not be easy to trick him—first, let us focus our efforts on the useless king and that impetuous Schneider.'"

Liesbeck laughed bitterly. "So those are the exact words of Tylus IV, eh?"

Liesbeck and Tylus were close to the same age and had been similar types of king. The main difference between them was that Liesbeck retired early, handing over the crown to his son, while Tylus preferred to keep the reins of power in his own hands and hadn't given a moment's thought to the question of royal succession. Or, put another way, he'd given up worrying about it, knowing that none of his sons had the intelligence required.

With a nod, Pikra continued, "According to the intelligence, Tylus is planning to send two documents, one each to King Evesrin and Lord Schneider. The one to King Evesrin will detail Schneider's plans for rebellion, whereas the one to Schneider will set forth how the king is trying to expel Schneider from the country by falsely accusing him of a crime; the word 'execution' will be mentioned."

Liesbeck snorted. "Hmph. Those rascals! If my son and Schneider were to receive these documents, they would not even be suspicious. They are both so blindly suspicious of each other right now that they would swallow every lie, get all riled up, and do something rash."

"Yes," agreed Pikra. "And furthermore, Tylus is trying to make them suspicious of you, as well."

"It is like throwing a bone to a starving dog. They will both bite happily."

"We will not be able to avoid internal struggle."

"And the Silver-Gray Castle of Orland will be dyed crimson with blood."

Liesbeck's eaglelike face darkened, the wrinkles between his brows deepening. He was sure Tylus was planning to invade Orland, waiting for these internal struggles to make the kingdom weak, ripe for the plucking.

The vision rose inside Liesbeck's head as though he were already there. He ground his teeth in frustration. He had never allowed an enemy such a moment of opportunity when he had been king. Perhaps he *had* retired too early. He'd thought that by giving up the throne to his son, he would encourage the development of kingly characteristics in Evesrin. Experience is the best teacher, he'd reasoned. He'd told himself that once Evesrin—who lacked confidence and was easily swayed—felt the weight of the crown on his head, he'd become more responsible and firm.

But it hadn't worked out that way. Luckily, in the end, Liesbeck had decided to retain some small grip on his former power, operating secretly, in the shadows, and putting counter-measures in place to ensure the safety of the kingdom. Despite his efforts, tensions were rising as internal and external threats multiplied. Perhaps he had been too indulgent.

Pikra looked on in wonder at the expression of self-derision that had twisted the features of the ex-king, who was laughing quietly to himself.

Liesbeck then sat silently, as if deep in thought. When he glanced up, he motioned for Pikra to come closer.

"I understand the situation," he said. "We must destroy those secret documents before they reach Schneider and the king."

"By what means?" inquired Pikra.

"You are the spy," Liesbeck replied. "You must have a plan for this sort of thing."

Pikra nodded deeply. "In truth, I expected you would order the documents to be destroyed, so I contacted the assassins guild some time ago. If you wish, we can take care of the problem that way. It is a rough method, but we do not have much time."

"I agree," said Liesbeck. "It is distasteful, but this is the only way. Hm. I wonder what Tylus will think when he finds out his messengers have been killed, his forged documents destroyed. . . ."

"He will guess that you are behind it, moving from the shadows, as usual."

"Yes. And in that case, will he not have planned his next step already?"

"I do not think he will be able to react so swiftly."

"I hope you are right, Pikra. Well, so be it. I will leave the rest to you."

Pikra bowed deeply. "Yes, sir."

On his way back to Ganau, the spy stopped at the private house of a certain manager of the assassins guild.

The house looked exactly like a normal house. The man Pikra had come to see lived there with his grandparents and his children. When the door opened to Pikra's knock, the man's wife smiled at him, her fat arms covered in flour; she had been kneading dough in the kitchen. Without a word, Pikra showed her a piece of red cloth, at the sight of which the woman's expression became much less sociable.

"Around back," she said, closing the door in his face.

Behind the house was a small shack. Pikra knocked on the door, and it swung open to reveal a nondescript, common-looking man. Silently, he beckoned to Pikra.

The inside of the shack was small. There was a square hole in the floor, with a ladder leading down. The man descended this ladder, and Pikra followed him to the basement. It was there that the man spoke for the first time.

"I'll take that piece of cloth."

The red cloth was like a ticket for passage, and Pikra had paid a high price for it. The arrangement was that one piece of cloth was good for the performance of one service.

Pikra was not unhappy to give it up. The cloth had a strange, slippery feel to it, and it was actually more dark brown than red, as if it had been dyed in blood.

Tucking the cloth into his pocket, the man asked Pikra, "How many?"

"Two," answered Pikra.

"Relate the situation to me in as much detail as possible."

Pikra gave him as much information as he had.

After he had listened to it all, the man spoke again. "It'll cost you ten thousand Gs a piece, half up front as a deposit."

"I understand," said Pikra. "I'll have it for you by tomorrow. However, what proof will I have that the men have been, er, dealt with?"

The man responded with a cold smile. "Do you need heads?"

Pikra realized suddenly that this ordinary-looking man, who resembled a common laborer, was actually a fearsome killer. Unable to speak, the spy shook his head from side to side.

The assassin grunted. "Good. Heads are heavy and draw attention. How about ears? They're easy to carry and to conceal. I'll give you ears from the two men as proof that they've been killed."

"Yes, that's fine," said Pikra, eager to get back into the sunlight. "Oh, and don't forget the secret documents. They must be destroyed. That's the most important part."

"Yes, yes." The man was no longer looking at Pikra.

"Hm. See you tomorrow then."

Pikra climbed the ladder and left the hideout of the assassin behind him without once looking back. But he couldn't get the vision of the man's yellowed teeth and evil, sadistic smirk out of his mind. They would give him nightmares for the next week.

The man dispatched by the assassins guild was a healthy-looking individual who did not look out of place in his travelers' clothes. After all, assassins have to blend in with normal people. No one seeing this man, whose looks were a perhaps a trifle condescending, would have guessed that he had the cold heart of a grim reaper and took people's lives without regret.

Such were the thoughts of Pikra when he saw the man, whose name was Land. At least, that's how he introduced himself, although Pikra felt sure it was an alias. The man was still young and had a slender physique, with brown hair and eyes.

At first, Pikra thought they would need two assassins for the two messengers, and he was surprised when a single man appeared. When he inquired about this, however, Land sneered, showing his white teeth.

"It's okay if you don't like it. After all, you're paying. But consider for a moment: The watchwords of the guild are 'discretion' and 'efficiency.' Members who can't live up to these ideals don't last long, if you get my meaning. So you better believe that if the guild managers sent one person, they've judged that one person is enough."

"Hm." Pikra considered. King Tylus' messengers were departing for Orland tonight or early tomorrow—there was no time to order another assassin. And he didn't really want to see the manager of the guild again. He sighed: There really was no choice. Nodding reluctantly, he handed the assassin a memo describing his two targets before he began relating his instructions verbally.

Land, who had been looking at the memo while he was listening, opened his eyes wide. "Hey, this Level 6 guy, Samuel, is fine, but what's up with this Clay Judah Anderson? Adventuring Level 16? And he's only twenty-four, a year older than me—how the heck did he get to 16 already?"

"If it's too much for you," Pikra began, but Land interrupted quickly.

"I'm not the sort of guy who takes the difficult route. There's no way in hell I'd tackle this monster of a fighter head on. But don't worry, I'll get him in his sleep or something. There's more than one way to skin a cat. Just make sure you have the rest of the money ready when I come back with the ears."

Pikra had been about to say, "Don't complain so much," but he realized that it might not be a good idea to antagonize an assassin. He decided it was time to take his leave.

Land didn't even look at the departing Pikra, instead continuing to study the memo and grumbling under his breath.

CHAPTER 18:

THE RED KNIGHTS' ARMY

iesbeck related this information matter-of-factly to Agnis and Charles. "By now," the ex-king concluded, "the two messengers are history."

It terrified Agnis that this old man could speak of such things so calmly. It was as if the lives of one or two people had no more weight than a scrap of paper when it came to the serious affairs of the nation.

Charles, who had been listening intently, only now understood how advanced the sickness was that had overtaken his country. One might even say that it was terminal. Perhaps it was necessary to undergo some surgery—to lose some blood and remove something—before there could be a cure.

"So, that is how diseased our country has become," said Prince Charles, speaking up for once. Yet it wasn't so much a statement critical of his grandfather as it was an expression of his own pain.

Liesbeck gazed inquiringly at his grandson.

My son Evesrin has grown up to be unbelievably selfish, self-centered, and paranoid, always afraid of how things might hurt him and never able to see the larger picture. But his son . . . Charles is not to be overlooked. From his appearance, the prince looks unreliable and definitely not suited to politics; but my, oh my, he seems far wiser than his father.

Just as Liesbeck started to see a little hope for the future in his grandchild, the door to the room opened with a loud bang. Liesbeck's followers tumbled in, shouting.

"Lord Liesbeck, it's terrible! Schneider has gathered soldiers and started a rebellion!"

Agnis and Charles leapt to their feet as another follower came running in.

"The Black Knights' Army is returning fire!" he reported breathlessly. "It's unknown whether King Evesrin is safe. The trouble may spread here, too. Please, escape!"

Liesbeck firmly gripped the arms of his chair. "So, it finally has begun."

Charles wrapped his arms around himself, his face deathly pale.

Seeing this, Agnis leaned close. "Charles, get a grip," she said. "We have to escape! Where would it be best to flee?"

The prince weakly shook his head. "N-no, it doesn't matter where we run, we'll still get caught. We're dealing with Schneider. He knows every corner of this castle, even the secret escape routes."

Now, they could hear the sound of explosions mixing in with the noise of the rain.

Agnis ran wide-eyed to the window and saw fires burning here and there about the castle grounds. She saw people running around in fear. She heard screaming and bellowing and the clashing of swords.

Then, all at once, soldiers dressed in red came barging into the room. They wore red full-face helmets and red armor. In fact, they were dressed top to bottom in red. This was not the Black Knights' Army. These soldiers belonged to the Red Knights' Army.

About twenty of them entered the room, kicking down the door and smashing the windows. Soon, Liesbeck and the others were surrounded.

CHAPTER 19:

A SURPRISE VISITOR

Olba, who had been nodding off again, jumped at the sound of explosions. "Whoa, what was that?!"

"It sounded like something blowing up!" Duan got to his feet and walked over to the jail cell's iron bars, trying to figure out what was happening outside. However, there was nothing to see but the filthy wall and floor.

"Cripes, they haven't started a war, have they?" came the voice of their neighbor.

"War?" echoed Duan. "Do you mean they've been invaded by another country? Is that a possibility? Has it happened before? We don't know anything about Orland—can you tell us?"

The man was happy to oblige. "Well, it's a long story—"

Olba cut him off. "Make it short."

"Hmph." The man sounded offended. "Well, I ain't gonna force you to listen to it."

"Why are you being so childish? If it really is a war, then we might be abandoned here," said Duan.

To which Olba added, "On the other hand, we could use it to our advantage and escape."

"You think? Could we really escape? I'm actually a father of three, and they're waitin' eagerly for my return. Just thinkin' about my poor tykes makes my heart ache 'n' ache."

"C'mon, just tell us," said Duan. "What's happening in this country?"

"Allrighty—if you let me come when you escape!"

"Well, if it's possible."

"Okey dokey, I'll tell you all I know."

Their fellow prisoner briefly explained the domestic history of Orland and the neighboring country of Ganau. But the man wasn't exactly a professional historian, and what he told them was full of gossip and exaggeration.

"So that means we're in deep trouble," the man concluded. "It's possible that our neighbors are invadin' and that we're havin' internal conflict. You know, civil war."

"What, both at the same time?" asked Duan.

Olba nodded thoughtfully. "It's probably the other way around: There were some internal problems, and then the neighbors started to invade."

"Hey, the jailers are runnin' away!" screamed the man next door.

"Really?" Duan clung to the iron bars and desperately tried to see what was happening.

"Really, truly. Shoot, the keys are right there!"

"You can see them? The keys?"

"Yup, they're hanging on the wall over there."

"Is there any way we can get them?"

"If there was, I would've done it already!"

"That's true." Duan turned away, disappointed. Then, like something out of a dream, he heard a familiar voice.

"Duan, Duan! Where are you? Gi-iis!"

"Check?!" He turned and clung to the bars again, putting one hand through the gap and wildly waving it. "This way, Check! Hey, we're over here!"

"Check see! Check come, cha!"

And seconds later, the little grinia flew between the bars.

"Wow, Check, am I ever glad to see you! I've been worried about you!"

"Check worried, too!"

"How did you find us?"

"Cha! Check smell!"

"Right."

Though winged-lizards don't have a particularly keen sense of smell—relying more on their eyes than their noses—they are deeply imprinted with their mother's smell upon hatching; and since Duan was the only one there when Check hatched, the baby grinia had been imprinted with *his* smell.

After he left Charles' room, Check had wandered about the castle looking at this and that, investigating everything that piqued his curiosity—which was, well, pretty much everything. In the course of this, he came across a familiar smell. This led him to a storehouse where Duan's and Olba's armor was being kept, packed away in a box. The grinia had realized that Duan must be somewhere nearby, and he began searching for his scent. Thus, Check arrived at the prison.

"Smell Olba, too, giis!" he added now. "Need bath, cha!"

At this, Olba laughed. "You've come at a good time, Check. We have a job for you."

"Check heal?" The little grinia always was eager to use his modest healing abilities to help his friends.

"Oh, right! No, no, that isn't it."

Duan immediately understood Olba's idea. Now, he said to Check, "Um, we want you to go get the keys to open this cell."

"Check go! Where keys?"

"Can you ask the person next door?"

"Check ask, gi–iis!" Check zoomed back through the bars.

Meanwhile, Duan called out to their neighbor: "This grinia is called Check, and he's my pal. Can you show him where the keys are? I think he'll be able to get them."

"What, this little feller? That's amazin'! But don't forget: You promised to take me with you."

"Of course."

"Hm. I ain't sure yer friend here's got the strength to—ow, ow!"

"Hey, Check," called Duan at the exclamations of pain from the neighboring cell. "What are you doing to him? Stop that!"

"Why, the little so-and-so pulled my ear!" cried the man. Luckily, he didn't seem angry. "Heh, heh. He sure is feisty! Okay, Mr. Check, have a look at that wall over there."

"Check see!"

CHAPTER 20:

CHECK TO THE RESCUE!

heck, you can do it!" Duan was cheering on the grinia.

However, all the keys to the jail were attached to a heavy iron ring, making them far too heavy for Check to hold as he flew. Even dragging them along the ground was taxing his strength to the breaking point. When he finally moved into Duan's field of vision, he looked completely worn out.

"Check!" Duan called to him again.

Check briefly looked Duan's way. The grinia was breathing heavily, his tiny shoulders jerking up and down, and he looked like he was in some pain. He repeatedly rubbed together his little hands and breathed onto them.

"Check, are you all right?" Duan asked worriedly.

Olba wasn't having any of that. "C'mon, Check! Don't stand there. Move it! Is that the best you can do?"

Olba's taunts angered Check. Taking another deep breath, he tightened his grip on the keys and dragged them inch by inch across the floor. When he finally got to the point where Duan could reach his hand between the bars and touch the keys, he collapsed onto his back.

"Yes, well done!" crowed Olba. "Here, Duan, gimme those keys!"

Olba took the keys from Duan's hand, picked out one key on the ring, and tried the lock. The door swung right open.

"Wow," exclaimed Duan, impressed. "You guessed well!"

Olba winked back at him. "That was no guess! I kept a close watch when they first locked us in here. The key they used was especially long, like this one, see? Remember, kid: Always keep your eyes open."

As they left the cell, their neighbor cried out desperately, "Hey, you haven't forgotten your promise, have you? You're supposed to be taking me with you!"

Duan was surprised when he finally saw the man in the next cell: His head was covered by a cloth mask.

At Duan's stare, the man said, "Oh, this. I can't remember for the life of me why or when they put it on me. Anyway, can't you get the door opened?"

Olba handed Duan the keyring. Duan tried key after key; on the sixth try, the door swung open.

"Phew, thanks," said the man as he stepped out. "Think you could take off this mask, too?" And he turned his back to Duan.

"Sure. How horrible! It even has a lock."

Sure enough, the mask was tied tightly at the back and secured by a lock.

"The key should be on that ring. The smallest one . . . yes, that one. C'mon, mister—please, get it off quickly!"

"Yes, yes. Stop squirming!"

It was difficult because the key was small, but Duan finally managed to unlock the mask and remove it.

"Phew," sighed the man heavily. "I feel alive again! Yeah, I couldn't figure out why they bothered to put that mask on me."

When Duan saw the face of the grumbling man, he was flabbergasted. The man had been saying all kinds of weird things, and he spoke in a way that made him sound like a lowly thief; yet he was very good looking and had real poise. He had silky, wavy black hair and an elegant, manly, slightly tanned profile. He also had a trimmed mustache. He was tall and looked to be in his late thirties. There was beauty in his broad chest and long arms and legs. He wore a white silk shirt and thin beige pants. They were slightly dirty (it was unavoidable after a long stay in a dirty jail cell!), but Duan could see from one glance that they were expensive.

As far as Duan was concerned, this only added to the mystery of why the guards had put a mask on him.

Olba regarded the man with suspicion. Then, he quickly turned, snatched up one of the torches hanging on the wall, and began to walk off with large strides. "C'mon, let's get going!"

Duan put Check on his shoulder and followed after him. He also took one of the torches.

"H-hey, wait! I'll come with you!" screamed the man who looked like a nobleman as he grabbed Duan's arm.

"Well, come on then," said Duan.

"I can't find one o' my shoes. . . ." The man was wearing only one black boot. He hopped back into his cell.

"What? Oh, please! Hey, Olba—wait!" Duan called to Olba. The big fighter had stopped walking and was peering into another cell.

"Is there someone there, too?" Duan asked.

"Yeah," said Olba. "Looks like he's sleeping peacefully."

When Duan looked in through the bars, he saw a small man wearing clothes that showed he'd been there for a while; he was curled up, sound asleep. In fact, he almost looked dead. It was a wonder that the explosions or all the other commotion hadn't woken him. His face was small and round—and bright red from drinking. If not for the circumstances, he wouldn't have seemed like anything more than a drunk.

"We should let him go," commented Duan.

"Y'know, we don't have time to help other people, get it?" shouted Obla. "We have our hands full protecting our own lives!"

Duan couldn't argue. He gave a little shrug and went back in the direction of the other man.

"Have you found your missing boot?"

"Yup. Sorry." The man had put it on and was standing up again.

Just then, there was another loud bang, like an explosion; they could feel the vibrations in their stomachs, and the floor shook.

"Argh!"

They clung desperately to the nearby pillars to keep from falling over.

The man let out a shriek that didn't suit his face. "Eek! Help!"

"Enough of that," cried Olba. "Follow me, on the double!" He ran toward the exit. Duan and the other man followed behind. But Olba suddenly stopped and turned around to look at Duan.

"What now?" asked Duan, perplexed.

"Throw the keys into the drunk's cell," Olba said.

"Oh, right. Yeah!"

Duan did as he was told and threw the bundle of keys into the cell where the small man lay fast asleep. He didn't budge and, for a moment, Duan thought the man really was dead. Then, he saw his chest rising and falling. He laughed in relief and hurried after Olba.

CHAPTER 21:

BEHIND THE SECRET DOOR

So, Check, how did you get here?" asked Duan. "Where's Agnis—er, were you *with* Agnis?"

Check tilted his small head. "Girl gone, cha!"

"Gone? So how did you manage to get here?"

"Check find way."

"Yes, but how?"

"Secret to K'nock."

"What?" Duan held his head in his hands. He couldn't understand what the grinia was telling him. He took a deep breath and tried again. "K'nock is here? This is really important, Check, so think carefully and answer."

"Gi-iis! Cat here!"

"And Agnis? Is she here, too?"

"Girl go somewhere."

"Somewhere? Oh, I get it. Um, Check, I'm asking you who you came to the castle with. I know that you probably came *here*, to the jail, by yourself."

Check tilted his head again at the question, only this time tilting it the opposite direction. "Check come with girl and cat."

"Right. And where is she now?"

"Don't know. Go with boy."

"What boy? What was his name, Check?"

"Name . . . whachamacallit."

Check's story was ambiguous, to say the least. However, Duan had found out that Agnis and K'nock were somewhere in Orland Castle. "Hm. Maybe that boy was the prince—you know, that childhood friend of hers."

"Probably," answered Olba.

Duan made a quick sigh. It was a strange feeling: He was worried and relieved at the same time. Suddenly, he looked up at Olba. "Olba, oh no! We can't dawdle!"

"What?"

"If Agnis really is with the prince, she's in danger! She'll be targeted!"

"Yeah, that's probably true," mused the big fighter. "They probably have a lot of bodyguards, though, like those Black Knights."

"Yeah, but what if Agnis was headed off on her own, and she accidentally went somewhere there were a lot of enemies? Knowing Agnis, it's not implausible. Even if he is a prince, he wouldn't necessarily walk around with bodyguards in his own castle. Then, what if they suddenly barged in and surrounded them? What should we do?!"

With difficulty, Olba swallowed the words "How the hell should I know." He saw how upset Duan was and realized that this wasn't a good time to be poking fun at him. So instead, he said, "Okay, okay. We can't do anything to help Agnis until we escape from here, though."

"That's true," agreed Duan. "Plus, we really should find our baggage. It wouldn't be too clever to rush off to her rescue without armor and weapons."

"Good luck finding our stuff in a castle this size," said Olba. "We have no idea where to start looking. We don't even know where we are now—or where we're going, for that matter."

This was all too true. They had escaped from the prison, but the paths from there were getting extremely complicated. They were dizzy from all the twists and turns they'd taken, all the times they'd had to backtrack from dead ends, all the stairs they'd climbed and descended, all the doors they'd opened into empty rooms with doors of their own, leading to more paths and stairs and doors.

"I think it'd be a stretch to ever get out of here," said Olba, wrinkling his forehead.

"Don't you think we'll get out above ground if we go through here?" asked Duan. They stood at the bottom of a stone staircase; coming from the top was the sound of falling rain.

"Yeah, maybe—if we make it through *here*."

What Olba was referring to were the iron bars planted in front of the staircase, blocking the way. There was a door set into the bars, but it was locked and didn't move one bit.

"If only we had a thief with us." Olba clicked his tongue, remembering the last thief he'd traveled with. The guy had been a jerk, but his skills were impeccable. He would've had this lock open in two seconds. He could have done it with his eyes closed.

"Right," sighed Duan. "I suppose it would be good to study locksmithing for situations like this."

Suddenly, the man they had freed from the neighboring cell, who'd been following them silently all this time, spoke up. "Stand aside and let me take a look."

Olba eyed him skeptically. "You can open locks?"

The man giggled. "Hee hee. I'm actually in the thieving business—thirty years now."

"Is that true!?" Duan looked at him wide-eyed. The man didn't look anything like a thief . . . not that Duan was sure what a thief should look like, exactly.

"Here we go," said the man meanwhile, bending over to work on the lock of the door. "Hm? Hm," he mumbled to himself as he probed and prodded, tilting his head this way and that.

At last, he sighed and straightened up. "It doesn't look like it's going to open."

"Some thief you are," said Olba. "A simple lock like this should be child's play for a real thief."

The man apologized again and again.

"If it won't open, it won't open," said Duan. "Look, why don't we try this direction?"

Finally, after many more wrong turns and disappointments, they made it above ground. In fact, they found a window and, when they looked outside, they saw that they somehow had managed to reach a height about two floors up.

"Shoot, how the heck can we get down there?"

As Olba was looking here and there in the narrow corridor, Check found a door—a secret door so well concealed in the wall that you could barely even tell it was there.

"Hey, Check's found something," said Olba, going over to take a look. He turned to the self-proclaimed thief. "You were examining this wall earlier, right? What kind of thief misses a secret door?"

Again, the man apologized energetically.

Ignoring him, Olba cautiously opened the door and peeked through.

On the other side, a pitched battle was raging between Red Knights and Black Knights.

CHAPTER 22:

THE RED AND THE BLACK

lba blinked in amazement. Then, with an awkward laugh, he quickly shut the door. "Er, I'm going to pretend I didn't see that."

"What did you see? You're acting suspicious," said Duan.

Olba stepped aside. "Go ahead, see for yourself."

"Okay, I will," said Duan.

"Me too, me too," said the man from the cell next door. "Gi–iis! Check look, too!"

Rolling his eyes, Duan opened the door and poked out his head. The others looked over his shoulder.

Bang! He slammed the door shut straightaway.

"W-what was that?" he stammered.

"Wow, that was scary!" exclaimed the man from the cell next door.

"Men fight, cha!" contributed Check.

"Right?" Olba said triumphantly, regarding Duan with his arms crossed over his chest and a smug expression on his face.

"I don't know why you're gloating," Duan said. "We're in the middle of a civil war, without any weapons or armor."

Olba's expression turned to a frown. "I haven't forgotten. I don't suppose there's any chance our baggage is somewhere nearby. . . ."

It certainly wasn't in the dreary landing where they now stood amid broken chairs and barrels lying on the dusty floor.

"There must be other exits, right?" asked Duan.

"The regular exit is probably where that locked iron lattice was back there."

Duan sighed heavily. "Then, there's no other way. We have to get out of here and look for our things."

"Do you really want to go out into the peak of that violent battle?" Olba asked, shaking his head. "I'll tell you right now, I ain't gonna do that. If we're attacked, we won't be able to deal with it."

"I'm getting more and more worried about Agnis," said Duan. "Can't we just break through all the fighting somehow?"

"No way," said Olba. "I'm not going out there bare-handed, and that's final. It would be tantamount to suicide." He glanced down in annoyance at Check, who had been tugging persistently at his boots. "What do you want, Check?"

The grinia was clenching a very small rock in his tiny hands, and he was looking up at Olba with sparkling round eyes.

"What?" the big fighter asked again.

Check grinned and handed the small rock to Olba.

"Huh?" Then, he understood. Check wanted Olba to use the rock as a weapon. "Are you crazy? A little rock against swords and armor?" He aimed a kick at Check, which the agile grinia dodged with ease.

Check glared up at Olba as if to say "Pah! To reject such kindness!" Then, he went to gather more rocks.

"Look, the only sensible thing to do is wait it out and see what happens." So saying, Olba sat down on the floor.

"How long should we wait?" asked Duan.

"How should I know? Thirty minutes, an hour? Sooner or later, the fighting will be over, and they'll either be gone or dead. Then, we can slip out."

"Hm. I guess that makes sense."

Duan crossed his arms and thought. There was reason in what Olba was saying. In fact, he knew that it was definitely the right course of action to take. But for some reason, he had a bad feeling about it. Something told him there wasn't time to dawdle.

Duan raised his head and said, "Listen, Olba, I think we should try to get past them now. It's just a feeling I have. I know that if something goes wrong, we could be in trouble, but I think we'll be okay. They're too busy battling one another to notice us creeping by. Of course, if you're scared . . ."

"What?" Olba shot to his feet. "Who said anything about being scared? Shoot, I don't want to be wasting time here any more than you do. Okay, let's go. Try not to draw attention to yourself—and that goes double for you, Check."

After extinguishing the flame from their torch, they opened the door again and quietly snuck outside.

Clinging and clanging metallic sounds resounded through the air. There were about ten Black Knights and twice as many Red Knights. Yet, despite the Red Knights' numerical superiority, the Black Knights' fighting skills were whittling down the odds. Even so, the Black Army definitely was struggling. It was a serious fight, sword to sword. But at least it seemed that Duan had been right: The combatants were so absorbed in the battle that they didn't notice the newcomers.

"Which way should we go?" whispered Duan.

They were at a place where the corridor changed direction, branching in three different directions. The ceiling was high, and it was almost spacious enough to be a room.

Olba pointed his chin to the right. It seemed there were fewer knights down that corridor. Duan nodded in agreement. They stealthily made their way behind a thick pillar at the corner of the corridor.

Breathing a sigh of relief, the harried group regarded one another. The man from the adjoining jail cell looked scared out of his wits. His talkativeness had vanished completely.

"What should we do first?" Duan asked, still whispering.

"Hm. I think we should either look for Agnis or try to find our baggage," Olba whispered back. "Not that we know which way to go, anyway."

"Let's get Check to show us the way," Duan suggested. "If he can lead us back to K'nock, K'nock probably can take us to Agnis."

"Makes sense," granted Olba. "Do you think Check is capable of finding his way back from here? Regardless, if he flies somewhere we can't follow, that's the end of it."

"I suppose so. But we should try, anyway. Hey, Check."

Check was surprised to hear his name. He glanced up at Duan as if to say, "What is it?"

"Um, do you remember where you were when you were with K'nock?"

"Check remember, gi-iis."

"You probably won't know how to get there from here, though—I don't suppose you remember this place, do you?"

"Check remember!" the grinia insisted.

"What? Really?"

"Check come here."

"Huh? Oh, right! You mean you passed this way."

"Cha! Smell Duan!"

"You caught my scent? From the jail, you mean?"

"From room. Olba, too, gi-iis!"

"Room?" mused Olba. "Do you think . . . ?"

Duan glanced at Olba, nodded, and then looked at Check again. "Check, this is really important. Can you guide us back to that room? Can you go there again?"

The grinia nodded proudly. "Check know way!"

"Great, Check! Let's go! I promise I'll give you a lot of nice food to eat later."

"Cha! Want malt liquor!"

Led by Check, the three men stepped into the corridor— just in time to find the way blocked by a large man in a full-face helmet and black, shiny, full-body armor. He was holding a halberd with both hands. One glance at that armor was enough to identify him as a member of the Black Knights' Army.

CHAPTER 23:

THE RED SORCERER

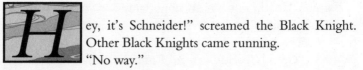ey, it's Schneider!" screamed the Black Knight. Other Black Knights came running.

"No way."

"Why would he be *here?*"

"Maybe it isn't him!"

The enemy Red Knights also were confused as they looked on from afar.

Olba, Duan, Check, and the man from the cell next door clumped together and looked questioningly at the Black Knights who stood around them with drawn swords.

The Black Knight who had spoken first, using the tip of his massive halberd, poked at the man from the adjoining cell—the man who said he'd been a thief for thirty years—and said, "Schneider, why are you running around and hiding? You coward! You started this rebellion, but it doesn't look like you have the stomach to stick around and finish it!"

Duan and Olba were shocked when they heard this.

"Schneider?" asked Duan, turning to the man from the cell next door. "Isn't that who you were talking about earlier—the important guy who was the head of the second-most powerful faction of the country?"

"Hey, you've tricked us, you rat!" cried Olba.

The man in question shook his head time and time again. "N-no! You've gotta be kiddin' me! Look at me—I couldn't be Lord Schneider in a million years. M'name's Carlos, and I'm just a worthless nobody."

His whole body was shaking, and he rubbed together his hands as he obsequiously bowed his head again and again.

At his attitude and accent, the Black Knights shot one another puzzled glances.

"Hm. Could this be a lookalike?"

"No, impossible. I can't imagine there would be someone who looked so much like Schneider!"

"What's going on?"

"We should take them with us. We can investigate later."

"That's true."

It looked as though Duan and Olba, along with their mysterious neighbor, were about to be captured once again.

"This ain't good," Olba whispered into Duan's ear. "Get ready to fight, kid!"

Duan couldn't answer at first because he was shaking his head so hard that he was getting dizzy. Finally, he pursed together his lips and said, "No, wait! It may be a good tactic to let them capture us. That way, we'll be taken to the Black Knights' base. Then, we'll be able to find out more information. And maybe we'll get some information on Agnis, too!"

"Hm. You may be right . . . but I don't like being captured so many times! It's tough on a guy's ego." Olba heaved a despondent sigh. "If only I had my weapons!" And so saying, he struck a pose as if he were holding a sword in his hands. He was a natural-born fighter, and being without weapons or armor was like being naked to him. He felt exposed and somehow inadequate.

Just when Olba and Duan had decided to allow themselves to be taken prisoner without a fight, a commotion arose among the Red Knights: "Look, it's the queen!"

Suddenly, Queen Milhene appeared on a landing about twenty steps up, nearly on the second floor. She seemed to have been captured by a pair of Red Knights and a strange man who wore a red robe with a hood that hid his eyes.

"Argh!" cried the queen. "What is happening here? Call Schneider—you will be sorry!" As she protested loudly, the queen was hitting and kicking the arms and legs of the Red Knights who held her. She was wearing a moss pink, lacy silk dress with a white gown; looking at her, Duan guessed that she had been lounging in her room when the conflict erupted and had been captured while she was running about in confusion. Her maids probably had been captured, too.

Sure enough, a moment later, her handmaids appeared, imprisoned by more Red Knights. Like their royal mistress,

they were fighting back and complaining nonstop.

"Release the queen!" shouted a Black Knight.

"It's cowardly to take women hostage!" called another.

The Black Knight next to him whispered, "Well, I suppose it's only to be expected."

At which the Black Knight standing behind him gave his helmet a thump to quiet him. "What should we do?"

"The queen comes first," spoke the Black Knight with the large halberd, who was evidently the company's leader.

"Roger. I'll guard Schneider."

"Good."

The Black Knights gathered beneath the landing. At that moment, the man in the red robe started to move his wrinkled lips and whispered something.

A bolt of lightning crashed into the Black Knights.

"Argh!"

A number of the Black Knights collapsed. Luckily, it didn't seem as though any of them had received a direct hit—but they were hesitant to attack now.

It's a sorcerer! Duan realized.

He and Olba stood helplessly, watching events unfold.

The Black Knights struggled to their feet again as the red-robed sorcerer tried to get his hands around the queen's thin white neck. She screamed at once.

"What are you doing? I said 'stop'! You filthy old man! I'm getting chills from your touch!"

The sorcerer weakened slightly at these words. Then, he extended his hands again.

"Aaah!" cried the queen. "Don't touch me! AAAH!"

Her scream, really more of a screech, resounded from floor, walls, and ceiling; it made Duan's ears ring.

The sorcerer looked like he was completely enraged now. He covered the queen's mouth, muffling her screams so that all that could be heard was a kind of grunting noise.

The sorcerer glared at the queen. His eyes were terrifying— the whites were completely red.

He started to chant another spell. This time, it was clear that the target would be the queen herself.

"Shoot!" whispered Olba.

The Black Knights screamed "Stop!" and rushed toward the sorcerer, but there was no way they'd make it in time.

The sorcerer smirked in triumph.

But just as he was about to poke his rough and bony finger into the queen's neck, they were both shoved from behind. Because it was unexpected, the sorcerer lost his balance and tumbled over, severely hitting his hip and the back of his head. At the same time, a bolt of lightning came blasting out from his finger: It struck the ceiling, dislodging a number of rocks, which came crashing down.

The queen also tumbled; in her case, she fell forward, right off the landing.

"Aiieee!"

Once again, the sound of the Queen's screech reverberated all around. It was so loud that everyone was too stunned by it to even think about rescuing her. Black and Red Knights alike winced and covered their ears.

Yet the queen didn't hit the floor.

A tall man appeared out of nowhere and caught her in his arms.

He wore a narrow sword at his hip, and on top of some flexible black leather armor, he wore special black metal armor. The man gave his head a shake, tossing back the luxuriant strands of black hair that had fallen into his eyes; in the process, he revealed a face that was thin but in no way weak-looking. His almond eyes were clear and warm.

The queen stared up at this mystery man in awe, her mouth agape.

He smiled at her and asked her in a deep voice, "I hope you aren't hurt?"

Her response was to start screaming again, as loud as she could. Although this time the screaming wasn't out of absolute terror. Her eyes moistened and her cheeks reddened as she screamed.

"Aaah! Aaah! Who are you? Who are you? Aaah! I don't believe this!"

The surprised man hesitated for one moment; then, after deciding it couldn't be helped, he shut the queen's mouth with one firm hand. "She's one noisy woman."

Suddenly, a slender, red-haired man appeared from the landing where the sorcerer still lay. He was the one who had slammed into the sorcerer and the queen. "Sorry," he said laughingly. "I was planning to give the old coot a good shove, but I guess I don't know my own strength—I wound up sending the queen flying, as well." He held his left hand behind his back, as if he'd hurt it.

This man's name was Land. The other man's name was Clay Judah Anderson; he later would become known as the Blue Paladin in legends told throughout the ages.

CHAPTER 24:

A WEIRD DANCE WITH A WEIRD SONG

eanwhile, the injured sorcerer stirred. Although unable to stand, he lifted his upper body from the ground and screamed, "Why aren't you doing anything? Fight! Kill them!" He once again passed out.

But his commands had their effect: The Red Knights, swords in hand, rushed to attack the Black Knights and Clay Judah Anderson. Others tried to recapture the queen. The sound of clanging swords commenced once more.

Clay Judah's movements were hindered by the queen, who was clinging to him for dear life. Even so, with just one hand, he fought off attacks from all directions. The Red Knights definitely were not skilled fighters. They easily dropped their swords, and their movements were sluggish. However, they were strong individuals, and there were a lot of them, and it began to seem as if they would never be exhausted. They were defeated time after time; but even when knocked unconscious, they would recover in a second or two, resuming their attack. On the other hand, the Black Knights slowly were being obliterated, despite their superior fighting skills.

"Friggin' heck," growled Olba through gritted teeth, "it burns my bacon to stand here like a wallflower at dance!" The Black Knight set to guard the man who looked like Schneider was holding Olba and Duan prisoner, as well. It would've been easy for Olba to grab the guard's halberd; but in the current circumstances, it may not have been the wisest move. Olba fretted over it for a few seconds before quickly making up his mind: *Heck, I'll leave the fretting to Duan!*

Olba was quick to decide and even quicker to act. He snatched the halberd from the startled guard and began to assist Clay Judah in the hard battle. With this additional new force, the Black Knights also were galvanized.

"Hey, you guys—which side are you on?!"

Duan tilted his head when the guard asked him this question. The Black Knights *had* captured them twice already, not something easily forgotten, but Olba was fighting on the side of the Black Knights, against the Red Knights. No wonder the guard was confused!

"We're on your side," explained Duan. "We actually came to this country because Princess Agnis asked us to."

"Princess Agnis? Of Fiana?"

"Yes. She's a childhood friend of Prince Charles."

"Oh? And why were you escorting Schneider?"

"We weren't escorting him; we just happened to escape together. And anyway, we didn't even know who this person was. In fact, we've never even heard or seen Schneider!"

The man from the adjoining cell broke in. "Like I told you before, Schneider is an important man in this country—even the king acknowledges that. He heads the leading opposition party, and—"

"Yes, we've heard that already," interrupted Duan somewhat irritably. "In fact, we heard it just a moment ago. What I wanted to say was . . ." Duan broke off, deciding the rest was too stupid to explain. It still didn't change the fact that they didn't know what was going on. Duan glanced at Check and sighed.

At that moment, the sorcerer who'd been struck down by Land regained consciousness and struggled to his feet.

"Finally awake?" Land called to him, mockingly. Without a word, the sorcerer raised his eyebrows and sprang at Land.

"Whoa, what the heck!"

Avoiding the clumsy attack, Land swept the sorcerer's feet out from under him. The man landed with a thud on his rear. As if suddenly realizing that he wasn't going to win this fight by strength alone, he started to chant another spell.

"Shoot," said Land, leaning down over the ledge. "Hey, this guy started chanting again! Yo, Clay Judah! What should I do?"

"Don't let him cast those spells!" cried Clay Judah as he fought. "Do something to stop him!"

Land pondered over the situation for a while. "Okay, got it," he said at last. He promptly started dancing around the sorcerer.

"Heehoo! Yayhoo! Eihoo! Come on, come on!" It was a weird dance with a weird song. He looked and sounded like a madman as he sang the melody and wildly swung his limbs.

The sorcerer wasn't able to complete his spell. Looking on, Duan thought the man was holding his injured head in agony when, suddenly, the sorcerer burst into laughter.

"S-stop it! Stop this man!" he screamed. "Agh, it's too ridiculous!"

However, the Red Knights were busy defending themselves from Black Knights, who were attacking with renewed energy now that Olba had joined the fray. The tide of battle definitely had turned; seeing this, the sorcerer, although still wheezing with laughter, managed to gasp out an order.

"Argh! Retreat! Retreat!"

Then, the strangest thing happened: The sorcerer's red robe billowed up, and a gust of hot wind surrounded the Red Knights. It lifted them into the air, spinning them around and around like leaves in a whirlwind. Before anyone could react, the Red Knights had disappeared.

CHAPTER 25:

WHY DO GENTLEMEN LOVE WAR SO?

After witnessing the sudden disappearance of the Red Knights and the sorcerer, the remaining Black Knights sat down on the spot, as though they were crumbling to the ground.

Only heavy breathing could be heard. Nobody spoke. Everyone was too exhausted to speak. Well, almost everyone . . .

"So, are you a knight, sir? Or just an adventurer?" said Queen Milhene to Clay Judah, still holding tightly to his arm. "Oh, I know. Perhaps you wanted to enter into the Black Knights' Army? If so, you can relax: I will give you a recommendation."

Clay Judah was pondering how to reply when Land answered for him.

"This fella—he's not here to join any army. He has a message for your king, and he's come to deliver it."

The queen looked suspiciously at Land, inspecting him from head to toe. "I . . . see," she said in a dubious tone of voice. "If you have business with the king, I can receive the message in his place. I am the queen of this country."

"We kind of figured that out," laughed Land.

"I-I have no business with you," stammered the queen. "Do not talk to me. I am speaking with this gentleman."

And she turned back to Clay Judah with a smile. "Oh yes, I haven't asked you your name yet. What is it? I am Milhene."

Clay Judah knelt on the spot, bowing his head down in front of the queen. "I beg your pardon for the delay. My name is Clay Judah Anderson. I am from Ronza, and I am on a training journey at the moment, as a fighter. Just as my friend Land here mentioned, I have brought a message for the king."

With this display of courteousness, the queen felt more and more attracted to Clay Judah. "Oh, I see," she said, blushing. "Why not tell me the rest of the story in my comfortable room?"

She aggressively tugged at his arm and started to lead him away, but the company commander of the Black Knights wouldn't hear of it.

"P-please wait a moment, Your Majesty! Your rooms are too dangerous now. Please, let us retreat to where the king is."

Queen Milhene had no argument. They *had* been attacked by the Red Knights, and she very nearly had been abducted— or worse. Still, she didn't have to like it. She puffed out her lips in a pout. "How boring. Why do gentlemen love war so?"

Seeing the queen accept his counsel, however reluctantly, the company commander sighed in relief.

"Should we take these men with us?" asked a Black Knight who was standing next to Olba. "This man—he put on quite a show. Who would have thought he'd reinforce our side?"

Olba wiped the sweat from his forehead and gave a laconic shrug.

"In fact," chimed in the Black Knight who was guarding Duan and the others, "these people say they are acquaintances of Princess Agnis of Fiana."

"What? Is this true?" asked the company commander.

Olba nodded with an unfriendly look on his face.

"Well, my, oh my. Why were you escorting Schneider?"

Olba shrugged again, at which point Duan stepped forward. "Er, about that . . . well, there's a long story behind it. To put it simply: We happened to travel with this man, not knowing that he was Schneider—and he seems to disagree with that assessment himself."

Check, who was sitting on Duan's shoulder, nodded seriously at this.

The company commander fell into thought, his arms crossed over his chest. After a moment, he shook his head. "You'd better come with us for now. We'll sort everything out later."

So it was that Queen Milhene, Duan, Olba, the man from the adjoining cell who happened to look exactly like Schneider, Land, Clay Judah, and Check, of course, were taken by the Black Knights to where King Evesrin was supposed to have retreated.

CHAPTER 26:

TEST FROM THE GODS

eanwhile, back in the meeting room of the mansion of ex-King Liesbeck, Sven Giesen and Liesbeck's guards had been fighting desperately to fight off the attacking Red Knights. they were outnumbered and steadily losing ground.

Agnis and Charles stood at Liesbeck's side, dumbfounded. The ex-king himself was sitting heavily in his chair.

I-I have to do something! Agnis thought. She gripped Charles' hand with one hand; with the other, she clutched her staff. However, she was so surprised and stunned that she couldn't think properly.

W-w-what should I do? Her heart pounded powerfully in her chest. Into her impatient head rose thoughts of the Star of the White Horse, the red-haired heroine who, disguised as a man, bravely fought against evil and injustice.

What would she do? Would she just stand here holding Charles' hand and trembling in fear? No, she wouldn't!

I'm the only one who can protect the ex-king and Charles. I'm not just a princess, I'm an adventurer! Yes! This is a test from the gods!

Agnis geared herself up and tightened her grip on her staff. She boldly stepped in front of a group of Red Knights advancing toward them.

The Red Knights looked at one another in wonder.

Agnis took another step forward, thrust her staff toward them, and said, "Hey, can't you see this staff? This staff isn't just for show. I may look like a beginner, but my Fire Spell packs a mean punch." She paused for a breath; then, with added emphasis, she said, "Basically, I won't go easy on you."

The Red Knights looked at one another again, repositioned themselves, and charged. In other words, they completely ignored Agnis.

"H–hey! Didn't you hear me? Do you want to feel the fearful power of my fire?"

There was no response.

"O–okay. Don't say I didn't warn you," said Agnis. She gripped her rod, closed her eyes, and began to chant her spell under her breath. Then, she quickly opened her eyes and looked at the Red Knights, her staff held high, ready to release the Fire Spell.

But she couldn't do it. She simply froze. Agnis realized suddenly that she had only ever used her magic against monsters. This enemy was human. They probably all had homes and families. Could she really unleash her Fire Magic on them? She knew how powerful the crimson flames were. Once, she had even burned a hydra! These men would be fried to cinders in an instant.

"Agnis?"

When she returned to her senses, Charles was standing next to her. Agnis crouched down on the spot as though she were crumbling.

"Hey, are you all right? It's dangerous to stay—aaagh!"

A Red Knight came up from behind them, charging at them with sword in the air. In a panic, Charles tried to grab hold of his short sword, but his hands were trembling and he wasn't able to draw it out of its sheath.

"Aaagh!"

He decided to give up drawing his sword and crouched down beside Agnis. The Red Knights mercilessly rushed toward them.

"Prince Charles!"

Sven Giesen ran to stand guard over Agnis and Charles. At the same instant, a Red Knight came from the side and slashed his arm.

"Argh!"

Sven slumped down on his knees. It was difficult to see any blood because of his black clothes, but he certainly had been cut. He clutched his arm, and the expression on his face was full of agony.

"Sven!" called Liesbeck in his sharp voice.

The wound was deeper than it seemed, and Sven was unable to stand up again. The Red Knight who had dealt the blow lifted his sword to finish the job.

At that moment, something sparked inside Agnis' head. Her vision went blank, and before she knew it, she had tightened her grip on her staff. Without a word, she thrust it toward the Red Knight.

Seeing this, the Red Knight abandoned Sven and came charging toward Agnis, instead. But Agnis didn't falter—she shut her eyes and chanted her spell.

Just as she finished chanting and thrust her staff forward again, the Red Knight brought his sword down in a killing blow.

CHAPTER 27:

A FIGHTING KING

ire came blazing out of Agnis' staff. The fierce flames first engulfed the Red Knight who was attacking her, causing his sword to clang to the stone floor. The fire spread to the other Red Knights, one by one.

However, using such large-scale magic in an enclosed room was dangerous; there was a high probability that the whirlpool of fire would spread to friends as well as foes. The castle, being made of stone, couldn't burn down, but the furnishings of the room were another matter: The curtains and carpets had caught fire, and thick white smoke was billowing into the air. To make matters worse, the Red Knights who had been blasted with a direct hit of flames already were returning to the fray. The tassels on their armor and helmets were singed, that was all.

Their deep red armor seemed to burn brightly, almost pulsing with a crimson glow.

Why? wondered Agnis weakly. *Why isn't my Fire Magic working?*

She tightened her grip on the staff to increase the strength of her magic; before she could begin to chant another spell, though, someone spoke in a strong, firm voice:

"Agnis, calm down. Stop the magic."

It was ex-King Liesbeck. He had risen from his chair and now stood beside her, reaching out to gently touch her hand.

The moment his hand touched hers, Agnis' body began to tremble. She stared at Liesbeck as if his touch had woken her from a nightmare.

"It will be all right," Liesbeck said soothingly, patting her back to calm her.

Agnis' eyes rolled up into her head, and she fell limply into the ex-king's arms.

He laid her down on a nearby couch. "Charles, this is no time to be cowering," Liesbeck said sternly to his grandson, who was crouching down and quivering like a lump of jelly. "Look after Princess Agnis."

At this, Charles finally returned to his senses. With a nod, he rushed to Agnis' side.

Liesbeck, meanwhile, threw off his cloak and grabbed a huge battle-ax that was hanging on the wall. He hefted it as though it were made of balsa wood.

The Red Knights retreated in surprise.

The ex-king laughed. "Did you think I was a senile old fool? There's plenty of fight in me yet! Here, have a taste!"

He started to swing the massive battle-ax in deadly arcs. In fact, long before he had assumed the throne, Liesbeck had been a famous military commander. Unlike the current king, his son, who was a piece of decoration protected by the Black Knights, the ex-king had taken the lead on the battlefield.

Liesbeck was a fighting king.

His well-trained muscles were a little slower now than they'd been when he was in his prime; even so, the Red Knights could make no headway against him. Again and again, they charged, only to be forced back by his unwavering presence.

Suddenly, a thick voice boomed out from the doorway: "Lord Liesbeck, Prince Charles, are you safe?"

It was Edward Zamut, the leader of the Black Knights' Army. Reinforcements had arrived.

Realizing they were now at a disadvantage, the Red Knights started to retreat out the windows. Edward ran toward Liesbeck and fell to his knees.

"Sincere apologies for the delay."

Liesbeck beckoned for him to rise. "No need for apologies, just tell me what the situation is."

"Yes, sir. As we had suspected, the attackers are targeting you, sir, and the prince, the king, and the queen."

"I see. What are their numbers?"

"At least fifty attacked the king, twenty or thirty attacked the queen, and it looks like you had about twenty to deal with yourself. How on Earth did Schneider manage to recruit so many soldiers?"

"A good question, but we will worry about that later. Right now, it seems we have about a hundred enemy knights on our hands."

"So far," cautioned Edward. "This may be just the first wave. There may be reinforcements coming."

"That is possible. Right now, our situation is not too bad, though. Our numbers are more or less equivalent. From what I've seen, these Red Knights are not skilled fighters; I suspect they are simply mercenaries hired for the job."

"That was my thought, as well. However, they do seem to have a few sorcerers on their side!"

"What? Sorcerers?"

"Yes, sorcerers that control lightning. One was involved in the attack on the queen, another in the attack on the king."

He glanced about the room, parts of which were still smoldering from Agnis' spell. "It looks like you had a taste of their magic yourself!"

Liesbeck shook his head with a laugh. "No, no. This was the work of an ally sorcerer."

"An ally sorcerer?" Edward looked around him in wonder. His gaze flitted over Agnis, who was lying unconscious on the couch, tended to by Prince Charles; but the idea that the beautiful princess from Fiana might be the sorcerer Liesbeck was referring to simply didn't enter his mind.

"I will explain later," said Liesbeck. "It is unfortunate that the enemy has sorcerers. Well, how many injured?"

Edward returned his gaze to the ex-king. "Fortunately, no deaths. Thirty or so are injured."

"And on their side?"

"Well, that is another strange thing. So far, we have not been able to find a single dead or wounded Red Knight. I think it must be the work of those sorcerers."

"You mean they hid them?"

"Yes."

"Hm, strange. But what of the citizenry? How are they reacting?"

"Not well. In fact, there is widespread panic. People are fleeing the city. There have been incidents of looting and a few scattered fires. If news of the sorcerers were to leak out, the situation would grow worse."

The ex-king grunted sourly. "Naturally, news of all this chaos will have reached King Tylus of Ganau?"

"Yes, quite likely."

As Edward answered, he couldn't help comparing the cool and collected response of Liesbeck with that of King Evesrin, whose only concern was his own personal safety. Liesbeck had first considered the situation of the battle, then worried about the state of the citizens, and finally turned his attention to the wider implications of relations with Tylus IV. Not once had he shown any concern for his own safety. If Orland was great today, it owed a large measure of that greatness to the skill with which Liesbeck had steered the ship of state.

How unfortunate it is, reflected Edward silently, *that at this precarious moment, with the future of Orland hanging in the balance, I owe my allegiance to the son and not the father!*

He could remember it as clearly as if it were yesterday, how Liesbeck had handed over his title to Evesrin. That had been when Edward was appointed leader of the Black Knights' Army. Liesbeck had taken him aside and given him a final command: "Look after the king." And that had been Edward's mission ever since.

Liesbeck had been silent for a moment, his brow furrowed; now, he looked up and resumed his questions.

"What of the king, Edward? Is he rallying the men?"

"Er, His Majesty has taken shelter in the Silver-Gray Tower."

"I see. And Schneider?"

"Unknown. The hour grows late, and the Red Knights seem to have retreated. They may be finished for today."

"I concur. I think we can expect another attack early tomorrow morning, though."

"Yes, most likely. However, there is one other matter of concern."

"What is it?"

Edward frowned and cleared his throat. "Although Schneider's whereabouts are unknown, we have captured a man who is absolutely identical to Schneider."

This news deepened the wrinkles in Liesbeck's brow. "What? What do you mean 'absolutely identical'? Are you saying there are two of them?"

"Yes, though this man denies that he is Schneider. He says he was in jail for a long time, that he is nothing but a thief."

"Hm. They say that everyone has a doppelganger somewhere in the world."

"This is more than that. On closer inspection, we found that the man was wearing a belt with Schneider's family crest on it. We think perhaps he is the real Schneider."

"What? But then who was that at the treasury?"

Edward frowned. "That was the genuine Schneider, no question about it."

"At that time, was this man in question in jail?"

"Yes. I spoke to the prison guard, and it seems he was in jail for quite some time prior to the confrontation in the treasury."

"Well, that makes no sense. A man cannot be in two places at once, can he?"

"It is a mystery we have yet to solve," Edward admitted.

Prince Charles, who had been listening intently to their conversation, suddenly raised his head. He looked at Agnis, who was still unconscious, resting her head on the prince's lap. Her face was pale, and droplets of sweat were forming on her forehead—she seemed to be in pain.

"In the southwest of the castle, behind the stone wall that can be seen from the third floor of the Silver-Gray Tower, the devil Senzrabur has been sealed by the Holy Dog. However, when the Dog leaves, the power of darkness will return . . . and the world will fall"

The prince was remembering those mysterious words.

There are two Schneiders?

Charles could feel his heart hammering away inside his chest like an alarm bell. He felt ill.

That's definitely it. Mother's opened the seal, and the devil has been resurrected. And after he was resurrected, he was looking for a moment to pounce. Maybe he was waiting for his power to return! Now, the time is ripe, and he's starting to wreak havoc!

His grandfather and Edward Zamut, who were sitting in front of Charles, were now talking about the battle situation. Listening to this conversation, Charles felt more and more pain in his heart.

Grandpapa, there's no use. You're fighting a devil. There's no way we can match his powers!

The prince looked at Agnis again. She had cheeks like smooth porcelain, and her long eyelashes made shadows on those cheeks. She almost might have been sleeping peacefully, except for the painful grimaces that occasionally contorted her lips. Charles wept as he stared at her beautiful face.

I'm sorry, Agnis. I'm sorry that I've involved you in this.

The violent wind and rain were coming into the room through the windows that had been smashed by the Red Knights. Sometimes, lightning would tear through the jet-black darkness of the sky.

Looking up at the same sky, Duan thought that there was something unnatural about the storm—something evil. He couldn't quite put a finger on it, but he had an extremely awful feeling.

Olba walked beside him. Behind Olba came Clay Judah Anderson and Land. How pleased the two of them seemed! Especially Clay Judah—he actually was whistling happily to himself as they walked along, as if things couldn't possibly get any better.

Clay Judah noticed Duan sneaking a peak at him and smiled back questioningly. Surprised, Duan quickly turned his head forward again, his face turning red. Olba shot him a look that said "weirdo" as plainly as if he had spoken the word aloud.

Clay Judah seemed like an unreachable being to Duan. Yet something about the man made Duan want to open his heart to him. His warm eyes seemed to invite confidences. He had never met anyone with such a mysterious presence.

Duan tried to calm his soul, which was filled with a mix of dread and anticipation. All at once, where earlier only a black sky could be seen, he saw a tower shining in dull gray, lit by many torches.

It was the Silver-Gray Tower.

CHAPTER 28:

THE SWORD OF SHIDO

lay Judah Anderson obtained the Sword of Shido two months before his arrival at the Silver-Gray Castle.

The legendary sword was said to have been the salvation of a number of countries on the brink of ruin. Yet, it also was said that countless adventurers had lost their lives fighting to secure it. Only the sword itself knew the truth of these legends, considering it had been sunk in the depths of the Saras swamps for centuries.

Clay Judah heard of the Sword of Shido in a song sung by a troubadour in a bar:

> Deep, deep in the Saras swamps
> A sword rests, bound in golden hair:
> The Sword of Shido.
> A spirit fills the sword, and it is dangerous to handle
> But its powers are infinite.

Only he who is chosen by the sword can wield it.
Just wait where the sun sets
And listen to the whispers of the Lagun tree.
Then, you will know where it lies.

His interest kindled, he left at once on a journey to find the fabled sword. It was on this journey he met Saras, the most wretched monster in the world.

Saras had been made by an evil sorcerer long ago. It had the beautiful face of a half-elf, but its body was that of an ugly, blood-sucking leech—the stark contrast served to make it all the more repulsive.

During his fight with Saras, Clay Judah almost drowned in the depths of the swamp. He had taken his last breath and, as his mind went blank, he'd felt a strange power spring forth. As though this power was guiding him, he found himself back at the surface of the swamp. He was surprised when he saw the sword he was holding—it wasn't the sword he'd been holding just a moment ago; instead, it was a sword he'd never seen, with a strange and marvelous design on its hilt: The Sword of Shido.

After that, he set off for new adventures, eager to put the legendary sword to the test.

What else can be said about this man, Clay Judah Anderson?

His home was a small town in the great country of Ronza, and he was born into a distinguished family that had served its king for many, many generations. He had grown freely, without want, until the age of fourteen, when he decided to become an adventurer.

This wasn't a decision the Andersons regarded as normal or even desirable. In Clay Judah's family, it was customary for boys who had come of age to go on a training journey before joining the Ronzan army.

Clay Judah was the third of four children. He had two older brothers and a younger sister. His two brothers had gone on their training journey together. They'd grown up handsomely, and they'd returned to their home country when they were both past the age of twenty. Now, they were the Ronzan army's most successful men.

Clay Judah left on his own. He'd chosen the path of sorcerer-warrior. Although there were times when he joined other adventurers, he mostly worked alone.

Now, at the age of twenty-four, he still hadn't felt the desire to return home. He figured there would come a time when he naturally would want to go back and decided to wait for it. He liked to have his own reason for doing things; he was not one to follow tradition simply because things always had been done a certain way.

Over time, his skills and levels also had increased. Ordinarily, the highest you could expect to reach by age twenty-four was Level 11 or 12. Once your levels hit double digits, adventuring became a whole different ball game compared to the amateur levels. And the path of the sorcerer-warrior often was more dangerous than that of an ordinary fighter.

But at twenty-four, Clay Judah was already Level 16. His body was sturdy, and his agility and dexterity were polished. These attributes were not enough, by themselves, to account for Clay Judah's success. The truth was, he was a natural-born adventurer. It was his destiny. Wherever he went, quests awaited him—following after him, even. And they were big quests—the kind that were passed down from generation to generation.

Countless monsters crossed his path—enough to kill him several times over—but he came out victorious in every fight.

And wherever he went, he earned the respect and good will of the people around him.

In fact, there was something charming about Clay Judah that made people want to help him. Although he was a quiet man, he held true kindness and compassion in his eyes. Just being around him, people would feel as if the depths of their souls were being warmed gently.

CHAPTER 29:

LAND

And what of Clay Judah's companion, the man called Land?

He was one year younger than Clay Judah. Up until two years ago, when he was twenty-one, he had been an adventurer. His current occupation was thief, but his skills were more focused on agile combat than the opening of locks and traps. In any battle, he would run riot in his light equipment. And there were many times that he enjoyed greater success than a fully armored soldier.

He'd stick out his neck as soon as there was a quest; and as soon as there was a monster in front of him, he would fight it down. His levels went up quickly, and he had reached Level 10 by the time he was twenty-one. To increase his levels, he did something rash. There was a quest everyone else in his party had given up on, but Land tried to clear it alone.

The heat had been strong enough to burn the hair of someone who merely stood there. And from time to time, the rock face that glowed crimson with heat would let out gusts of steam. The valley near the summit of the mountain literally was a valley of fire. And his opponent had been a breed of fire-breathing dragon: the salamander.

Luckily for the reckless young adventurer, this salamander was itself a fledgling, still learning the ropes. The fight to the death between the two was lengthy; by the end, they both were injured deeply. When Land fell beneath the fire dragon's fearsome claws, the monster loosed its Breath of Fire on him.

That would have been the end of Land, had he taken a direct hit. However, an old woman who happened to be there had thrown a fire-protection amulet on the brave but foolhardy young man's unconscious body. The salamander, shocked by the unexpected appearance of the woman, widened its eyes and tried to flee. But the woman, with a speed that belied her years, threw a magic knife at the retreating beast, cutting off its tail.

This was a greater shock to the fire dragon. It wasn't the first time the monster had lost its tail, which would grow back, but the dragon still felt confused and upset, humiliated by an old woman. So, when the salamander saw the old woman advancing toward him again, its courage crumbled, and it fled in tears.

The old woman slowly climbed the rocks and grabbed hold of the severed tail, which was squirming like a great worm. She stuffed it into a cloth bag that she slung over one shoulder. Then, she picked up Land as if he were a baby and slung him over her other shoulder. Thus encumbered, she descended the mountain.

The old woman was the shopkeeper of the magic store at the foot of the mountain. She made medicines and various magic items, selling them for a high price. Salamander tails were necessary for the preparation of magic staves capable of casting Fire Spells; it was for this reason that she had climbed the mountain in the first place. It was nothing more than luck that she happened to be there in time to save Land's life.

That was good fortune for Land, yes, but what happened next was not: As soon as the old woman had brought him back to her shop, she sold him to a certain guild, as if he were one of her magic items, not a human being. This all occurred while Land was still unconscious.

When he awoke, he couldn't determine where he was or how he'd gotten there. After a while, he slowly figured out that the place was some kind of guild. The house looked as if it belonged to a regular farming family, and several other people also were living there.

Finally, he recovered enough to sit up. Then, he heard that the place was an assassins guild from a strangely sexy woman who brought him scraps of food. Surprisingly, the beautiful woman, Misty, was one of the assassins. Using her attractive body, face, and voice, Misty charmed her clients with conversation as she sneakily served them poison. As she told Land this, he thought that her deep red lips seemed all the more venomous.

The manager of the guild taught Land that any assassin with a success rate of ninety percent or more was a very accomplished one. When Land tried to thank the man for saving his life, the manager interrupted him with a laugh: "It's natural that I'd want to look after my goods!"

Land puzzled over this remark until later, when a man with sunken cheeks and a face that looked like a skull explained the details of the sale to Land. Without knowing it, Land had become a member of the assassins guild.

Two years passed in the blink of an eye. At times, Land thought of escaping the guild and returning to the life he'd known as an adventurer—but this was merely a dream. Once you were in the assassins guild, there was only one way out: death. That was the law of the guild. Knowing he'd be targeted by a group of cold-blooded professional assassins if he tried to escape somehow made his new life at the guild more bearable.

So it was that Land decided to stay. Really, it wasn't such a bad life. The fact that he and Misty had become lovers might have had something to do with his decision. . . .

CHAPTER 30:

AN UNLIKELY PAIR

his particular assassins guild was the very guild that ex-King Liesbeck's spy, Chris Pikra, had commissioned to kill the messenger from Ganau.

Shortly before this commission, Misty left Land for another man. When he found out, Land put on a brave face and showed no regrets; in fact, he accepted things calmly and wished Misty good luck. In his heart of hearts, however, he was ruined. He started to spend his days drinking and gambling to such excess that the guild manager—who never stuck his nose into other people's private affairs—had to take him aside, gently cautioning him.

And then, this job had come along.

"A Level 16 sorcerer-warrior?" Land had commented, his eyes practically bugging out of his head.

His manager snorted in laughter. "What? Feeling intimidated?"

"Nah, not me. There's another one, too, right?"

"The other one's nothing—you could finish him with your eyes closed."

"The pay's awful."

"Don't do it if you don't want to. There are plenty of others. I made the effort to ask you first because I knew you were in trouble. I thought this might take your mind off that business with Misty."

Pah, thought Land. *Why is he looking at my feet?*

Glancing down, Land noticed all the gambling tickets stuck to his boots. He sighed. He needed some cash to pay off those debts; although the pay scale for this job was low for such a high degree of difficulty, it was better than nothing. Land looked back up at his manager and reluctantly nodded his head.

I never get a choice. . . .

Grumbling under his breath, Land went to meet the client, a man of good personal appearance called Pikra. Pikra told him that the King of Ganau had entrusted copies of a secret document to two men, one bound for the King of Orland, the other for Lord Schneider; both men were on their way to Orland. Land was to assassinate these messengers and retrieve the documents.

Land guessed immediately where this commission had come from. The domestic conflicts of Orland and the prickly relationship between Orland and Ganau were well known. It also was known that ex-King Liesbeck still kept an oar in the political waters, so to speak. So Land had a pretty good idea about what was going on and who Pikra took his orders from.

The first target, like his manager had predicted, proved an easy dispatch, thanks to Land's skill and a little luck. By pure coincidence, the assassin checked into the same inn as his target—and booked the same room. When the messenger, who didn't suspect a thing, fell asleep, Land smoothly terminated his employment. He searched the pockets of the dead man's clothes and found the secret document intended for Lord Schneider. And he fulfilled the terms of the contract by cutting off the man's ear as proof. Actually, he didn't quite fulfill the terms: Land had been instructed not to look at the secret document; human nature being what it is, however, he couldn't help taking a quick glimpse.

He heaved a sigh. Its contents were just as he had expected—the document set forth in excruciating detail how much King Evesrin of Orland looked down upon Lord Schneider. On top of that, the document requested that Lord Schneider see to it that the messenger who had brought the document be "terminated" as swiftly as possible, to ensure confidentiality. Land couldn't help a cold smile at the irony: The messenger had been a dead man already, before Land had killed him.

Despite his smile, Land didn't exactly find this amusing. On the contrary, the man's fate seemed utterly wretched to Land now. He told himself that, after the next job, he really would start thinking seriously about his future.

Then, he headed off for the next target: Clay Judah Anderson, who almost certainly was carrying a bogus document detailing how Lord Schneider had outwitted the King of Orland and was trying to start a rebellion.

Land finally caught up with his prey on a road that separated Ganau and Orland, deep in the forest. Dressed as an ordinary traveler, he approached the messenger.

However, his plan failed. Thinking about it later, he wasn't quite sure how he'd given himself away. Somehow, Clay Judah had been on his guard and had stabbed Land in the shoulder. The next thing Land knew, he was opening his eyes inside a cave. It seemed he hadn't died, after all. No, he'd been rescued and bandaged up. In fact, Land's rescuer was right there, waiting for him to awaken: It was Clay Judah Anderson!

Not only had Land's intended target nursed him back to health, the man actually had walked miles in a thunderous downpour to find a particular medicinal herb that would speed the healing process.

Far from being grateful, Land was angry at these inexplicable acts of kindness by a man he'd been hired to kill in cold blood. He recognized that he was in the man's debt, though; so, more in desperation than anything else, he confessed everything—not only his own role, also how the secret document the other messenger had been carrying really had been a treacherous death sentence for its bearer. He was relatively sure that the document Clay Judah was carrying to King Evesrin held a similar message, and he strongly urged Clay Judah to look for himself.

Clay Judah refused.

"I'm doing the job I was asked to do," he said in a calm voice, adding that he meant to deliver the bogus document to King Evesrin even if it meant his own death.

Late in the evening of the next day, Land and Clay Judah arrived in Orland. They had no chance to deliver the document, though, because the rebellion already had erupted. Fires flamed all around the castle, and people were running aimlessly in terror. Even in the face of this situation, Clay Judah stated that he still intended to deliver the document, although events had overtaken its contents and rendered them all but meaningless.

Upon hearing this, Land groaned. "Stop this idiocy! What's the point of delivering the document now? Do you want to die for nothing?"

Clay Judah wouldn't change his mind, though.

"I'm not the one who decides whether there's a point to it," he said as he set out for the castle.

Land hesitated a moment before following him.

Clay Judah paused and gave the assassin a curious look. "There isn't any point in following me," he said, "unless you still plan to kill me?"

"Pah, you seem to have the gods looking out for you. I'm not the sort of guy who tries that hard! But I'm not going to miss out on watching how things unfold. I'm coming with you."

When the unlikely pair reached the Silver-Gray Castle, the fight between the Red Knights and the Black Knights was reaching its peak. . . .

CHAPTER 31:

THE SILVER-GRAY TOWER

ow, let's rejoin our story already in progress. . . . Duan and the others were being escorted by Black Knights to the Silver-Gray Tower, where King Evesrin was said to have taken refuge.

Queen Milhene was accompanied by her maids. Every few steps, the queen would heave a big sigh and moan, "Why must this happen to *me*?"

In response, her maids would sympathize dramatically and comfort her.

Duan and the rest were way behind them. Next to Duan was Olba, and on his shoulder stood Check. Behind them were Clay Judah and Land. Black Knights followed after, also flanking them on both sides as though to sandwich them.

The man who looked like Schneider, who insisted his name was Carlos, was in front of Duan, arms held by a Black Knight.

Nobody knew where the Red Knights and their sorcerers had retreated to, but there was no sign of them now.

The Silver-Gray Tower stood in the southwest of the castle, looking down on the inner gardens. The corridor that connected the castle to the tower was roofed, but this was scant protection against the heavy rain, which was being blown sideways by the wind. Although they all narrowed their shoulders and hurried along, everyone was drenched quickly.

Before they went inside, Duan glanced up at the tower, blinking his eyes against the driving rain. The tower had an oppressive look to it that was very different from the luxurious splendor of the castle. In fact, it seemed cold and dejected, like some ancient ruin.

They entered the tower and found themselves in a small room. Three wooden chairs were lined against one wall, but there was no one present. The Black Knights swiftly marched them through, straight into the next room. This one was fairly large, with a big pillar in its center. Black armor and helmets hung on the walls. Torches burned brightly on the walls. Toward the back of the room was a set of stairs laid in stone.

As they climbed those stairs to the second floor, Duan looked out the windows located here and there along the walls. Because of the heavy rain, however, he barely could see anything. Every so often, a flash of lightning would illuminate figures in the darkness. Roaring thunder always followed the lightning, without so much as a heartbeat of space between them. Duan already was lonely and apprehensive; every time the thunder roared out, he felt his entire body clench up.

The third time he glanced out a window, lightning flashed and a great boom of thunder rang out at the exact same moment, startling him. His foot slipped off the step.

"Aah!"

Bang! He fell backward, hitting smack into the chest of Clay Judah, who was walking right behind him. It was like hitting a brick wall. Crumpling to the floor, Duan looked up at Clay Judah, who was quite tall, and blushed.

I look pathetic, so pathetic!

Clay Judah helped Duan to his feet. "That lightning sure is is amazing," he said with a smile. Thanks to that comment, Duan didn't have to make any excuses. The comment also triggered the line of people who'd previously been silent to start talking.

Land was the first one to voice his doubts. "Does anybody think it's strange that they'd flee into a tower?"

Olba nodded. "Yeah, definitely. Once you're holed up in here, there's nowhere left to run. What if the enemy lights a fire down below? How are you gonna escape? Sprout wings and fly away?"

"Yeah, exactly," said Land. "And why take refuge here so quickly? Surely, the tower is a last resort! I mean, under normal conditions." At this, Land glanced over his shoulder at the Black Knight following him. "Hey, are you guys low on numbers or something?"

The Black Knight was caught off guard. "Er, that's classified information. We'll ask the questions around here. All you lot need to do is obey."

"Right. I guess that's all you can say."

Land and Olba shot each other a glance as if to say, "It can't be helped."

The mystery was soon solved. They found King Evesrin on the third floor of the five-story tower, where there was a relatively spacious hall. This section of the tower was wider than the rest; later, Duan learned that the tower had been constructed for just such emergencies as this one. In order to make it a functional command center for the army, the tower had been built so that the entire castle and its surroundings could be seen. To defend against attacks from below, there was only one entrance—which was also the sole exit. The slits of windows through which Duan had glanced as they climbed the stairs made it possible to shoot deadly storms of arrows at enemies below. And in case of a siege, the tower had been well stocked with food, water, and other necessary supplies.

In the center of the hall, one section was higher than the rest, and a red carpet laid there, along with a simple wooden chair. Upon this chair, as though it were a splendid golden throne, sat King Evesrin, flanked by a pair of Black Knights. The king wore a disturbed expression.

It seemed there were more rooms at the back of this one, but they were hidden behind thick curtains.

As soon as they entered, Queen Milhene ran toward the king, issuing complaints.

"Dearest, what is all this? I nearly died!"

"I-I'm sorry," stammered the king. "I'm sure it must have been terrifying. Poor thing!" As he spoke, Evesrin squeezed the queen's hand and stroked it.

Puffing out her red cheeks, the queen brushed aside his hand. "I'll tell you more about it later, but a horrifying sorcerer wearing a red robe cast a spell on me!"

"W-what? Is that true?"

One of the Black Knights by the king's side answered. "Yes, Your Majesty. As I reported to you a moment ago—if you will recall—it seems there were a number of sorcerers aiding the Red Knights."

Suddenly, the king caught sight of the mystery man—the one who looked exactly like Schneider. He shot to his feet and cried out, "It's Schneider!"

The man shrieked in terror and threw himself to the floor, where he bowed and groveled before the king. "N-no, no, sir. Not me. I'm just a thief named Carlos. Please sir, I'm not asking something impertinent like being set free or anything—just send me back to my cell!"

King Evesrin looked at the Black Knight with an expression of incredulity. "W-what's happening? What is this pitiful state? Where is Edward?"

"The commander has gone to rescue Lord Liesbeck, Prince Charles, and also Princess Agnis, who is visiting from Fiana. According to our recent reports, he is escorting them here now."

At this, Duan and Olba looked at each other in relief.

"I guess Agnis is fine," Duan whispered to Olba.

"Of course she is," the big fighter whispered back. "She's been through worse scrapes than this. We all have."

At that very moment, the subject of their whispers, Agnis R. Link, was ushered into the hall, along with ex-King Liesbeck and Prince Charles. Edward, who had been conducting the group, immediately hurried toward the king.

"I apologize sincerely for the delay, Your Majesty. I have brought Lord Liesbeck and Prince Charles."

As Liesbeck entered the room, all the Black Knights stood to attention. The king fell silent, a nervous expression on his face. Duan, who had not yet made the ex-king's acquaintance, didn't know exactly who he was at first—but he quickly figured it out.

That must be the previous king. What an amazing presence . . .

Agnis was right behind Lord Liesbeck. When she recognized Duan and Olba, she opened her eyes wide and raised her eyebrows, but she didn't say a word, simply following after Liesbeck and Prince Charles as they approached the king.

"Pah, what's with that stuck-up attitude?" whispered Olba to Duan.

"Yeah, she could have said 'hello' or something!" Duan whispered back.

"I guess we're too common for the likes of her now that she's with her royal friends!"

"Exactly!"

This moment of rare agreement between Olba and Duan didn't last long; the Black Knight who was guarding them gave them both a rough shove.

"Be quiet, you!"

Duan, who was hit in the back of the head, crouched down on the spot, whereas Olba instinctively threw a punch at the Black Knight. "You be quiet!"

As his opponent was fully armored, this was not the wisest action. Olba's fist crumpled against the man's breastplate.

"Oww . . ." He shook his wrist as though he could fling the pain away like so many drops of water.

The Black Knight smirked.

"What the heck are you doing?" asked Land, who stood beside him.

Next to Land was Clay Judah. He seemed as if he were thinking about something else, resting easily against the wall with his eyes closed.

Meanwhile, a full-scale argument was raging at the center of the hall.

CHAPTER 32:

THE WORK OF MONSTERS

re you certain this man isn't Schneider?" King Evesrin demanded.

"Yes, sire," Edward Zamut confirmed. "It is impossible. The prison guard has sworn that this man was locked away in his cell while you were meeting with Schneider in the treasury. Granted, this man—who calls himself Carlos, I believe—was made to wear a mask for some reason . . . still, his voice is unmistakable. He has been in the prison for some time now, never having been released before today."

"But they're so alike! And those clothes look like the clothes of a nobleman. If, as he says, he's a thief, then he wouldn't be wearing clothes like that."

"Yes, he wears the Schneider family crest on his belt."

"Then, he must be Schneider."

"We thought so at first, as well—but it would be easy to dress someone in these clothes."

"For what possible reason?"

"It's incomprehensible, Your Majesty."

Normally, when King Evesrin was in front of his father, ex-King Liesbeck, he was silent and shy. But with the queen and his servants looking on, he was desperate to look good. He thought he had succeeded pretty well, too, and his mood was on the upswing . . . until Liesbeck spoke.

The ex-king, who sat on a chair that had been placed hastily next to the king's, said bitterly, "Well, this is all your responsibility, falling prey to Schneider's trap!"

Upon hearing this, King Evesrin realized that his father knew everything, and he felt himself becoming depressed again.

Exactly who *do they think is king around here?!*

"It is pointless to cast blame now, though" Liesbeck continued, turning to Edward. "Instead, we should be planning our strategy."

The king listened, simmering with resentment. *No point in casting blame? Then, why did you just cast it, you old fool? Listen to him! Whatever he says, he still can't let go of the throne. Can't he see how unfair that is? If he didn't think I could be trusted to reign wisely, he shouldn't have retired. Then, I still could be having fun.*

If the king had uttered these thoughts out loud for Liesbeck to hear, who knows what kind of lightning would have dropped! But the current king kept silent. It wasn't from fear of his father. (He was used to being lectured by the ex-king and could tune him out in a second.) No, it was the queen he he feared. He didn't want Milhene to become fed up with him. His greatest concern was that she would one day reach the end of her tether and simply leave him. When Evesrin thought about this possibility, his blood ran cold, shivers went down his neck, and he was unable to stop himself from trembling.

Yes, these were the kinds of thoughts running through the mind of King Eversrin at this moment. Rather than thinking about the plot against his crown, the domestic crisis, and the ramifications for international relations, the king was brooding about his father and his wife. He was so caught up in the past and the future that he had no thoughts to spare for the present.

In the king's silence, Liesbeck had taken charge. He spoke to Edward as if he were still his liege lord. "It will be necessary to ascertain whether this man is Schneider, Edward. Depending on this, our enemies' objectives will change; and thus, our strategies will change."

Before Edward could respond, King Evesrin stood up and moved between them.

"I believe this is all the work of monsters," he stated. "Schneider's treason, this man's story, all of it. In fact, I think Schneider was originally the reincarnation of a monster. Yes, it's all making sense now!"

No one said a word in reply. They were too dumbfounded to speak. Every eye was trained on the king, wondering what he would say or do next.

When he'd finished speaking, even Evesrin wondered what had possessed him to make such a bizarre accusation—which had failed to convince anybody, including himself. What evidence was there? What proof? None. But he couldn't take it back now. What would his father think? What would the queen do? No, a true leader never admits he's wrong.

King Evesrin quickly glanced at the queen. He was worried about what sort of expression she would be wearing when he met her gaze. He was afraid that he'd behold the same confusion and lack of respect that appeared—or he imagined he saw—on the faces of the others. But Queen Milhene was not looking at him at all. With a dreamy gaze, she was staring off somewhere completely different . . . toward the wall.

What? The king followed her gaze, and blood rushed to his head. *W-who is that man?!*

The object of the queen's gaze was a tall and handsome fellow who was just the type Queen Milhene found most attractive. He was wearing light armor, and his black leather clothes—along with a mantle to keep out the cold—showing off his thin but strong body to his advantage. He also wore a slender silver sword and long black boots. . . .

I've never seen his face before. Is he a soldier from somewhere?

The man's long black hair fell over his shoulders, and his blue eyes shined impressively. On top of that, he seemed completely confident . . . but in a natural way, not a snobby or pretentious one. He had charisma to burn. The king noticed that *everyone* kept sneaking glancing at the silent figure.

Beside the dark-haired man was another sturdy-looking if slender man, as well as a delicate boy, who looked almost like a young girl. Finally, there was a slight man with flaming red hair.

Who are they? Why are they here?

Lord Liesbeck cleared his throat. "Son, you must be tired. Why not delegate your authority to me and rest a while?"

The king returned to his senses as soon as his father spoke to him. "Thank you, Father, but this isn't really your concern anymore. After all, you're the one who should be resting, now that you're retired and everything."

The ex-king raised his eyebrows. "I wish a thousand times over that I could rest. Unfortunately, the king of Orland just said, straight-faced, that the crisis threatening to engulf our nation is the work of monsters! How can I leave things to him?"

King Evesrin bit the inside of his cheek. "Then, how would *you* explain it, old man? How would *you* explain Red Knights that revive time and time again, no matter how often they've been struck down? And sorcerers that command lightning?"

This was too much for Liesbeck. "Shut up, shut up, you useless imbecile! We have no time to quarrel now." Standing up, he turned toward Edward. "From now on, you will report directly to me. Is that understood?"

But King Evesrin also had reached the end of his tether. His face was bright red, and the veins of his neck were popping out. "Useless imbecile!? How dare you call me that . . . in front of everyone!"

Inside his head, some switch flipped. Evesrin went deathly pale. Then, somehow, the silver-haired man in front of him seemed to grow bigger and bigger. Or maybe he was shrinking. Yes, he felt like a little boy again. Yet no matter how angry he was, Evesrin couldn't hate his father. If only he *could* hate him, he'd probably feel a lot better. Something in his nose stung, and he felt moisture in the corners of his eyes.

Edward stepped forward and laid a gentle hand on the king's shoulder. "Stop, Your Majesty. Calm down. It is a silly thing, nothing to cry about."

The king heaved his shoulders, took a few deep breaths, and glared at his father with reddened eyes.

Seeing this, Liesbeck sighed deeply. "How many years . . . how much experience and responsibility do you need before you start acting like an adult? I expected more from you, son. It is truly disgraceful. . . ."

After these words had been spoken, silence fell over the hall. No one moved; no one even dared to breathe. The only sounds that could be heard were the violent rainfall, the moaning winds, and the loud booms of thunder, along with the sizzling of the torches burning high on the walls.

CHAPTER 33:

BEHIND THE CURTAIN

his is awful.

Duan raised his shoulders and started to sigh . . . only to realize at the last moment that it wouldn't be appropriate. He swallowed, trying to get rid of his breath in three or four short bursts without anyone noticing.

Eek! Honestly, what are we gonna do? The tension in the air—everyone's holding their breath! Don't they realize there isn't time for this? Not that I have any idea what's going on or what to do about it. . . .

Duan glanced at Olba, who was leaning against the wall and looking up at the ceiling with a bitter look on his face.

That's when Duan heard his name being called. . . .

"Duan, girl come, cha!"

It was Check, and though the grinia perched on Duan's shoulder spoke quietly—quietly for Check, that is—Duan felt himself flushing red with embarrassment.

"Be quiet!" he whispered harshly.

When he saw who was coming, his jaw dropped. It was a young woman with long, flaming red tresses that cascaded down her back and eyes like sparkling purple jewels. Duan thought he'd never seen anyone so lovely.

It was, in fact, Agnis, all dressed up and looking every inch a royal princess. She'd been trying to make her way over to Duan without drawing attention to herself.

Duan shot her a questioning look, and she replied by jerking up her small chin in an imperious "follow me" signal.

Follow her? Where the heck is she going?

Agnis strode over to a bay window and ducked quickly behind the curtains. Duan wondered what on Earth she was up to—and there was only one way to find out. He slid in behind her.

"Ouch!"

"Argh!"

Because there was so little room behind the curtains, the two bumped into each other. Agnis lost her balance and clung to Duan to keep from falling. Her cheek pushed against his chest.

Whoa, I can't believe how close we are in here! He could feel her breath on his face. She was soft and warm, and she smelled very pleasant. His heart was pounding in his chest. The nearness of her was so intoxicating that the blood rushed to his head . . . and to his face, which turned beet red.

Agnis, who probably wasn't aware of any of this, grabbed Duan's hand and drew him toward the bay window, where they would be able to exchange whispers.

As he was being pulled along, Duan realized that her hand was as cold as ice. "Agnis," he began in a low voice.

"We should be fine here," she said. "Duan, it's been ages!"

"Agnis . . ." Duan took both of her hands in his.

"What are you doing, you pervert?" She recoiled, slapping at his hands.

"Owww! W-what do you mean, 'pervert'? I was just trying to warm up your hands. They're like ice!"

The earlier pounding of his heart began to settle. *Pah! What was I thinking? I forgot the sort of girl she is!* Duan pushed aside his "perverted" thoughts, though he couldn't help looking a bit disappointed. Not that Agnis noticed.

"We don't have much time, so I'll just summarize," she began. "Um, to start with, um, well, it's going to be a complicated story, anyway, but how much do you know about what's been going on?"

"Er . . . well, we were attacked while we were sleeping, and then we were falsely accused of a crime. We were in prison until a short while ago. As we were escaping, the Black Knights and the Red Knights started to fight. . . . Oh yeah, there was also this guy in the next cell who looks exactly like Schneider! And this Schneider is the guy who's fighting against the king, right? And then—"

Agnis shushed him by pressing an ice-cold finger to his lips.

"That's fine," she said. "I'll explain everything later. But can I ask you to believe everything that I'm about to tell you now?"

"Er, o-okay . . ."

"Good boy."

Duan bristled at this. *Good boy? I'm older than you!*

Before he could object, Agnis continued, "I'll get right to the point: The bad guy is a devil."

"Huh?"

Lightning flashed through the window from time to time, illuminating their faces; but for the most part, they were speaking in total darkness—which was lucky for Duan, because he had never looked so dumbfounded in all his sixteen years.

They were interrupted when a loud uproar commenced on the other side of the curtain.

"I wonder what's up?" asked Duan.

Agnis responded by taking Duan's hand again and pulling him back through the curtain and into the room. As they went, she continued to whisper to him.

"The prince has started his explanation. Listen, Duan. There's only one person here that can help us, and that person is . . . you!"

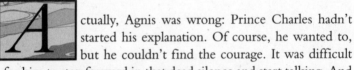

CHAPTER 34:

OF MONSTERS AND MAGICIANS

Actually, Agnis was wrong: Prince Charles hadn't started his explanation. Of course, he wanted to, but he couldn't find the courage. It was difficult for him to step forward in that dead silence and start talking. And as he was dawdling, a Black Knight rushed into the room and gasped out his report.

"The enemy has started to move!"

Ex-King Liesbeck nodded calmly, as if he'd expected this news. "So, they have come."

King Evesrin reacted much less calmly. "EEEK!" the king screamed pathetically, holding his trembling hands to his mouth, his whole body shivering as if with cold.

"How many? Do they know our location?" asked Edward Zamut.

The Black Knight answered, "Sir, it seems they are still wandering the area. In fact, I think they are finding it difficult to move about freely in this rain. We do not have accurate numbers yet. There was a report, however, that there were three sorcerers wearing red robes!"

"What? Not two?"

Edward and the others furrowed their brows as they looked at one another. There were a few knights whispering at first, and then the room filled with noise again as they all burst into speech at once.

"Where the heck are they coming from?"

"One is difficult enough, but three . . ."

"Yes, especially considering we have no sorcerers of our own!"

"Hrmm . . ."

Edward turned to these knights, who couldn't hide their trepidation, and spoke in a low, resounding voice, "Do not falter. You will tarnish the reputation of the Black Knights if you show any hesitation or doubt."

Hearing this, Land immediately protested. "Nah, hesitation and doubt are normal!"

"Yeah," said Olba in agreement. He stood next to Land, his arms crossed over his chest. Glancing at the man who had occupied the adjoining cell in the prison, who was standing as if forgotten in one corner of the room, he added, "I wonder what's gonna happen with that guy who looks exactly like Schneider."

"Who knows?" answered Land. "He just might drop dead from sheer fright. I mean, look how pale he is, and his trembling is worse than the king's!"

When Land made this teasing comment, Clay Judah, who had been silent up until that moment, suddenly spoke. "I think he's under some kind of magic spell. He's had his memory exchanged with someone else's."

"What? How can you tell?" asked Land.

Clay Judah replied: "He has no substance."

"Substance?" growled Olba. "What the heck is that?"

Clay Judah studied Olba for a moment before saying, "I learned this from my old master, who schooled me in the ways of magic. People have a permanence at the root. That is *substance*. It's like the latent momentum of being human. People whose bodies are truly connected with their minds have this quality in abundance. If, however, someone were to leave their mind someplace, then this quality becomes diluted."

"Hm," said Olba, rubbing at his chin. "I get it, but I don't get it."

"Yeah, I didn't think you would."

"What's that supposed to mean?" demanded Olba in a fed-up voice.

Clay Judah only laughed.

At that moment, Agnis emerged from behind the curtain with Duan in tow. She took in the scene before her. "I'm glad you guys are taking the situation so seriously!"

Clay Judah and Land looked a little surprised at this comment, but Olba shot right back: "About time you showed up, Princess. Because of you, Duan and I have been eating smelly food while you were being treated like a VIP."

"I-I was worried about you two," she stammered in reply, blushing a bit because, after all, she had forgotten about them for a moment . . . well, actually a little more than a moment! She followed with a shushing gesture, indicating they all should pay attention to the activity going on around ex-King Liesbeck and Edward Zamut.

Preparations were underway to fight off the Red Knights. Black Knights with bows were lining the bay windows—though heavy, wind-swept rain made it difficult for them to see clearly or fire effectively. The most powerful Black Knights already were assembling downstairs at the entrance to the tower, where they would bar entry to anyone in red, whether soldier or sorcerer.

King Evesrin had his own plan. "Er, I suppose it would be best if I withdrew. Here, Milhene, come quickly."

At this, Liesbeck cried out in a thunderous roar. "What kind of example are you trying to set? A king fleeing before the battle even begins?! Sit down and be quiet!"

"B-but, it's all the doings of monsters," protested the king, red-faced. "Monsters and magicians! How can we fight against that?"

Liesbeck shouted back, "Will you shut up about the monsters, you dolt!"

Reluctantly, the king sat down.

As Prince Charles watched his father's humiliation, his chest pricked with pain.

I should speak up now.

He still couldn't find the right moment, though.

Even if I tell them about the devil, who's going to believe me? Oh, what should I do?

He clutched his blond-haired head in an agony of indecision.

Agnis chose that moment to step forward. Her cool voice rang through the room.

"Excuse my interruption, but I beg you all to listen to Prince Charles."

A shocked silence ensued. Everyone there looked at her. And then, they looked at Charles.

As the seconds ticked by without a word from the prince, Agnis screamed silently in her mind: *Charles, come on! Now's your chance!*

CHAPTER 35

LIKE FATHER, LIKE SON

Prince Charles, meanwhile, stared at Agnis in surprise. For the first time, he took note of Duan, who stood beside her.

Hm. He must be that guy Duan she's been talking about. . . .

Duan was completely different from what Charles had imagined. Because Agnis, whom he'd been friends with since childhood, had chosen to rely on Duan instead of him, Charles expected Duan to be manlier and more skilled. Until this moment, he'd actually assumed that Duan was one of the high-level men who stood close by.

But, no: He was the little guy standing beside Agnis, looking at Charles with a worried expression!

He's not much different from me: He's slight, like I am, and his face is as pretty as a girl's!

Agnis clutched Duan's arm. *Come on, Charles,* she thought. *What are you doing?*

"Ow!"

Duan let out a loud yelp as Agnis's sharp fingernails dug into his skin. Now, *he* was the center of attention. Edward and Liesbeck looked at him with questioning faces.

"Er, no, I . . ." As Duan turned bright red, stammering uselessly, Prince Charles finally summoned up the courage to speak.

"Excuse me," he said. "I have an idea about what may be happening."

He took a step forward to start his explanation, drew a deep breath, threw out his chest, opened his mouth . . . and hesitated yet again. Who would believe him if he just launched right into explaining away all this chaos as the work of a devil? But he had to say it. He glanced quickly at Duan and Agnis—who were watching him worriedly—gritted his teeth, and began:

"To tell you the truth, this began some time ago, when I was reading in the library one day and found an odd book."

The prince did his best to explain in a frank manner. However carefully he chose his words, though, there was no disguising the absurdity of his story. It was better than the explanation (to use the term loosely) that Agnis had given to Duan behind the curtain; but in the end, it did nothing more than render Liesbeck and the others speechless. They gaped open-mouthed at the prince and at one other, wondering why in the world Charles would come out with this insanity now.

The prince, realizing that he was losing his audience, ran desperately to one of the windows of the tower and flung open the curtains. "In the inner garden that can be seen from this very window . . ."

Unfortunately, it was pitch black and raining outside. Nothing could be seen. Now, the prince grew more desperate.

"Um, in the inner garden was a statue of a dog. I mean, a man with the head of a dog! No, a dog with the head of a man! What I am saying is true, right Mother?"

Queen Milhene was confused by the sudden question. "I-I think so, but I cannot be certain. . . ." Her voice seemed almost tearful.

"It's all right, my dear. There's no way you could know." King Evesrin ran over to the queen to comfort her. He was the only one thankful for the prince's words. The king believed the prince had started to talk like this to defend him, after all. For the first time in a long time, he felt proud of his son. Although, to tell the truth, he did think that this business of a devil was going a bit too far, and Charles should have stopped at monsters.

"You think all this was caused by a . . . a devil named Senzrabur?" asked Liesbeck, who finally returned to his senses.

The prince nodded with utter certainty. "I understand this story is not exactly easy to believe. With the Red Knights, the sorcerers, and then this man who looks exactly like Schneider, though—there are an awful lot of strange things going on!"

"Hm."

Liesbeck fell into silence. He wasn't thinking about the explanation, however, he was remembering that he had at one point thought Prince Charles might be more responsible and more useful than the king. *I had small hopes in that boy. Now, he's talking straight-faced about how this is all the work of a devil. Hmph. Like father, like son.*

Liesbeck sighed in frustration.

"Excuse me," said a warm, comforting voice.

When Liesbeck glanced up, a man all dressed in black stepped forward.

"My name is Clay Judah Anderson. I will prove my identity later—"

"Speak up," Liesbeck called out impatiently. "I hope you're not going to spin another fairytale!"

Clay Judah smiled. "No fairytales. I have a little experience with magic, and I've seen a situation like this one before. I think I can explain what is going on with this man here."

At this, the man who called himself Carlos, who looked exactly like Schneider, became the center of attention.

He looked on with a blank expression and took a step back.

Clay Judah paced toward him. He stood in front of the hapless man, closed his eyes, and seemed to concentrate very hard. Then, without a word, he opened his eyes and delivered a quick punch into the pit of the man's stomach.

"Urgh . . ."

The man collapsed slowly to his knees.

"Where am I? What is happening? What? Huh?"

Still on his knees, the man looked up nervously.

"Who are you?" asked Clay Judah.

The man looked around in puzzlement. "Why, Lord Liesbeck . . . Your Majesty! Where am I? Who is this fellow?"

He scratched his head, registering his filthy clothes with an expression of distaste. Then, as though asking for help, he looked at Liesbeck, Edward, King Evesrin . . . and then at the man who had awakened him, Clay Judah.

Ex-King Liesbeck found his voice at last and addressed the man in a commanding tone. "You—what is your name?"

The man answered simply. "I am Schneider Deks."

Before anyone could reply to this statement, a Black Knight came dashing up from below and burst into the room.

"Commander! The enemy has started to gather and is heading for the tower! On top of that, it seems that their numbers are much greater than we had predicted!"

Edward and Liesbeck quickly exchanged a glance.

"Right, I will take care of this," said the ex-king. "Edward, I want you to take personal command!"

Edward saluted and made to leave with the knight who had come in with the report.

Before he could go, the man who now claimed to be Schneider stopped him.

"Wait, Edward. What is this? What enemy?"

Edward brushed past him and out of the room. "Excuse me, there is no time—"

Schneider looked to the ex-king.

"Lord Liesbeck, please tell me what is going on! If we are being attacked by some enemy, I also will help!"

"Hm . . . How should I explain this? To summarize, somebody is trying to overthrow the nation of Orland, and he is commanding knights all dressed in red and sorcerers that can use lightning magic."

"Oh my! Who is it?"

"Who is it?" Liesbeck pointed his finger straight at Schneider. "You."

"What?"

"It is a man named Schneider Deks."

The man stared, opening and closing his mouth. Then, without warning, he screamed, clutched his head, and curled up on the floor.

Looking on, Land was excited. "This is fun! What's gonna happen now? Ooh, I can't wait!"

Olba gave a bitter laugh. "The prison food was inedible, but I guess I can't complain when I get to see a floor show like this one."

CHAPTER 36:

SHU AND EV

As Clay Judah had suspected, the man from the prison, who soon convinced everyone that he was the real Schneider, had been the victim of a soul exchange. Because the magic wasn't particularly strong, easily dispelled by a single punch from Clay Judah, there probably were no aftereffects to worry about. Yet even so, Schneider couldn't relax. In fact, the more he found out about the current situation, the angrier he grew.

"To use my name and threaten the king is outrageous! I will protect His Majesty with my very life!"

King Evesrin and some others were awestruck when they saw Schneider affirm his loyalty to the crown. What had caused this change in his mental state?

"Schneider . . ."

There was something warm rising up inside King Evesrin's chest. When he and Schneider were small, they used to play together often. Then, things had become strained between them, and they'd gotten on less and less well as the years went by. It didn't help matters any that the king had difficulty honestly stating his feelings and made comments to Schneider that the other man took as sarcasm, responding in kind as a result. This angered the king and made him want to punish Schneider. And so, the vicious circle continued.

In truth, the king was still quite fond of Schneider. Being king was a lonely business, and he missed the friend of his youth. Why, he could remember as if it were yesterday how the two of them had run around the castle together!

Now King Evesrin took Schneider's hand. "Schneider, I'm sorry that I've been mean to you for so long. . . ."

Schneider also was feeling overwhelmed. Thinking about the last few years, he was filled with regret at how childish he'd been.

Just imagine how stressful and difficult it is to be a king, Schneider thought to himself. *The menace from other countries, the constant threat of domestic troubles . . . What pressure to have to protect the nation always! And how tiring to be the focus of attention every second of every day. Wouldn't it be natural for someone under that kind of stress to mouth off and take it out on close friends? Really, it's just a sign that I was his closest friend. That's why he took it out on me. And instead of understanding, I took it personally and turned all rotten inside. Why, I used to call him Ev, and he always called me Shu! When did that stop?*

"No, I retaliated in a childish manner!" Schneider said now, brushing away a tear. "Please forgive me."

"Shu!"

"Ev!"

The two clasped hands and embraced.

"I kept on thinking that you were trying to overthrow me. . . ."

"I would never do such a thing! I was merely reacting childishly."

"Oh, you should have told me!"

"And you, Your Majesty, should have told me what was on your mind!"

The two acted as though they were boisterous teenage girls, patting each other on their shoulders and hands and laughing together through their tears.

All the others looked on with complicated expressions, laughing bitterly.

"Well, heck," sighed Olba.

"This is so funny! Too funny!" Land leaned against Olba, trying to suppress his laughter. He had tears in his eyes, which he wiped away with one finger.

Clay Judah, who was standing to the side, watched for the reconciliation between the king and Schneider to wrap up before stepping in front of the king to present him with the letter from King Tylus of Ganau.

"W-what is this?" stammered the king.

"I was asked to give this letter to the King of Orland from King Tylus of Ganau."

"Hm . . ."

King Evesrin took the letter and read it at once. The color of his face changed in seconds. He thrust the letter out to Schneider. As Schneider read it, the color of his face changed, too.

"W-what is this? This nonsense has gone too far!"

"Schneider, that letter sets forth in detail the means by which you planned to overthrow the nation," said Liesbeck.

"I swear by the gods of heaven and earth that I have no idea what this letter is in reference to. I'll do anything to prove my innocence," Schneider stated, red-faced.

Liesbeck laughed in response. "No, no. I never thought you were capable of fashioning a grand plan like this and executing it in secret. You and the king were not on the best of terms, and I worried about that; but I was more concerned with Tylus. He knew you two weren't getting along and was planning to use that to his advantage. There should be another letter, one that would report in detail how King Evesrin was trying to implicate you, Schneider, in a plot against him."

At this point, Land promptly stepped forward, producing a second letter. "That would be this letter," he said.

Despite his surprise, Liesbeck took the letter without a word. He did not open it but handed it straight to the king.

The king and Schneider ripped open the letter and read its contents. Once again, the color of their faces changed.

"W-what is this? It's lies! All lies!"

"Tylus, how cowardly . . ."

"Indeed—is he not embarrassed to be the king of a great nation?"

"Exactly!"

The two of them held hands again and expressed their indignation.

Watching this, Liesbeck sighed dramatically. "You two have no right to talk this way about Tylus—think carefully about why we are in our current situation."

The men appeared downcast.

"Anyway, we should concentrate on what to do now," said Liesbeck, at which Prince Charles stepped forward.

"Grandfather, if you think there might be a small possibility that all of this is the work of a devil, please give me a chance to prove it. I will research this as fast as I can and find the devil's weakness. In fact, if he was imprisoned once, there should be a way of imprisoning him again."

Liesbeck considered. *Hm . . . Strange things are happening; the prince is right about that. Maybe it's all fairytales! A devil—no, I can't believe this is all due to a devil! Perhaps there is something inhuman up to mischief, though. . . .*

"All right, Charles," he said. "We should do everything in our power. How do you intend to research this?"

"Well, I am concerned about the missing statue and the strange dog represented there. Also, I think I should have another look at the book and try to decipher the code. Agnis has promised to help."

Hearing her name so unexpectedly, Agnis hiccuped.

Liesbeck nodded, looking at the two of them.

"Hmph. I suppose it cannot do any harm. The two of you can leave by the secret escape tunnel. Meanwhile, Schneider, you take the king and queen to the secondary shelter room. Charles, make sure you are cautious and take some guards with you, do you understand?"

"Yes, I understand."

When the prince lowered his head, Liesbeck softened his usually hard features, revealing the face of an old man who couldn't help but adore his grandchild.

"Who will guard you, though? Ah, I know. You men there. You have come with us this far—can you continue to help us a little farther?"

He was addressing Olba, Land, and Clay Judah.

"If my eyes aren't mistaken, you are all very skilled soldiers," ex-King Liesbeck added. "Needless to say, there will be a reward. Well, what do you say?"

There was certainly nobody with a reason to say 'no.' In particular, Olba had been asked to go to Orland by Agnis in order to help Charles, so he couldn't leave now. And Land had come too far to turn back; in fact, Land didn't have any money at the moment, so it was too good a deal to pass up. Clay Judah didn't especially benefit from the plan, but he rarely refused anyone who asked anything of him. In the end, everyone gave ready consent and joined the prince as his guards, exactly as the ex-king had requested.

Well, he hadn't actually requested anything of Duan. To tell the truth, Duan was feeling out of the loop, as if he'd turned invisible. He hadn't appeared on Liesbeck's radar, and the prince didn't seem to see him, either, even though he was talking to Agnis, who was standing right next to Duan.

Finally, Agnis acknowledged his presence. "By the way, Charles," she said, "this is the guy I was telling you about, Duan."

The prince replied rather indifferently. "Oh, right."

Agnis and Duan looked at each other, tilting their heads but saying nothing.

Preparations were completed swiftly, and the two groups headed toward the secret passage, which was located under the throne on the platform in the center of the hall. A narrow spiral staircase led down into darkness.

"I guess I'm coming with you guys, then?" Duan asked in a timid voice.

Check, who was clinging to his shoulder, slapped him on the side of the head with one gauzy wing. "Duan come, gi-iis! Check too!"

CHAPTER 37:

DUAN UNDERGROUND

Single file, they descended the narrow spiral staircase. Around and around and around . . .

Duan was beginning to feel sick. Agnis too. And Charles, who hadn't done any regular training, almost sat down a number of times.

To go down three floors of spiral stairs took a lot more effort than you'd think. And these stairs went down three floors and kept going. There was no way the king and queen could do this without complaining; for the first three floors, that's exactly what they did, nonstop. After the fifth floor, they practically were having temper tantrums. Fortunately, Schneider somehow managed to cheer them up, and they pushed onward.

Olba and the two other high-level adventurers didn't even change their expressions.

"Hurry up, kid!" Olba, who was behind Duan, shoved him in the back.

"Aah! Stop it, Olba! I'm about to slip as it is."

"Pah, pathetic. That's because you need more daily training."

"Check train! Help Duan, gi–iis!"

And so, while being moaned at by Olba and cheered on by Check, Duan kept descending. When he thought they'd reached the bottom, though, he found that he was being too optimistic.

"Darn! There's more?"

Yes, the first staircase led to a second, which led farther down into the basement below the tower. At least this one wasn't a spiral staircase—but each step was high and narrow, which was hardly an improvement.

When they finally reached the bottom of this staircase, they entered a passageway. The ceiling was so low that they all had to stoop over. A pair of Black Knights took the lead, followed by Schneider, the king and queen, and then Agnis, Prince Charles, Olba, Duan, Land, and Clay Judah.

The passageway seemed like it continued straight ahead, but it wasn't lit at all; the only source of light came from the Black Knights in the lead, who were carrying torches—and that illumination barely reached Duan and the others at the back.

As usual, the king's and queen's complaints loudly bounced off the walls.

"This secret tunnel is cool!" Land commented excitedly. "I've never been in one like this before. Wow, its structure is excellent! I guess it figures they'd build well for a royal escape route. . . ."

Duan was about to say something when he smacked his head on something.

"OWWW!"

He could see flashing lights; at the same time, there was a sharp pain deep inside his nose.

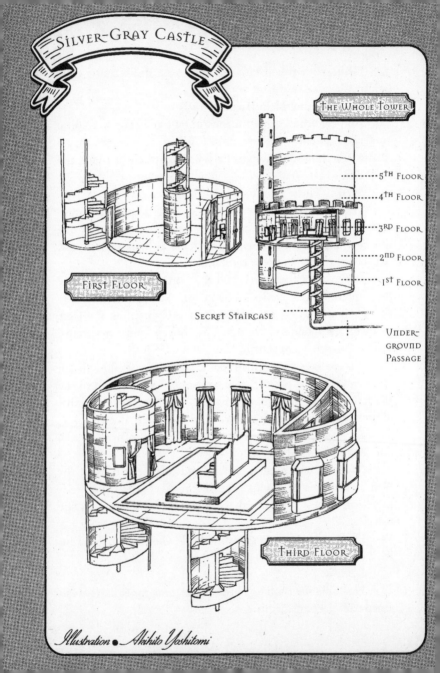

Olba, who was standing to his side, frowned at him. "What the heck are you doing?"

"I-I . . . bumped into something. . . ."

Land giggled and pointed up ahead. Although you couldn't really see it, there was a protrusion in the stone. "When you're walking through places like this, you have to keep checking ahead of you and above your head. I was just about to say that, actually. Unlucky. Poor you. Hee hee!"

Duan bit his lip in embarrassment. He knew it was the most basic of basic adventuring rules.

I was walking carefully in the Red Dragon's dungeon! Darn it! I've been a little . . . no, really unlucky lately.

As he sighed, someone patted him on his back; he looked around and saw Clay Judah.

"Are you okay?" he asked.

Duan went bright red again. Luckily, it was so dark, there was no worry that anyone could see him.

"S-sorry to be trouble."

He lowered his head and ran to catch up with Olba.

"Watch out for your head!" called Land from behind. "Heh!"

Oh yeah, oh yeah.

If I were to hit the same place again, I don't think I could look at people. I'd be so embarrassed. I don't think I'd want to stay here. I'd dig a hole and hide!

Someone was patting his back again.

"Yes?" He replied respectfully because he thought it was Clay Judah, but it turned out to be Check.

"Don't worry, gi-iis. Check see. Check warn, cha!"

"Thanks, Check."

Urgh, there's something wrong with me. I mistook Check's hand for that guy's! Duan dropped his shoulders lower.

After a while, they came to an intersecting passageway, but they kept straight on. Then, they came to another intersection; this time, they turned to the right. This led to yet another intersection. . . .

"Wow. This dungeon is like a chess board!" Duan said appreciatively.

"If the enemy did follow us, they'd get lost on this grid, see?" said Land from behind.

"Oh, right. And I guess we just need to remember when to turn, so it's easy for us. Even if it's your first time, as long as you know where to turn, you're fine," commented Duan.

Land grunted. "Kid, you may be clumsy, but I guess you're smarter than you look."

Duan felt his cheeks rising into a smile. He hadn't exactly distinguished himself thus far, so a moment like this really meant something to him. Melodramatic as it sounds, he felt as though some of his shredded pride had been knit back together again by Land's words, even if the compliment was kind of backhanded. Olba's next comment shredded his pride all over again:

"Smart? Pah, he wouldn't have anything left if you took that away from him! Just his pretty face."

Before Duan could object to this remark, Agnis, who had been walking ahead, spoke up. "Olba, you didn't have to say that. As usual, you've taken it too far."

U-urgh. I'm happy that you're defending me, but . . . in this situation, you really don't want to be defended by a girl! I look so pathetic.

Duan could do nothing but laugh bitterly. Someone patted him on his shoulder again. This time, it was Land.

"C'mon, move on. You're blocking everyone else!"

"Oh, sorry!"

As he apologized, Duan felt like Land was Olba all over again.

Great, just what I need: two Olbas!

CHAPTER 38:

A TIME OF CRISIS

fter turning a few more corners, they came to another staircase, this one heading up.

At the top of the stairs was a door that opened into a spacious room with luxurious furnishings and a comfortable-looking sofa. At the back of the room, there were two more doors.

King Evesrin immediately went to lie down on the sofa. "Dear me, I couldn't have taken it much longer—all that climbing!"

Schneider lowered his head and said, "I apologize profusely. When this is over, I'll see that the passage is rebuilt so it's more pleasant to walk through."

The king beamed at that comment and looked at the queen, who was sitting beside him.

She held a silk handkerchief to her small nose. "I do hope this commotion is dealt with quickly," she said. "If I don't go to bed soon, my skin will suffer."

Agnis couldn't believe her ears. *"My skin will suffer?"* *When there's a possibility you could die . . . ? Do people who live in high society not understand the situation around them?*

She herself was also royalty. Though Agnis thought she was down to earth, she wondered if maybe other people thought she was disconnected from reality, like the queen. It occurred to Agnis that maybe, in her own way, she was out of touch. It was something she would have to think about. Meanwhile, she realized there was no point in getting angry at the queen. She sighed deeply.

"What's wrong?" asked Prince Charles, looking at her worriedly.

"Oh, nothing. I guess I'm a little tired. We should get going, though. We have no time!"

"Yes . . ."

Charles snuck a peek at Duan.

Duan, who noticed him looking, peered back with a questioning smile.

Charles looked away in a hurry.

Agnis, who saw all this, tilted her head.

"What's wrong, Charles? Is something bothering you about my friend?"

"N-no, not at all. I'm shy, though. Unlike you, I can't chat and be friendly with just anyone."

Agnis was too surprised to reply. The prince had spoken quite rudely. This was a rare event. In fact, even Charles himself was surprised by it.

"Oh, s-sorry! I didn't mean to be rude. Anyway, it's nothing, so don't worry about me."

"I guess we don't have time to discuss it now, anyway."

There was something dissatisfying about it, but Agnis blew out her cheeks and decided to ignore it for now.

211

Oh yeah! We have to think about the devil first!

She paced toward Duan and the others.

"I'd really like to get go—" she stopped with a start.

Everyone was focused on her, especially Clay Judah. He looked at her with eyes of true kindness. At once, Agnis' heart began to race.

W-what was that? Silly me!

She pressed her hand against her rapidly beating heart. Then, she took a deep breath and started over: "I'm afraid we don't have much time, so I'd appreciate it if we can depart as soon as possible."

She was looking at Clay Judah when she said it, so he answered for everyone.

"Of course. We can go anytime." He gave her a pleasant smile.

Agnis smiled back at him. All her tense muscles loosened. Her heart returned to normal, too.

Ha ha. That's it. It's because it's a time of crisis! Both Charles and I are feeling hot-headed and not normal. I should relax. You always should be calm in times like these.

"So, where would you like to go first?" asked Land, who was standing beside Clay Judah.

Agnis turned around and looked at Charles. "Where that book is—right, Charles?"

"U-um, yes. I think it's necessary to have another look at that book," answered the prince in a small voice.

"Where is it now?"

"It's in my room."

"Okay."

Then, when they seemed ready to depart, Olba remarked, "By the way, it's going to be kind of hard to fight in these clothes. We need armor—and weapons, too."

"We have some here. Let us lend you some."

It was Schneider who spoke. Who knew when he had managed to change, but he now wore luxurious lacy clothes beneath gleaming silver-plate armor. His helm was decorated with flashy tassels.

"This is the special armor of the royal family," the king said proudly. "You may borrow it."

Olba grimaced. "Urgh, how gaudy is this armor? Gold decoration patterns on top of silver? Gimme a break!"

"It can't be helped," said Duan. "We don't have time to search for our own stuff now. C'mon, Olba, let's borrow these." Duan tugged at the big fighter. Check tugged, too, fiercely flapping his little wings.

"Okay, okay!" Olba, pulled along by Duan and Check, looked up at the ceiling and sighed.

CHAPTER 39:

TERROR ON THE STAIRS

lba was wearing silver-plate armor and held a matching shield and longsword. He clinked and clanked as he walked, and Agnis and Land giggled at him.

"You won't have to swing your sword in that outfit," said Land. "You'll blind the enemy, it's so bright!"

Olba snorted at Land's sneering comment. He had been offered a full-face helmet, as well, but he had declined politely, as had Duan.

Duan's armor was so large that it was difficult to move in. On top of that, it was heavy. He was wearing undergarments with chain mail (also very heavy), as well as boots, knee-protectors, thigh-protectors, a neck-protector, a breastplate, and shoulder plates.

Duan had heard somewhere that the total weight of full-plate armor could be anywhere from ninety to one hundred thirty pounds. He felt weary when he remembered this.

That's practically the weight of an adult!

A vision of himself carrying Olba on his back and almost collapsing in exhaustion entered his head. Although the armor couldn't possibly weigh as much as Olba. Could it?

Urgh . . . It sure is difficult to move in.

When Duan actually tried to walk, he was surprised— it was worse than he'd imagined. "U–urgh . . . W–what? N–no way!"

Oh dear. He couldn't take a single step. *You've gotta be kidding me!* Unfortunately, it was the absolute truth.

"What are you doing? It's pretty heavy, eh?" commented Olba, who was moving around freely—looking completely fine—and checking his longsword.

"U–um . . . I actually think it's better for me not to wear this," said Duan, trying to act as natural as possible because he couldn't possibly say that he couldn't move.

Olba wasn't fooled. "What's the matter, kid? Can't you walk in it?"

"What? No, it's not that . . ."

"Okay then, why don't you stroll on over here?"

Duan felt every eye in the room upon him. His face burned as though it were on fire.

Even Check, who had been repeatedly checking the armor, was watching him with judgmental eyes.

Urgh. Olba didn't have to say that here, now, in front of everyone. . . .

Duan glared at Olba. Olba glared back at Duan. Clay Judah stepped forward.

"You don't have to wear it all. First, take off the knee- and thigh-protectors. . . ."

Clay Judah helped Duan change into light armor.

"Th–thank you."

"It's okay. It's difficult to wear full-plate if you're not used to it. I don't like it, either."

"Really?" *Oh yeah, this guy's wearing really light armor.*

Clay Judah's armor was black, but Duan couldn't figure out what it was made of. It looked like it was strengthened with some kind of special magic.

"So, I think this will be all right." He had his boots, breastplate, and shoulder-protectors on over his chain mail undergarments. *Yeah, I can move in this!*

After that, Schneider asked him whether he'd like to borrow a longsword. Duan politely declined and took a small short sword instead.

Then, the party made a swift exit from the secret room by pushing past a hidden door at the end of a narrow corridor.

They were now located in the corridor in front of the king's room. Rooms lined one side of the corridor; the other side overlooked the grand hall beyond a handrail.

In fact, it was a super-grand hall! The scale of the place was overwhelming. It wasn't just wide: The height of the ceiling was about five times that of an ordinary castle. And the pillars that dominated the hall were so large in girth that it would've taken three or four people holding hands to encircle one. Each was separated by about a pillar's length of space.

It was possible to descend into the grand hall by either of two staircases. One was the grand staircase, which happened to be near their current location. It had stone handrails with carvings engraved into them to act as protection against evil spirits. The other staircase was at the end of the corridor, and it was a plain stone staircase that meandered down.

Small windows lined the grand hall. And every so often, lightning brightly illuminated the place. The storm was still going strong.

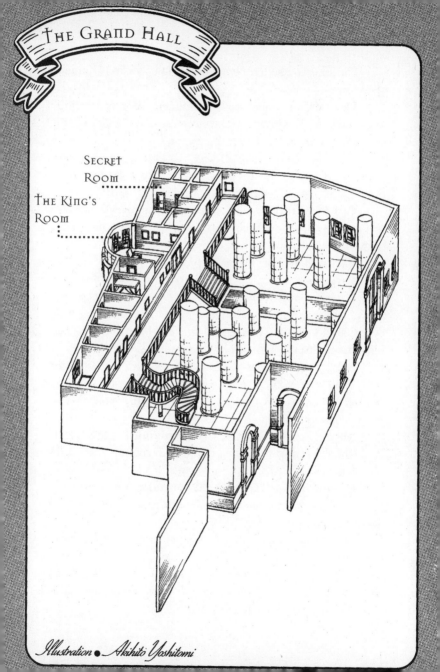

The Grand Hall

Secret Room

The King's Room

Illustration ● Akihito Yoshitomi

"So, this is where it comes out." Agnis looked around in appreciation.

Duan didn't appreciate her comment because he didn't know where "this" was. He concentrated on standing still, trying not to make a sound in his armor.

I wonder where Charles' room is? Duan's thought was interrupted by a pat on his shoulder—although it was more a clank than a pat. When he turned, he saw Clay Judah.

Clay Judah thrust out his chin and, using his eyes, signaled to Duan to look down into the grand hall. Everyone took a cautious peek, leaping back the very next second.

They're there! They're there!

Red Knights were wandering around the grand hall!

I suppose they wouldn't leave the king's room unguarded, thought Duan. And then, moving swiftly, he clamped a hand over Check's mouth. The baby grinia had been about to start screaming in panic. That would have been a catastrophe.

Meanwhile, Charles glanced at Agnis with a questioning expression. Agnis knew what he was trying to say: It wasn't possible to get to the prince's room without having to pass through the grand hall.

Seeing the two of them, Clay Judah nodded toward the Red Knights and said softly, "I take it your room is that way?"

Charles nodded.

Clay Judah quickly whispered something into Land's ear.

Land gave a thumbs-up sign and began quietly creeping down the grand staircase.

"Get to your room while we keep them busy," Clay Judah told Charles.

Charles opened his eyes wide. He looked around at Duan and Olba in their gaudy armor. Then, he vigorously shook his head and squeezed Clay Judah's arm.

Clay Judah shot Charles a questioning look.

"N-no, you've got to come. Grandpapa said you'd come!"

Clay Judah turned a gentle gaze toward Charles, who seemed like he was about to cry. "I understand," he said. "In that case . . . Olba, was it?"

Olba, hearing his name, pointed at his own face, as if to say "Who, me?"

"Yes. I'm sorry, but do you think you could keep them busy with Land? I will escort Prince Charles."

Olba looked down his nose at Prince Charles and Clay Judah.

Without thinking, Charles squeezed Clay Judah's arm.

Finally, Olba raised one eyebrow and shrugged. "Whatever. Okay, Duan, don't do anything stupid!" And with that, he ran down after Land.

"Let's go," said Clay Judah.

The prince nodded. Agnis and Duan already had started walking toward the stone staircase at the end of the corridor.

"Agnis!"

Charles began to run toward Agnis, but Duan put his finger on his lips in reaction to the somewhat-loud call.

"We'll be in trouble if they see us."

Charles replied angrily, "I know that already, without having *you* tell me!"

This time, it was Duan who got angry. *What was that about? Why is he so uptight? If he knows, then he should keep quiet!*

"Duan, gi–iis! Hurry, cha!"

At this reminder from Check, Duan quickly followed after the others.

After a while, a commotion began at the bottom of the grand staircase.

"I think they've started to run riot," said Clay Judah. "We should get going now."

Led by Clay Judah, the group made their way down the winding stone staircase. The prince told them they had to take the back corridor on the right side of the grand hall to get to his room.

The small party dashed through the hall, hiding in the shadows of the big pillars. As they ran, Duan caught glimpses of Land and Olba fighting a bunch of Red Knights on the grand staircase.

"Are they all right on their own?" Duan asked, hesitating slightly.

Check gave him a small punch on the side of his head. "Remember, cha! Olba say don't do anything stupid!"

This was indeed true, but having to hear it from Check made Duan exceedingly angry.

At last, they made it safely out of the hall. Although there were lit torches on the walls, it was still fairly dark. The party was led by Clay Judah, and Duan took the rear; Charles and Agnis were in between.

"If you turn the second corner, there's a staircase. The corridor to my room is at the top," Charles said after they had turned a few corners and ascended and descended a few staircases.

It was such a bizarrely complex castle that if they didn't have Charles, who lived there, they would've no doubt been lost.

As Charles had said, there was a stone staircase when they turned the corner. Each step was eroded and rounded down.

They were about to run up the stairs when Check started yelling, "Danger! Danger!"

"W-what?" gasped Duan, but then he gulped.

Someone was descending the stairs. It was someone wearing a blood-red hood that came down low over the eyes. In short, it was a sorcerer.

CHAPTER 40:

A FAMILIAR VOICE

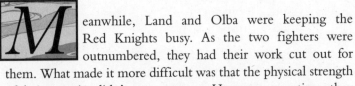eanwhile, Land and Olba were keeping the Red Knights busy. As the two fighters were outnumbered, they had their work cut out for them. What made it more difficult was that the physical strength of their enemies didn't seem to wane. However many times they were beaten down, the Red Knights eventually got up again.

And then, reinforcements began to arrive.

"This is bad," said Land.

"Yep," Olba agreed.

Although the secret room was sectioned off with a hidden door, King Evesrin and Queen Milhene still were only a hair's breadth away from capture. And now, more and more Red Knights were being drawn toward the Silver-Gray Tower.

"Let's try and lead them someplace else," said Olba as he avoided the sword of one Red Knight.

"Roger!" Land quickly sped around the Red Knight he was fighting, kicking him with all his strength from behind. The Red Knight crumpled onto the ground, making a racket as he fell. Land then lightly jumped over him. He moved so swiftly that it was hard to believe he'd been injured on his right shoulder.

"Okay, then. C'mon, c'mon, dearies! Er . . . which way should I go?" Land asked Olba.

He tilted his head. "Dunno. Outside would be good."

"Outside? It's still raining. And the lightning is strong.

"Even better," Olba said. "They'll lose us soon enough. Then, we can come back here."

"Boo—I just got dry! And I'm still injured, y'know?"

"C'mon, let's get going. I'll listen to your complaints later," said Olba as he fought off three Red Knights with his borrowed longsword, hurrying toward the left side of the hall, where a large door led outside.

He kicked down the door with a bang; at once, rain fell like a waterfall against his cheeks. "Hm . . . maybe that's not such a good idea, after all. . . ."

When he shut the door, the Red Knights that had followed Land and him came surging up behind them.

"I-idiot! Why did you shut the door?!"

"Oh? Okay, here you go."

With exaggerated courtesy, Olba opened the door for Land. Land ran through it, the Red Knights right behind him. After about ten minutes, he came rushing back.

They quickly shut the door, Land panting desperately. After he had calmed his breathing, he started to shout at Olba.

"W-what the heck were you doing?"

"I didn't want to get wet."

"Jerk!" screamed Land, standing on his toes to get right up into Olba's nose. Raindrops dripped onto the floor from his long hair. He was completely soaked.

"Calm down. So, what happened to them?" asked Olba.

Land replied moodily, "I lost them out there. They're probably still looking for me in the rain."

"Wow, you're good."

"Who do you think I am?" asked Land, straight-faced.

Olba whispered simply, "Dunno."

"What?" asked Land.

"No, nothing," replied Olba, and he laughed bitterly.

"Well, shall we follow the prince?"

"Yeah."

No sooner had they started to move than the door crashed open with a loud bang. The Red Knights had returned, soaked to the bone and making a racket as they walked.

"Shoot, you guys came back?" laughed Land in annoyance.

"I thought you lost them!" shouted Olba, who already had started to fight them.

"Maybe they're smarter than we think," answered Land, avoiding a strike from a sword coming down in front of him.

At that moment, another group entered the scene.

The newcomers were dressed completely in black; like the Red Knights, they were soaking wet.

"Whoa, I thought they were more reinforcements—but look, here come the good guys!" cried Olba.

"Great, maybe we can relax a little," said Land.

Olba was about to reply "yeah" when he looked up the grand staircase and said in a weary voice, "No, it doesn't look like it."

Land followed Olba's line of vision and groaned. The corridor overlooking the grand hall was lined with Red Knights, about twice as many as the newly arrived Black Knights. And to make matters worse, they were armed with crossbows. Arrows began to fly.

Land and Olba fled outside their range.

"Don't they even care if they shoot their own men?" asked Land. Arrows rained down on the Red Knights, too; some of them had been hit and fell to the ground.

"Whoa, they've pierced the plate armor! What's happening?" asked Land again.

Olba replied with a bitter look on his face, "I don't think they're human."

At that comment, Land looked around in surprise. "The thought did cross my mind. You think so?"

"Yeah. Can't you feel it? They have no life force."

Land, with terrified eyes, replied in a quivering voice, "You mean, they're ghosts?"

"What're you talking about? No, I'm saying they're monsters! They're controlled by a puppet-master; they're probably a type of golem," explained Olba.

Land's expression changed to one of relief. "Oh! Don't scare me like that! If there's one thing I'm scared of, it's ghosts. Monsters are easy-peasy. C'mon, you monsters!"

With that, Land leapt amid the Red Knights.

Watching this, Olba shook his head. "The guy can't do ghosts, but he's okay with monsters? What a weirdo! Well, in any case, it's a waste of energy trying to kill them if they're golems."

"True."

Olba immediately went on guard when he heard the voice speak behind him. When he turned, there stood a Black Knight. He was wearing a full-face helmet, so Olba couldn't tell who he was.

"Olba, that's flashy armor you're wearing," the Black Knight said.

"What?" Olba recognized the man's voice, but it was a long-lost memory, in the depths of his mind. "Who are you?" he asked.

At that moment, the Black Knight turned to clash with two Red Knights. He was quite skilled.

A Red Knight came charging aggressively at Olba, a war hammer in his hand.

"Whoa!" Olba dodged with ease. The Red Knight continued running—it seemed he couldn't turn around very quickly in his full-body armor. When he finally managed to do so, he came charging at Olba again; this time, the big fighter tripped him.

The Red Knight yelped and tumbled to the floor. He lay there struggling, making a huge clatter as he unsuccessfully tried to rise. Olba couldn't decide whether to strike at the fallen knight or search out a new enemy, so he took a quick look around. There were Black Knights and Red Knights fighting everywhere; he couldn't tell which was the knight he'd been speaking to, the one with the voice that was somehow familiar.

Olba gave a shrug, cracked his neck from side to side, and returned to the battle.

Chapter 41

Not A Moment Too Soon

At that same moment, on the other side of the grand hall, Clay Judah raised his hands as if to protect the others and shuffled backward, retreating before the figure in the red robe, who continued to descend the steps, smirking and sneering.

"Where is King Evesrin?" the sorcerer asked in a muffled voice.

Duan and the others remained silent.

"By the time I'm through with you, you'll be begging to tell me all you know!" The sorcerer's wrinkled mouth started to move as he began to chant a spell.

"Shoot. Prince Charles, please run! Duan!"

"Y-yes!"

Duan had been frozen to the spot like the others; now, he came back to his senses.

He tugged the two beside him. "Come on, Agnis, Prince Charles!"

He pulled their arms and tried to go back down the stairs. Before he managed to do so, however, a coil of light shot from the sorcerer's fingertips.

"Aah!"

Duan turned his back to protect Agnis and Charles, but the light scattered before it reached Duan.

Huh? What's happening?

I shouldn't analyze this now. We have to run. Otherwise, we'll get in Clay Judah's way.

Duan grabbed Agnis' and Charles' arms again. As he hurried them down the stairs, he slammed against a hard wall.

"Ow!"

"Ooow!"

"Whoa!"

The three fell on their behinds. There was a slightly shiny, semi-transparent wall in front of them!

Agnis and Duan looked at each other and screamed at the same time: "Magic Wall!"

They looked behind them. Another coil of light was beginning to form at the sorcerer's fingertips. This time, the light flew toward Clay Judah. Another semi-transparent wall appeared, like the one behind Duan and the others. Magic Walls enclosed them. The sorcerer started to chant another spell.

"Here it comes," said Clay Judah.

When Duan and the others looked up, they saw something like an arrow made of light in the grip of the sorcerer's hand.

"Gra-ha-ha . . ." With an eerie laugh, he threw the arrow at them.

It was, of course, a Magic Arrow. The arrow penetrated the Magic Wall and started to chase Duan and the others.

Clang!

A metallic sound reverberated through the place. It was the sound of Clay Judah's slender longsword slamming against the Magic Arrow, which shattered in an instant.

The laughter disappeared from the lips of the sorcerer. "That sword . . ."

He bit his lips in a loathsome way and raised his hands above his head. This time, he made a bunch of Magic Arrows and temporarily raised them so that more than ten arrows floated mid-air.

He unleashed them in one go, aiming at Clay Judah. The arrows seemed like they were alive as they moved about in different directions. They pierced the Magic Wall and came right at Clay Judah.

Clang! Clink!

With a minimum amount of body movement, Clay Judah knocked them down one after the other.

He can't keep this up forever, thought Duan as looked on helplessly from behind another Magic Wall. *Clay Judah's concentration will slip sometime, no matter how skilled a soldier he is.*

Duan looked at Clay Judah's armor-clad back and felt his chest tightening. He had no idea what he could do to help.

"Argh!"

One arrow of light zipped past in front of them. Clay Judah, who turned back once to check that they were okay, glared at the sorcerer again (striking down another Magic Arrow as he did so).

The sorcerer's eyes, hidden under his red hood, sparkled spookily. He started to concentrate as if he were planning a stronger attack. His body slowly was becoming enveloped in a reddish light. When this red light was shining so brightly that it hurt to look in his direction, the sorcerer thrust out both his hands.

At that moment, Clay Judah raised his sword again and struck at the Magic Wall. There was a sound like a pane of glass breaking, and the wall was gone.

The sorcerer's jaw dropped. He stood frozen in position, his hands out in front of him. It was as if time had stopped. When it started again, it seemed to Duan that Clay Judah must have teleported; there was no other way he could have moved so quickly. Suddenly, there he was, standing before the sorcerer, his longsword buried in the man's stomach.

The robe floated down, and the sorcerer's face was revealed. He collapsed onto the floor with an expression of disbelief.

Duan, Agnis, Charles, and even Check gaped at this scene in shock. Unable to believe their own eyes, they were at a loss for words.

"Duan, don't just stand there—go, quickly!" called Clay Judah.

"What?!" replied Duan, wide-eyed.

"Quickly!" Clay Judah tugged him.

"Come on, you two."

Agnis and Charles also were pulled up.

In their shock and confusion, the three somehow found their way to the top of the stairs.

Oh yeah, we have to get to the prince's room, thought Duan. As they reached the landing, he looked back. "What about you?" he asked Clay Judah. "Aren't you coming?"

Clay Judah looked at him without a word.

Behind him, where the Magic Wall had formed at the bottom of the stairs, a red robe started to float into the air.

"What?!"

The sorcerer Clay Judah appeared to have killed actually had regenerated in a different location. Now, he was creating dozens of Magic Arrows at once, unleashing them at incredible speeds. Even Clay Judah couldn't deflect them all; some of them were damaging his armor.

"Aaah!" screamed Agnis with a pale face. She started to cry at the sight of fresh blood dripping down Clay Judah's forehead.

"Go!" cried Clay Judah. "You must bind the devil that's controlling them! It's the only way. Duan, I'm counting on you. I know you can do it!"

Duan gritted his teeth and nodded. He looked at Prince Charles, who, like Agnis, was shaking, his face pale and tearful.

Olba and the others probably are fighting an endless battle now, too. The Red Knights and this sorcerer aren't human. . . .

"Okay," said Duan, coming to a decision. "Charles, Agnis, follow me: We're getting out of here."

Agnis, still looking pale, shook her head. "No."

Duan couldn't believe his ears. "What?"

"I'm not going. I can't leave him here to fight all alone. I simply can't do it!" As she spoke, she gripped her staff.

Oh no! Duan quickly pinned back her arms. "You can't cast your Fire Spell in an enclosed space like this, Agnis! You'll fry us all. Besides, you heard him: There's no end to this! If you kill the sorcerer, he'll just regenerate again, right? We have to stop this at the source, and that means finding the book in Charles' room! It's our best weapon against the devil at this point."

"I can't just leave him here!" Agnis protested. "He'll die. I don't want that!"

Her cheeks, wet with tears, gleamed as she stared at Duan. It became clear to Duan as he looked into her purple eyes. "Agnis, are you . . . ?"

Agnis, who understood why Duan swallowed his words, blushed brightly. She bit her lips and turned away.

Just then, Magic Arrows started to chase them. An instant later, they'd both been pushed down by something, something that came down the stairs in the blink of an eye.

It floated down and landed in front of them, flexing its supple muscles. Dazzling white fur with beautiful, elegant, floating black spots . . .

"K'nock!" screamed Agnis.

The snow leopard had been waiting patiently in Prince Charles' room for Agnis' return. Now, hearing her scream, he'd rushed to her rescue. Agnis clung to his neck and felt warmth fill her soul.

"I know, K'nock—I'm happy to see you, too. But don't look after me. I want you to look after that person." Agnis indicated Clay Judah.

K'nock glanced toward Clay Judah. He leapt up without a sound, this time landing in front of the sorcerer with the red robe.

"Grrrrr . . ."

The snow leopard growled, approaching the sorcerer.

"Good cat, gi–iis!" Check cried out in excitement.

K'nock leapt toward the sorcerer, crashing into a Magic Wall.

"Get down," said Clay Judah.

K'nock obeyed. With his sword, Clay Judah struck at the wall, which shattered like the other wall had. K'nock didn't wait for the glow to fade; he again leapt at the sorcerer and began chasing him down the stairs.

"Your friend looks like he'll be helpful," commented Clay Judah with a more relaxed expression. He hurried after K'nock.

"Agnis, he's all right now," said Duan. "Come on, let's do our part."

Coaxing along Agnis, Duan led them up the stairs. Agnis still was worried about K'nock and Clay Judah; but after looking back two or three times, she put aside her worries.

"Come on, Charles, let's go!"

Hurrying the prince along, Agnis ran up the stairs. Their destination, Charles' room, was right in front of them.

CHAPTER 42:

THE DEVIL AND THE SORCERERS

To the north of the Silver-Gray Castle was a steeple about the same size as the Silver-Gray Tower. The tower could be seen from the steeple, and it was right above where Duan and Olba had been imprisoned. Oppressive black clouds stormed around the top of the steeple, pressing against it. Every so often, a flash of lightning starkly illuminated its features.

On the very top floor was an ice-cold room. In that room, dressed in magnificent blue clothes beneath a deep, red cloak was Schneider Deks . . . although, technically speaking, it would be more accurate to call this man an exact duplicate of Schneider Deks, at least on the physical level. Marbles of sweat glistened on his forehead, and he breathed with difficulty as he pressed a hand to his chest and dropped heavily into a chair.

That chair was the sole piece of furniture in the room.

Apart from the man who looked like Schneider Deks, the only person there was a sorcerer dressed in a red robe. He tightly clasped the robe around him with rough and bony fingers as he said through chattering teeth, "F-f-f-freezing. Th-this room is p-powerfully c-c-cold."

The man who looked like Schneider did not answer him, simply continuing to breathe with difficulty. Watching this, the sorcerer shrugged.

"Lord Senzrabur, perhaps you've used too m-much of your magic p-power? M-magic power is something you should keep charged to the max at all times. If you d-don't . . ."

He spoke like a teacher reprimanding a poor student. But he quickly shut his mouth when the man he'd addressed as Senzrabur glared at him hatefully. The man's eyes shone red, and a small flame appeared on the hood of the sorcerer's robe, right next to his cheek. In the blink of an eye, the fire spread.

"Argh! Aah! Hot! Hot!"

The sorcerer frantically slapped at the hood until the fire was out. "W-what are you doing!?" he demanded angrily.

Senzrabur sneered, "Didn't you say you were cold?"

The sorcerer looked back in astonishment at Senzrabur, making a small sigh and patting down his hood. The sorcerer's name was Kojey Crawley. He was the second oldest of the three sorcerer brothers that Senzrabur had employed. That said, the three of them all were very old, with deeply wrinkled faces and muffled voices. They looked and dressed the same, so Senzrabur couldn't tell them apart unless they wore different colors of robes.

They were not human. They were citizens of darkness. At root, they were monsters.

The Crawley brothers were mercenaries. As long as they were paid, they'd appear anywhere, do anything.

The one fighting Clay Judah was the eldest, Ojey. The one fighting at the Silver-Gray Tower was the youngest, Tajey.

Kojey's talents, to put it politely, didn't incline him toward rough-and-tumble, hand-to-hand combat. No, his talents lay more in the accounting line. Someone had to stay at home and keep the books all neatly balanced while Ojey and Tajey were out on business!

The brothers' specialty was electricity-related magic, but they weren't particularly powerful. At the moment, they were borrowing Senzrabur's magic power, which was why they were so strong.

While Kojey was sulking, Senzrabur stood up, his deep red mantle fluttering, and peered out the window at the Silver-Gray Tower.

"Where is that fool of a king?" he muttered. "Is he really not in the tower? No, he must be hiding there somewhere!"

Around the Silver-Gray Tower, Black Knights and Red Knights were fighting in the rain. Fires billowed out from the tower windows, telling the story of a hard battle within.

Kojey, who also was watching the scene, said, "According to my younger brother Tajey, the king definitely is not in the Silver-Gray Tower, only the ex-king, old man Liesbeck, who's proving to be quite a robust opponent and apparently is quite a handful for Tajey."

Kojey cackled; though, who knows what he was laughing about.

At this, Senzrabur glared at him again with a look of utmost displeasure.

Kojey, in a panic, laughed weakly and said, "N-no, it really isn't the time to be laughing, is it? Ha ha ha . . ."

Senzrabur sighed deeply, as if there were no point talking to him anymore. He turned his back on the window. Then, he rounded his back to gather the power in his body. A red light began to envelop him, growing steadily brighter. When it was bright enough to light his surroundings, he started to chant a spell in a wheezy, low voice.

"Iikonokei, iikotode, iiikooo, tedeeee . . ."

Abruptly straightening his back, he brought up his hands. The red light gathered there, swirling. When it had grown to the size of a large ball, he threw the light onto the floor with a loud grunt. Immediately, the red light transformed into different shapes. The light slowly faded, and the outlines became clearer.

Kojey gave a melodramatic sigh. "What, another Red Knight? They're all strength and no brains. Can't you make something else for once?"

Senzrabur glared at Kojey and, as though spitting out the words, said, "All we need to do is stall them. My real powers will awaken any moment now. And when they do, *He* will awaken, too. But we must have a sacrifice ready, and the sacrifice must have the rank of king. You—if you have time to linger around here, go and look for him, too. We must find the king, at any cost!"

"Yes, of course I'll go," said Kojey. "That's our contract, after all. Please, remember to keep your end of the bargain."

Without replying, Senzrabur opened the door for the newly born Red Knight and issued instructions in a gruff voice: "Go to the Silver-Gray Tower and find the king. He's definitely there somewhere, or . . ." Here, Senzrabur paused before nodding meaningfully. "Or maybe not. Yes, I'll wager there's a secret room or passage leading out of the tower! Find it, and you'll find the king. Understood?"

The Red Knight nodded wordlessly and stomped down the narrow staircase.

Kojey waved his hand at the retreating form. "Good luck! Bye-bye!"

Senzrabur kicked him in the rear. "Useless imbecile—you too! Go and find the king!"

CHAPTER 43:

THE RIDDLE OF THE HOLY DOG

eanwhile, Duan, Agnis, and Charles had made it to Charles' room. Charles and Agnis reached to open the door, but Duan stopped them.

"What?" asked Agnis, looking doubtfully at Duan.

Duan gently laid his ear against the door and listened. Then, he ushered Agnis and the prince back down the corridor.

"There's someone inside," he whispered.

"What?!" exclaimed Agnis. "It must be Red Knights, waiting in ambush!"

Duan tilted his head. "Maybe. Or another sorcerer."

"Hm. Are there that many sorcerers?"

"That Black Knight reported multiple sightings."

"Oh right, now I remember. What shall we do?"

Duan thought over things for a while before making up his mind. "I'll open the door first. If there are any enemies, I'll run out quickly. If it's a Red Knight or a sorcerer, they'll follow me out, won't they? So, I'll lure them out to buy us some time. You two hide in the shadow of this door. When the room is empty, go inside and get the book—only the book—and then hide somewhere safe."

"I know the perfect place," said Charles. "There's a spare bedroom at the back of the room. Hardly anybody knows it's there."

"Okay," said Duan. "Ready?"

Nodding, the prince and Agnis held hands and hid themselves in the shadow of the door.

Duan gulped. After taking a deep breath to steel himself, he placed his hand on the doorknob. The door opened with an echoing clank—a sound that was bad for the heart. With one hand on his sword, Duan entered boldly.

In the center of the room, someone peered at him with large round eyes. It wasn't a sorcerer or a Red Knight but a gentleman sporting carefully combed silver hair and an elegant white mustache.

It was Charles' butler, Loren Bator.

Duan bolted upright. Agnis and Charles poked their heads around the door.

"Oh," sighed Charles in relief, "it's Loren!"

Loren bustled over with tears in his eyes. "Your Highness! Thank the gods you are safe!"

The butler seemed to be dragging his feet.

"Loren," asked Charles, "what has happened to your leg?"

"Oh, this? I was attacked by some Red Knights. But I was so worried about you! And somehow, I managed to get back to this room. I was at a loss about what to do next, of course. Oh yes, until a moment ago, Princess Agnis' snow leopard was here with me, but he looked like he wanted to leave, so I opened the door."

"Yes, we know," said Charles. "In truth—"

Duan interrupted. "Excuse me, Your Highness, but we don't have much time. I'm very sorry, but could you show me this book of yours?"

Charles creased his beautiful forehead and glared at Duan. Ignoring him, he gently placed a hand on Loren's arm. "Loren, I'm very sorry, but I don't have time to explain."

"Oh no, not at all. If there is anything you need, please do not hesitate to ask."

After Loren bowed his head, Charles stepped past him into the room, heading toward his desk. He got the book and thrust it out without a word. It seemed as if he wasn't ready to talk to Duan yet.

Duan was getting a little irritated by now. *What is he sulking about? Doesn't he understand this is an emergency? Never mind. I don't have time to worry about that now.*

Before inspecting the book, Duan turned to Check, who was perched on his shoulder, already craning his little neck to peer curiously at the contents. "Check," he said, "this man has hurt his leg. Can you cast a Heal Spell on him?"

"Man hurt, gi–iis?" Check made his round eyes even rounder as he looked at Loren.

"Oh no, please, pay me no mind," the butler responded, not wanting to trouble anyone. "Please, finish whatever you need to do."

"Cha! Check not mind!" And with that, the baby grinia flew over and extended his little arm to shake the hand of the somewhat mystified butler. Then, Check brought together his hands and started to chant. Loren and Charles looked on in amazement.

Satisfied that Check had matters under control, Duan focused on the book.

Although to tell the truth, it wasn't really a book at all: It was more like an empty box. When Duan turned it upside down and shook it, a small piece of paper came floating out. He picked it up and read:

In the southwest of the castle, behind the stone wall that can be seen from the third floor of the Silver-Gray Tower, the devil Senzrabur has been sealed by the Holy Dog. However, when the Dog leaves, the power of darkness will return . . . and the world will fall

Duan read over this paragraph many, many times, pondering its meaning.

So the queen, to make her garden, must have taken down the stone wall and had the Holy Dog removed. But where? The Dog is gone now.

Does that mean the world is going to fall into ruin? Or can we just replace the Holy Dog? No, that would be too easy. It says that the devil was sealed by the Holy Dog, so it has to be sealed again. Er, if that's even possible! In which case, the way to seal it should be written down somewhere.

At this, Duan remembered a book he had read ages ago. It was about a cat that tricked a giant who could use magic; the cat got the giant to transform into a mouse, and then he trapped him in a small pot.

Hm. I can understand how the giant was sealed inside the pot, but how do you seal something with the Holy Dog? Is there a cavity within the statue of the dog?

CHAPTER 44:

REMEDIAL PUNCTUATION

Charles and Agnis watched quietly as Duan studied the message. Charles looked at him half in doubt . . . well, in fact, he had no faith in Duan whatsoever.

What can this useless, incompetent guy do? Compared to Clay Judah, he's . . . well, he doesn't compare!

In fairness, Duan hardly could be compared to the Level 16 Clay Judah!

It never would've entered Duan's mind that Charles was thinking such thoughts. Duan just read the paragraph over and over, concentrating hard enough to burn holes in the paper with his stare.

He tried turning it over and also illuminating it with a candle. He closely inspected the book the paper had been found within.

Check, as if to say, "leave any checking to me," inspected the paper and the book with close attention, as well, his little face screwing up in concentration.

"Um, you're not going to find anything else, however many times you look," said Charles at last. "I read it about a million times myself, you know."

Duan thrust out a hand to stop Charles, who was looking displeased, and said, "W-wait, there's something I was stuck on. What was it again? What was I stuck on?"

"How should I know?" Charles asked huffily.

"What were you looking at? The first line?" asked Agnis, who ran over next to Duan and looked at the paper, too.

Duan shook his head. "No, that's not it."

"Well, what about the second line?" asked Agnis.

Duan shook his head again.

"The third line?"

Duan's eyes sparkled. "That's it!"

"What, the third line?"

"Well, no, after that."

"After that? There are only three lines!"

"Look closely. It says, 'However, when the Dog leaves, the power of darkness will return . . . and the world will fall' . . ."

"Yeah, so?"

"There's no period at the end of that line!"

"Um, okay. I guess. So?"

"What does a period mean?" Duan asked in turn.

"What is this, third grade? It shows where a sentence ends, of course," said Agnis.

"Right. If there's no period, that means . . ."

Charles whispered excitedly, "If there's no period, it's not the end of the sentence! There must be more!"

Duan smiled triumphantly. "Yup, exactly!"

"Hmph," said Charles, frowning again. "I thought that myself already, but I couldn't find a missing piece of the message anywhere."

"Are you sure?"

Duan placed the book that had contained the piece of paper on top of the desk and took out his short sword.

"What are you going to do?" Agnis asked nervously.

Instead of answering her, Duan smiled at Charles and asked, "I'd like to dismantle this book—is that all right?"

CHAPTER 45:

THE PLOT THICKENS

harles immediately gave his permission.

It's a national emergency. No, a world emergency! Under the circumstances, who could object to destroying a book or two?

Exercising the utmost caution, Duan started to dismantle the ancient book, using his short sword to make a series of small incisions in the cover and binding. Paper from the old, frail book started to flake off like dust.

Duan paused to blow off the loose paper before slowly making another incision. He patiently continued this work until the book lay in pieces.

When they saw the insides of the book, they all were surprised. Concealed in the interior was another piece of paper with a short paragraph written on it.

"There it is!" Charles' face sparkled.

I was looking for it for ages—all that searching and worrying. Who could have guessed it was right there?

Duan and Agnis gave each other a high five.

"What say, gi-iis? What paper say?" Check eagerly stuck out his neck.

Duan pushed him back and picked up the paper, squinting his eyes. It was difficult to read because it had grown discolored over the years. At last, he made out the words.

"*. . . but do not despair. Remember that it takes time for the power of Darkness to return. For a short period after his release, before the full portion of evil magic seeps back into Senzrabur, the devil will be weak. That is your chance to seal him once again with the Holy Dog.*"

"I see," commented Charles. "It completes the sentence and continues the message!"

Agnis quirked an eyebrow. "So it reads . . . let's see . . . 'However, when the Dog leaves, the power of Darkness will return . . . and the world will fall . . . but do not despair.' Hm. That's a strange line, don't you think?"

"Yeah," said Charles. "It gives you hope, but it doesn't tell you anything of importance! Pah—my ancestors . . ."

"Right," Agnis agreed. "I mean, 'seal him once again with the Holy Dog.' How the heck are we supposed to do that? What does it mean?"

As Agnis complained, Duan took the corner of the piece of paper and fiddled with it using the tip of his short sword.

"What is it now?" asked Charles.

Agnis tuned in. "Oh, be careful, Duan. Charles, I don't think it was just one piece of paper; there are two stuck together! Your ancestors really were quite mischievous."

Charles looked at Duan in surprise.

"I'd like some water. Is there any water in this room?" asked Duan.

Loren, who had been leaning against the wall, rushed over with a jug of water. "Will this do, young sir?"

"Thanks, it's fantastic. I'm sorry to trouble you. I know you're injured."

"Oh no, please. Thanks to Check, I feel no pain."

Check, hearing himself praised, ducked his head under one wing. "Aw, gi–iis!"

Meanwhile, Duan took the jug from Loren and poured water over the mysterious passage. After a moment, Duan rubbed the corner of the paper with his short sword. The water must have loosened whatever had stuck the papers together, because the upper sheet peeled right off. And as Duan had predicted, there was another passage underneath!

"To tell the truth, Senzrabur is not anything as monstrous as a devil—he is just an underling. No common man without substantial magic power could seal a real devil, but Senzrabur can be managed quite easily. He can be sealed with a book like this one, only true, and the Dog of Truth. But do not go unprepared: Senzrabur is skilled at manipulating thoughts. And the more time that passes, the stronger his power of Darkness becomes. When it is strong enough, he will be able to awaken a real devil. Then, this country—no, the world will fall to ruin."

"I see." Duan nodded. He turned his attention to Charles and Agnis. "So, our priority is to find the other book and the statue of the dog."

CHAPTER 46:

SPLITTING UP

e should put this book back together again. It wouldn't be good if the enemy saw it," said Duan as he looked at the dismantled book.

Loren nodded. "I will take care of it with some glue. . . ."

"It doesn't have to be that tidy," said Duan, "just enough to make it look like it hasn't been taken apart."

"Of course," said Loren, bowing his head.

Duan looked straight at Charles. "Now, in regard to the other book . . ."

Charles fell silent before Duan's intensity. Duan wasn't thinking at all about what had happened earlier and the awkward problem he'd had with Charles, though, he was focused on the mystery, filled with excitement at the challenge of solving it.

"Your Highness," prodded Duan, "do you have any ideas?"

"Um . . . I-I was trying to remember, but I can't think of anything."

"I see. Well, what about the library where this book came from? Maybe the other book is there, too."

"Yes, that makes sense."

At this, Agnis broke in. "What does it mean, 'a book like this one, only true'?"

Duan nodded. "This book . . . well, it isn't a real book, is it? I mean, it has no pages! It's just a box made to look like a book. So I think the message is referring to a real book—with pages—with exactly the same binding."

"Wow, good thinking, Duan!"

"How is this, young sir?" Loren handed Duan the reassembled book.

Duan examined it and pronounced himself satisfied.

Then, he turned to Charles. "Um, this library. Is it near here? Or is it—"

Charles interrupted him and answered immediately. "It's right here. Turn right at the end of the corridor, and the library is the second door."

"Okay. And this statue of the dog . . . any ideas where it might be?"

Charles pondered for a while. "I think it probably is near the gardener's house. He said he threw it away on the back hills, but I looked there and couldn't find it. Maybe he found it first and hasn't managed to get it back to me yet."

"Hm. Is this house on the castle grounds?"

"Yes."

"Can you take me there?"

Charles stood with his mouth agape. *You're asking me, a prince, to guide you through a downpour in the middle of the night, through a castle under siege?!*

Before Charles could put his thoughts into words, Loren stepped forward, still favoring his injured leg. "What you ask is impossible! Prince Charles, a common guide? And in this weather? Why, he could catch a cold! I will take you there myself."

"Are your sure your leg is okay now?" asked Duan.

"Yes, yes, it is much better."

"It doesn't look like it," commented Duan.

Loren tried to show he was fine by standing up straight, but he overdid it, further injuring his leg. His face showed a pained expression. Through this pain, he forced a laugh. "Ha ha! It is nothing! I will guide you even if I have to crawl!"

Duan sank deep into thought.

I can appreciate your devotion; but to be honest, you'll just slow us down. And if Red Knights attacked, we'd have to stay and protect you. You're right about one thing, though: We can't put the prince in danger. What should we do?

It's a complicated castle—if we don't have someone who knows the grounds, we'll get lost for sure. And we can't delay much longer!

Meanwhile, Charles placed his hand on Loren's arm and spoke decisively. "It's all right, Loren. This is a national emergency. I have to protect the country, not worry about my royal dignity. I'll take Duan to the gardener's house. Meanwhile, you can search the library for the book with Agnis. You remember where I found this one, don't you? On the shelves to the left. So you probably should look there first."

Loren opened his eyes wide and gazed at Charles in something like shock. "Your Highness!"

"Don't worry—if it gets dangerous, I'll make sure this person protects me. You *are* a fighter, aren't you?" The emphasis Charles placed on the word "are" seemed to indicate some doubts on the matter.

Duan didn't let himself rise to the provocation. He pretended not to hear and just replied, "Well, first let's decide what route to take to get there. I have a general idea of the layout. Where on the grounds is the gardener's house located?"

CHAPTER 47:

PRIORITIZING

f you look out this window," began Charles as he led Duan toward a small window on the left side of the room. Unfortunately, all they could see outside was darkness and rain.

"Er, you can't see it now. Usually, you can see a red chimney," Charles continued, blushing slightly. "That's where the stove is for the servants. Their living quarters are to the right of that."

"I see. How long will it take to get there? Is it far?"

"No, not really. But it's night, and the rain hasn't stopped, and there's all this thunder and lightning, and it's cold, and—"

Because it seemed as though the prince's list of complaints might go on forever, Duan interrupted him. "What's the quickest way there? It would be best if we could avoid the rain and the Red Knights."

"What's our top priority?" asked Charles.

This question surprised Duan.

Hey, this prince is actually pretty smart!

"Um, well, first, we want to avoid the enemy. Second, we need the shortest route. And avoiding the rain is last."

"Okay, then. In that case, we have to go in the opposite direction to the library, making a left turn at the end of the corridor. There's a staircase there we'll have to go down. Those stairs are narrow and not used often, so I don't think there will be any enemies there. After that . . . oh yeah, it'd probably be better if I were to draw a map!"

Charles went to his desk and got out a pen and piece of paper.

"We are here now," said the prince, quickly sketching a map of the castle grounds. "If we go down the staircase, we'll come out toward the back of the castle."

"What do you mean the 'back'?"

"Well, you can't see very well now, but it's the south side of the castle. This way—we'll get out this way."

"Okay."

"I don't think there will be any enemies there, either. And so that we don't get wet, I think we should use the outer corridor here."

"The outer corridor. Right."

Charles filled in a patch near the line he drew to represent the outer corridor. "There's a tall hedge here. I think the only way is to get over it somehow. The other places are war zones at the moment. It's tricky, and we'll get soaked, but . . ."

"We won't go through the war zones."

"Then, it's simple." Charles drew out a thick line.

"Okay. We should get going. We'll definitely get wet in this rain, so you'll need a cloak. Loren, can you get the prince a cloak?"

"Yes . . . but you will need one, too, no?" asked Loren.

"Oh, yes. If there is a shabby one I can borrow, I'd be very grateful."

Loren snorted at Duan's comment. "This is the prince's room. It would be difficult to find a shabby cloak here!"

Duan shrugged. "Well, never mind. It isn't like I'm going to die from a little rain."

Charles whispered to Loren, "It's okay, Loren, lend him one of mine."

Loren bowed. "The prince's kindness is boundless." Then, he went off to find the cloaks, a big smile on his face. He still was dragging his hurt leg, but Check's Heal Spell had helped a little, because he definitely was able to put more weight on it than at first.

It hadn't been easy for Agnis to hold back as the other two were talking, but she'd concluded it would be best to let them plan things on their own, hoping her two friends would grow to like each other better if they worked together.

Duan will protect Charles. I'm sure they'll become friends! After all, they're so much alike.

Agnis was confident of it.

When Loren finally returned with the two cloaks, Duan and Charles put them on.

"Do you have something like a lantern?" Duan asked. "It's pitch dark out there."

Still smiling, Loren brought out a lantern. "I thought you might ask. It is a small model, but it is very good. It will not extinguish in heavy rain, and it is plenty bright but not too heavy. I put it in Prince Charles' room for emergencies. I never would have imagined it would come in so handy!"

Duan had a look at the lamp. "It's very nice, indeed. Thanks, Loren! Oh, I'd also like to borrow a rope. If we're to climb over this tall hedge, we'll need one."

"Yes, yes, we have one," replied Loren. "Why not carry this emergency rucksack? You can tie the lantern to the side, and it has water and dried meat inside—although, I am sure you will have no need for that."

"The first rule of adventuring is to expect the unexpected," said Duan, gratefully accepting the rucksack. He took off his cloak, put the rucksack on his back, and then put on his cloak again.

"Okay, prince, shall we go? Agnis, good luck with your end."

Agnis responded with a double thumbs-up. "Same to you two. This guy's pretty delicate, so don't let him do too much."

Charles sulked at the word "delicate."

Duan laughed gently. "I was quite delicate, too, you know. When I was young, I got fevers all the time. I'm a lot stronger now . . . although, I guess I'm still weak compared to my partner, Olba."

Partner?

A vision of Clay Judah rose into Charles' head, but he soon shook it away. In its place rose a vision of Olba October's manly face.

CHAPTER 48

AN OLD FRIEND

round that time, Olba and Land were trying to lure the Red Knights outside again. In the time they'd been fighting, the number of enemies had almost doubled, and more were appearing every moment.

Fortunately, some Black Knights had appeared, as well, and Land and Olba began to think that, with their help, they might survive this battle.

"Hey, you're coming with me this time," said Land, gripping Olba's shoulder.

"What do you mean?" asked Olba, feigning innocence.

The last time Olba had proposed leading the Red Knights into the rain, Land had dashed out the door, but Olba had stayed put . . . and dry. Now, even though Olba was playing dumb, he was worried about Land's wounded shoulder, which was oozing blood.

He'll last only a little while longer. I have to get him to rest somewhere so I can stop the bleeding.

"Okay, okay," said Olba. "I'll go this time. You wait here."

"What?" Land widened his eyes as he avoided the blows from the Red Knights.

Olba was wearing silver full-body armor with delicate golden designs. In his hand, he was holding the royal longsword. It was a gaudy outfit, but Olba was getting used to it. Kicking the Red Knights around him, he approached a Black Knight who'd been making bold moves.

"Hey, you."

The Black Knight was surprised to be called out. Still in his full-face helmet, he looked at Olba.

"We're at a disadvantage if we continue like this. Is there a place we can lock them up for a while? It doesn't matter if we can't get them all if we can decrease their numbers," said Olba.

The Black Knight gave a big nod. "Yeah, I was thinking the same thing."

Olba recognized his voice—it was the mystery Black Knight from before. "Hey, who are you?"

"Me?" asked the Black Knight, taking off his full-face helmet. A black-haired young man appeared. He wasn't gorgeous, but he had elegant features.

"Y-you!" exclaimed Olba, pointing to him as if in disbelief.

The young man smiled and looked at Olba.

Land approached them, wondering what was happening. "What's up? Do you guys know each other?"

"What was your name again?" whispered Olba.

At that moment, one of the other Black Knights came over to the disappointed young man and said, "Hey, Sven, is your wound okay?"

"Yeah, it's all bandaged up. It's fine."

"Don't overexert yourself," said the Black Knight as he returned to fight with the Red Knights.

As soon as he left, Olba made a fist and gave the young man a punch in the stomach.

"Urgh . . ."

It must've hit his wound, because he wrinkled up his face.

"Oh, I'm sorry, I'm sorry. You're Sven! Sven Giesen. I remember!"

Yes, it was Sven Giesen, who had been wounded by a Red Knight back in ex-King Liesbeck's room.

Sven laughed painfully and said, "Olba, you haven't changed a bit."

"Ha ha! Well, you sure have! You've been successful—the royal guard!"

"Yeah, well, it hasn't been that long."

"But the Black Knights' Army—you have to be skilled. I hear they're strict with the background check, too."

Sven laughed and shrugged off the question.

It wasn't something Olba was interested in or wanted to pry into. Anyway, they had their hands full, so Olba just responded with a shrug himself.

"Who would have thought we'd meet here?" commented Sven.

Olba nodded. "Yeah. A little while ago, I was telling my partner about you—we were locked up in your jail here."

"Yeah, I heard. That's why I said you haven't changed. I'm sick of prison cells and jails myself."

"Same goes for me. Who gets into prison 'cause they want to? We were dragged into your conspiracy—it's been a major hassle. Never mind that, though, we don't have time to talk about the old days now."

Yes, it was Sven Giesen whom Olba had been telling Duan about. He was the man who knew about Olba's past—the prison guard who had rescued him moments before death and the mystery man who had joined up to form a party with him.

Now, it may seem odd that Olba and Sven would chat in the middle of a pitched battle. Of course, as they talked, they hadn't paused fighting—and not just against one opponent, either. Sven and Olba were up against at least two or three enemies a piece. It was clear that the two old friends were of more than ordinary strength!

"Man, you two are just like the red guys—monsters with bottomless strength," whispered Land with an awed expression.

"What?" growled Olba without a moment's delay.

"No, no, nothing at all. So, what are we doing again?"

"Yeah, things could get hairy if a sorcerer came out now, so we should act before then. Sven, like I said before, can we lock up these Red Knights somewhere? If you tell me where, I can make a quick dash and lead them all someplace."

"Hm, I was thinking about it, too, but I can't see a good place for that. All I can think of is inside the riding grounds."

"You have something like that?"

"Yeah, it's behind the stables and the barracks. If you can lure them out there, I think we can keep them there for a while."

"How long is 'a while'?"

"Well, they'll probably try to escape by any means. And it's not like a prison cell, so the exits aren't that sturdy. There are windows, too, which aren't barred."

"I see. Well, we could use a break. I'm sure my partner's doing something about things while we're busy down here."

As he said that, Olba looked toward the corridor Duan and the others had gone down.

Sven quickly glanced that way, too, tilting his neck. "Is your new partner that reliable? I've heard that he's a young boy, as thin as a girl!"

"Heh heh, that's true. But he's not just a weak kid," Olba replied with a satisfied grin.

Land, wanting to brag, too, put his hand on Olba's shoulder and said, "I dunno about that kid, but Clay Judah, the guy who went with him, is one heck of a guy. He's only twenty-four, and he's already Level 16. He has this weird charisma thing going that—"

"Level 16!?" interrupted Olba and Sven at the same instant.

Land looked back at them with a smug expression.

Olba blankly commented, "My partner is Level 3!"

This time, it was Sven who screamed. "Level *3?!*"

Olba snorted. "Never mind. Either way, it seems like we need to concentrate on buying time. Land, I'll guide this gang to the riding ground with the other Black Knights. You get Sven here to stop your bleeding."

Then, he turned to Sven. "Listen, Sven, this guy's Land. I can make a better introduction later. Like you, he has a wound, and it's quite serious."

Sven nodded. "Okay, I'll look at it as soon as possible."

"What about your wound, Sven? Are you okay?"

Before Sven could answer, a Red Knight came charging at him.

Sven calmly took a step back, tripping the Red Knight as he did so. The knight lost his balance, and Sven delivered a brutal kick as he tumbled by. Another Red Knight aimed an arrow at him, which Sven dodged with ease. He whipped out his short sword and threw it at the Red Knight, hitting him directly in the throat and causing him to collapse with a thud.

"Er, I'll take that as a 'yes,'" said Olba.

"Wow," said Land. "Your friend fights better injured than I do healthy!"

"Lucky, I guess," said Sven, sweat dripping from his forehead. "You two wait here while I go tell the others about the plan!"

With that, he ran toward the other Black Knights.

CHAPTER 49:

SUPERHUMAN

lease, escape!"

How many times had Edward Zamut's voice echoed through the third floor of the Silver-Gray Tower?

They'd been invaded by the Red Knights, and even the platform on which the king's throne stood had become part of the battlefield.

Ex-King Liesbeck was there, holding off a large number of Red Knights.

The ex-king was swinging a big battle-ax from side to side as if it weighed no more than a feather. With each swing, screaming Red Knights were flung away. Yet for some reason, no fatal wound had been dealt to any enemy; no sooner did they hit the ground than they rose again and came back for more.

"What is happening?" shouted Liesbeck to Edward. "Could it be that Charles was right, and this is all the work of a devil?"

"I don't know!" gasped Edward as he fought off a pair of Red Knights.

Liesbeck pinned a Red Knight to the floor with the broad blade of his ax. "You—confess! Who is your master?"

The Red Knight didn't answer.

"Take off your mask!" yelled Liesbeck. When the Red Knight didn't seem likely to comply, he ripped it off himself.

A chill ran down Liesbeck's spine. The Red Knight had no head. As Liesbeck looked on in terror, the headless Red Knight clumsily groped around for his helmet, found it at last, and put it back on his head—or rather, where his head should have been.

"Aaargh!"

At that instant, there was a scream from downstairs. Edward ran toward the stairs as Black Knights came running up the stairs in full retreat.

"Keep it together, men!" Edward shouted. "What's happened?"

But the knights all had gone into a state of shock. One was bawling his eyes out.

"Hey!" Edward put out his hand to place it on the man's shoulder, but he quickly drew back. The man's armor was bubbling and smoking.

"This isn't good." Edward turned to some of the other Black Knights. "You there—help them get this armor off! Put on gloves and be careful while you do it."

He started to run down the stairs; but before he had taken more than a few steps, he saw a figure climb into view—a sorcerer wearing a red robe. Edward instinctively cowered back.

The sorcerer, who grinned eerily with his wrinkly mouth from underneath his hood, advanced toward Edward.

"I will not let you pass!" said Edward, readjusting his grip on his sword.

The sorcerer merely laughed, still advancing.

"Don't you dare, you fool!" Edward thrust his blade forward. The sword's point plunged into the sorcerer's chest.

The sorcerer remained standing. He drew out the sword with ease, hardly pausing to glance at it, and dropped it to the floor. Then, he passed by Edward, who was now quite paralyzed with shock.

In less than a heartbeat, Edward's consciousness returned—but when he woke, his body still refused to move. He couldn't even twitch a finger. *He put a Paralyze Spell on me!*

"Lord Liesbeck!"

He could hear his soldiers' voices from behind him.

"Aaargh!"

He also saw powerful flames and heard screams that chilled his soul.

"Come on . . . !"

Summoning up every ounce of will-power he possessed, Edward broke free, shattering the Paralysis Spell—which, luckily, wasn't all that powerful.

Now that he was free again, Edward ran back up to the third floor, avoiding the flames. There, he saw something more difficult to believe than anything he'd witnessed so far: On the platform, Liesbeck had grabbed hold of the sorcerer by the nape of his neck and was poking him with his battle-ax.

"Edward, this one is not human, either. We need to finish off their master, or this fight will never end." He gave the sorcerer another poke. "Right?"

Unable to bear the pain, the sorcerer nodded repeatedly.

"They are looking for the king."

"The king?" asked Edward.

The ex-king tightened his grip on the sorcerer's neck. "Right? That is what you were asking a moment ago when you swaggered in, 'where's the king?'"

The sorcerer couldn't respond; he breathed with difficulty as he held back tears. Watching him, Liesbeck continued, laughing bitterly, "Pah—I guess you will escape as soon as you have the chance, anyway."

At this, the sorcerer nodded as if to say 'yes' and promptly disappeared, leaving only his robe behind.

Liesbeck pinched the red robe with his fingertips, as if the merest contact with the fabric was vile, and said, "Edward, it seems we will need to stay here to buy some time—to protect the king."

"Yes, sir," replied Edward, marveling at the ex-king's strength and stamina.

Lord Liesbeck is truly superhuman!

CHAPTER 50:

TIME TO RENEGOTIATE THE CONTRACT

nfortunately, something was just about to happen that would make all Liesbeck's and the others' struggles and sacrifices seem meaningless.

The second of the three sorcerer brothers, Kojey, was wandering about the castle. He had been told off and thrown out by Senzrabur; but, being a coward, he didn't much feel like going to fight. So, he ambled at random through the castle, pretending to search for the king but actually just doing a bit of sightseeing.

Humming softly to himself, he strolled along the balcony above the grand hall, where the Red Knights, Black Knights, Olba, and Land had been fighting so desperately. As he paused to take a breath, he thought he heard people speaking.

He listened carefully.

The voices seemed to be coming from behind the wall. There was a high-pitched woman's voice complaining about something and other male voices trying to placate her. Kojey immediately became more alert. He had heard this voice before;

it belonged to the woman he hadn't managed to finish off earlier: Queen Milhene.

Oh, I see—there's a secret room here!

He smiled with his deeply creased face and started a thorough inspection of the wall. As he suspected, he found the indentations of a door. Although it had been disguised cleverly using pictures and the patterns of the wallpaper, it was definitely a secret door.

Ha ha! What have we here?

Kojey had no intention of charging through the secret door on his own. If King Evesrin was inside (which seemed highly likely), there undoubtedly would be many guards to face. No, he would charge in with plenty of allies in front of him.

But how to profit most from this information that had fallen into his lap?

Senzrabur was desperately in need of the king for sacrifice.

Maybe I should offer to tell him the king's whereabouts in exchange for a substantially increased payment? Yes, now may be the time to renegotiate our contract. . . .

Kojey's financial instincts kicked in. As he walked back to the north tower where Senzrabur was, he felt as though he'd already received the large sum of money he hadn't actually earned yet, and he was unable to contain his smug laughter.

▭

Meanwhile, the plan to lead the group of Red Knights inside the riding grounds to lock them up was in serious trouble.

No sooner were the Red Knights locked in than they started to break out by kicking down the doors and windows.

"Stop them!" rang Sven's voice.

But it was futile. When the Black Knights focused on one escape route, another two would open up.

"Wow, they've got a heck of a lot of determination!" commented Land. Though he spoke casually and with ease, he didn't look well, and he actually was struggling to even stand upright.

It wasn't only Land. Olba was suffering badly from fatigue, and the Black Knights' movements were getting slower and clumsier. The Red Knights from the riding ground just kept on escaping and attacking them, one after another.

"Graa! They just keep on comin'!" Olba struck away one Red Knight who had come flying toward him. Even though the knight fell to the ground, though, he jumped right back up and charged at Olba again.

It's like a never-ending nightmare. . . .

At that moment, Land managed to avoid an attack from a Red Knight but collapsed into Olba's arms.

"Hey!" Olba called to him. His face was pale and his eyes were closed.

"It's g-getting a bit painful now," he whispered.

The cold rain didn't seem like it was stopping anytime soon. And although he should have been ice cold, Land, lying in Olba's arms, was burning up with fever. Olba knew from his long experience that Land was in grave danger of losing his life. Even as he realized this, however, Red Knights kept leaping at him.

Olba saw that Sven's wound wasn't doing too well, either. His movements weren't as swift and strong as they had been only moments before. As he supported Land's body, a somber mood fell over Olba.

Cripes. At this rate, we're all gonna die. . . .

CHAPTER 51:

MIND MANIPULATION

rince Charles and Duan put on their cloaks and, as silently as they could, cautiously ran through the castle. Because they didn't want to get spotted by the enemy, they hadn't lit a lantern and relied only on the torches burning at intervals along the walls. Duan realized there was no possible way he would've been able to navigate through the castle without Charles to guide him.

On top of that, the rain was still coming down hard. Although they were wearing cloaks, the cold was so bitter that their fingertips were frozen.

First, they went toward the passage that Charles had spoken of. If there were no Red Knights here, they would be able to cover quite a distance without getting wet. If there were a guard, they would have to climb over the tall hedge, which would be difficult and dangerous in this storm.

Will the prince, who looks so delicate, be able to do it? It's an emergency, but I don't want to push him too hard. I'd rather not take that route.

Pacing down the passage, Duan met a strange group of people. At first, he thought they were enemies. But the five or six figures were of grand personal appearance, and they looked at one another with worried faces, shaking in their boots and hiding in the shadows of the pillars.

There was one chubby man with thinning hair who looked like a nobleman. The rest would've been better suited to military uniforms.

As Duan stood speechless, Charles called to them.

"Aren't you Schneider's men? And aren't you Lord Shimul?"

The men nodded a few times. They had pale faces and vacant eyes as though they'd been sleepwalking. When they looked at Charles, they didn't recognize who he was. They had terror in their eyes and stood petrified, like zombies.

"They're being manipulated by Senzrabur," whispered Charles in horror.

"And his control is slowly breaking them down," said Duan as he looked at them with pity.

It was written that Senzrabur could manipulate the thoughts of men. The sight of these men convinced Duan that to have your mind manipulated for even a short while was an abominably cruel thing.

"What shall we do?" asked Charles with an anxious face. "We can't just leave them!"

Duan hardened his soul. "Prince Charles, we have to focus on sealing Senzrabur as soon as possible. It's not easy leaving these men behind, but we don't have the time or the strength to transfer them to someplace safe."

Charles gulped and nodded. "Yes . . ."

That must've been difficult for him, Duan realized as he led the prince down the corridor, away from the mind-controlled men.

We have to seal Senzrabur for their sake, too! If his real powers awaken, we'll be in real trouble. If Senzrabur is this powerful, who knows what would happen if a real devil were awakened!

Duan shook his head free of bad thoughts and prayed there would be no enemies in the outer corridor.

CHAPTER 52:

WHEN IT RAINS, IT POURS

Unfortunately, Duan's prayers were not answered. In the shifting light of many torches, they saw an indeterminate number of Red Knights, their armor blazing as though it were molten steel.

Duan stole a sideways glance at the prince and saw that he was turning paler and paler. He quietly spoke to Charles, "It looks like we won't be able to use this route. There are others that are worse. Please, guide us to the hedge route."

Duan tried his best to cheer up Charles as they retraced their steps, but the prince seemed lost in thought.

At last, Charles stopped and pointed. "There it is," he said.

In the direction he was pointing stood something that looked as sturdy and dark as a rampart, as stagnant and lonely as a petrified forest.

"Y-you call that a 'hedge'?"

"I said it was big," Charles replied somewhat defensively. "Don't you think we can climb it?"

"Er . . ." Duan accidentally fell into silence and pessimistically clicked his tongue.

Uh-oh—I can't be the one to lose his nerve! Charles is depending on me!

It was already too late. With a groan, Prince Charles crumpled to the ground. "It's impossible! What was I thinking?" He looked like he was about to burst into tears.

His shaking isn't due to the cold alone, Duan thought to himself. *Of course he's scared—there are terrifying enemies all around him. Monsters too!*

The rain and wind were strong, and they were frozen to the core. Charles was still very young, and in his everyday life, he was used to being catered to by butlers and servants.

He's lived his whole life without a care. This new situation must be harsh for him. The responsibility must weigh heavily on such slender shoulders!

It was a strange feeling. In the dark and cold corridor, in the heavy silence, Duan felt almost as if Charles were a younger brother. Something hot rose up inside him.

I have to help this person!

Duan was overwhelmed with this thought.

"Prince Charles," he began, crouching down beside the prince and taking his hand. It was, as he had suspected it would be, ice cold. "Listen, Charles, let's do the best we can, okay? I'm sure there'll be things we can't do. When that happens, we'll find another way. I swear to you that I will protect you the very best I can." He spoke from the heart.

And Charles may have understood this. He listened without responding; then, he glanced up at Duan as though he were seeing some kind of miracle and slowly nodded. Sniffling, he gripped Duan's hand and pulled himself to his feet.

"Let's go!" said Duan.

Charles' reply was almost enthusiastic. "Okay!"

The two of them leapt determinedly into the rain. It fell with so much power that they barely could keep their eyes open. They were soaked in an instant.

"Prince Charles!"

"I'm fine. Duan, this way—this way is quicker."

"Okay! Watch out for your feet!"

Supporting one another, they walked through the wind, defying it. When they were almost at the bottom of the hedge, there was a big flash and a rumble of thunder. Charles closed his eyes and clung to Duan.

Holding Charles close to his side, Duan continued toward the hedge, dragging his sodden cloak, which seemed to weigh a hundred pounds. He caught a glimpse of something in another flash of lightning and stopped. He looked behind him.

Was he just imagining things, or . . . ?

He strained to see. It was as he suspected. And now, Charles saw it, too. In the pouring rain, for some reason, stood a solitary Red Knight.

CHAPTER 53:

LAUGHTER IN THE RAIN

he Red Knight didn't seem to have noticed them yet.

What should we do?

Charles clung to Duan's arm. It would be difficult to climb the hedge without being noticed. Fighting the Red Knight wasn't a good option, either. Duan carried a short sword, whereas the Red Knight held a destructive-looking battle-ax. He wouldn't have a prayer. And the noise of any battle likely would draw other Red Knights.

That would be awful.

Thinking quickly, Duan took the rope out of the rucksack and handed it to the prince. Charles gazed up at him with a questioning look.

Duan whispered, "I'll jump on him from behind. That massive battle-ax is a bit dangerous, but we could use it to our advantage and bind his arms behind his back. Your Highness, you'll need to tie him up with the rope."

"I-I can't do that. Anyway, are you going to be able to hold him down?"

"If we catch him off guard. Like I said—"

Charles interrupted him. "All we can do is to try our best, right?"

Duan laughed and answered, "Yes. That's right."

Now the wind and rain were a stroke of good luck. The Red Knight didn't notice their presence as they crept closer.

Duan jumped on the Red Knight from behind and used the battle-ax to throttle his neck.

"Your Highness!" he called to Charles, who was completely focused on tying up the Red Knight and tightening the rope. When Duan called to him again, Charles came back to his senses.

"Charles! Look at him!" screamed Duan, whose head was being beaten down by the rain as if by a waterfall. Duan was pushing the battle-ax against the Red Knight's neck to hold his head down. However, they couldn't see anything above his neck: His head was missing.

Charles and Duan never had felt closer to death.

The prince hadn't been so nervous in his life—or ever used so much of his bodily strength.

Yet instead of panicking or giving up, they redoubled their efforts.

The headless Red Knight, held down by Duan and tied up by Charles, was brought to a standstill. Duan grabbed the battle-ax and threw it to the ground.

"Your Highness, let's get him down. Then, let's take off his boots. Help me!"

"What?" For a moment, Charles couldn't comprehend what Duan was telling him, but it soon became clear. He gave a sly grin and a thumbs-up.

The duo rammed into the headless Red Knight and started to work on his boots. It was quite difficult to hold down his kicking legs and take off the boots with their hands slipping in the rain. Oddly enough, though, they were oblivious to the wind, rain, and cold now, while desperately tugging at the boots. When they finally came off, they both cheered without a thought and hugged each other.

Like they had suspected, the boots were empty inside. In other words, the Red Knight had just lost both his legs. Now, he couldn't walk.

"What shall we do with this?" asked Charles, who was holding one boot.

"Why don't we do this?" Duan answered, throwing away the boot in his hand with all his might.

"Sounds good!" Charles threw his boot with all his strength, too. His boot didn't go as far as Duan's, but it was still out of the Red Knight's reach.

They both found the situation incredibly funny, and they started to laugh, slapping each other on the shoulder. As he laughed, Duan thought what a strange sight they must have made, laughing like two maniacs in the middle of the pouring rain.

Taking a deep breath, he said, "Okay. Now for the hedge. Charles, would you hand me the rope?

Strangely enough, the tall hedge that had seemed like an insurmountable obstacle a moment ago was now a challenge they felt confident attacking.

CHAPTER 54:

THE GARDENER'S HOUSE

nlike a normal wall, the hedge had footholds and places to put their hands, so it was relatively easy to climb. On top of that, there were some sturdy branches meshed in, making it almost as solid as a wall.

We can do this! thought Duan as he started to climb.

Once he started, however, he became overwhelmed by the height of the hedge and the stinging, relentless rain. His hands and arms soon were covered in cuts and grazes from sharp thorns and branches. It occurred to him that he should have asked Loren for gloves, if only for the prince's sake.

At last, Duan managed to get to the top. He tied one end of the rope to the base of the thickest branch he could see and slung the other end down to Charles. Duan knew from experience that at times like these, the number one rule was to put your head down and just do it. One shouldn't stop to take a breath or look down.

"Take that rope and tie it around your waist!" he called down to the prince. "I'll pull you while you climb, too, okay?"

Duan wished he could see Charles' face. With the driving rain and darkness, he couldn't see more than a few feet in front of himself. A vision of a worried-looking Charles rose into his mind.

A heavy weight tugged at the rope. Although the prince was delicate and slight and probably weighed about ninety pounds, Duan still found himself straining to pull the prince to the top of the hedge, even with Charles helping from below.

"You're almost there!" he called encouragingly to Charles, not knowing if he could be heard over the wind and rain. "You can do it!"

He felt like he'd been hauling on the rope for hours already. Would it ever end? Yet, when he reached out his hand and finally felt the prince's slim fingers, it was as if mere seconds had passed. A flood of happiness rushed through him as Charles took hold of his hand and squeezed back firmly.

Duan hauled Charles to the top of the hedge, almost embracing him. They looked at each other and laughed.

"Okay, Charles: This time, you go first. Like we did before; I'll hold the rope."

Charles nodded. It was much easier going down than up. Once Charles reached the ground, he tugged on the rope to let Duan know, and Duan climbed down.

"I think it's all right to turn on the lantern," said Charles when Duan had reached the bottom and was coiling the rope to place it in the rucksack. "I don't think our enemies will see us now."

Duan nodded and, after stowing away the rope, turned on the lantern. As Loren had claimed, the small lantern cast a bright enough light to shine through the heavy rain.

In front of them was a line of private houses, almost like a town. There was a narrow cobbled street lined with flowerbeds.

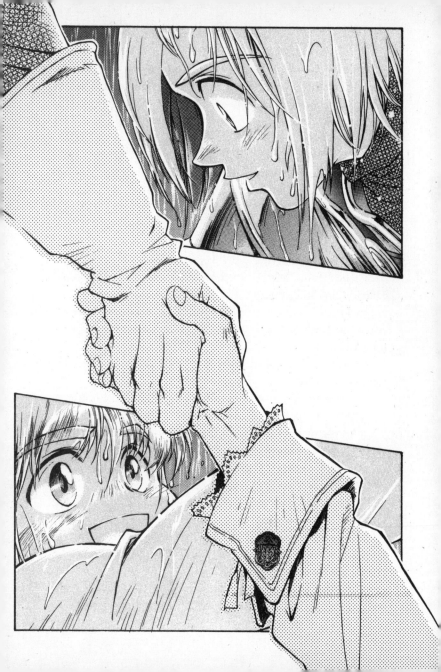

Farming tools and wheelbarrows hung outside the houses. Everything was so peaceful and orderly that it was hard to believe that Black Knights and Red Knights were in a fight to decide the fate of the whole kingdom on the other side of the hedge!

"It's this way," said Charles.

They ran down the cobbled street, led by Charles. After he passed by a number of similar-looking houses, he stopped. "I think it's here. They all look the same in the dark, though, so I'm not sure."

"Well, there's only one way to find out," said Duan. "Hello! Anyone home?"

No one answered.

They cautiously entered through the front door and called again. Still no reply. The light of the lantern showed an empty kitchen. In fact, the whole house seemed to be deserted. After investigating for a while, however, they heard a noise from the back.

Duan and Charles looked at each other and headed toward the noise.

There was a narrow bedroom at the back of the house.

"Anyone there?" called Charles.

An old man jumped from the room, making things rattle.

"Aah!" screamed Charles.

"Aah!" screamed Duan.

"Aah!" screamed the old man.

Then, the three of them stood stock still, panting and staring at each other with fear.

The gardener—for it was him—was the first to regain his senses. Recognition flooded his eyes. "Your H-highness," he began, before bursting into tears.

"What's wrong?" asked Charles. "Don't cry! I want to ask you something. Listen, have you found the statue of the dog?"

The old man continued to sob.

"I can't understand you if you cry!" exclaimed Charles in frustration.

At that, a girl of about ten stepped out of the shadows and stood in front of the old man.

"Don't you be mean to my grandpa!" she said sternly, her hands on her hips and her eyes blazing. "Aren't you the prince? I've seen you before. We were really scared, you know. What happened to the castle? The grown-ups all were talking about it. They said Lord Schneider and the king were fighting. Everyone's preparing to leave. The whole town's gone crazy! But Grandpa isn't well, so we can't go. Please, don't get us involved!"

Once she finished her speech, the girl tightly pursed her lips, her face bright red.

Charles was at a loss for words. He glanced beseechingly at Duan.

Duan crouched down in front of the girl and looked her in the eyes. Her lips were still tightened, but she wasn't shaking anymore. She looked at Duan with curiousity. He smiled and introduced himself.

"Hi, I'm Duan Surk. I'm in the middle of an adventure; right now, I'm helping Prince Charles."

The girl stayed still, watching him with wonder.

"Yeah," he continued, "there's a lot of trouble at the castle. In fact, it's a war zone. At first, everyone thought, like you said, that it was because Lord Schneider and the king were fighting. But Prince Charles noticed that wasn't the real reason."

The girl tilted her head in further wonder. She couldn't understand why Duan was giving her such a detailed explanation.

"Your grandpa found a statue of a dog in the garden—do you know it?"

The girl shook her head.

"Well, this whole business started because of that statue."

"Is it Grandpa's fault? Is that why you're here—to take Grandpa?" The girl opened her eyes wide and raised her hands as if to protect the old man.

"Oh no," Duan assured her, "nothing like that. Anyway, I heard it was the queen who ordered the statue to be moved."

This time, the old man behind her nodded and said, "Yes, that's true."

Duan addressed the old man. "Please, don't be afraid, sir. Prince Charles knows this, too. To put it simply, the reason why we're in this trouble now is because that statue was moved."

The gardener gave a shudder. "Was it cursed, like I thought?"

Duan smiled grimly and said, "Perhaps, although I think it's a little bit different than a curse. Basically, to bring the situation back to normal, we need that statue of the dog. That's why Prince Charles and I came here. Prince Charles said that he'd asked you to look for it."

The old man stood up hurriedly. "Yes, I found it a few days ago. It was so dirty and disgusting, I thought I'd wash it before I brought it to the prince. It's standing in the shed outside!"

Duan and Charles looked at each other and nodded.

CHAPTER 55:

THE THOUGHT OF ARISTOCRAT GIRLS

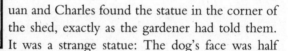

Duan and Charles found the statue in the corner of the shed, exactly as the gardener had told them. It was a strange statue: The dog's face was half woman, half man, and the beast was positioned as if half-lying on the ground.

They wrapped it with a cloth the gardener had given them before placing it in the rucksack Duan was carrying. The statue was so heavy that it caused the straps of the rucksack to cut deeply into Duan's shoulders.

Thankfully, the duo were lucky enough not to meet any enemies on the way back to the castle.

"Your Highness, let's change out of our wet clothes before we go to the library," suggested Duan. "We'll catch a cold otherwise."

Charles couldn't have agreed more. "Wow—it's so warm in here!"

"I feel so revived!"

Crackling in the fireplace of the prince's room was a warm fire, thoughtfully lit by Loren before he'd left with Agnis. Duan and Charles, frozen to the core, stood as close to the fire as they could get to unthaw. But they couldn't remain carefree for long.

"Where do you keep your clothes?" asked Duan.

"Er . . . I don't know," Charles sheepishly admitted. "Loren does all that for me."

Duan decided to look in the same place Loren had brought the two cloaks from, so he headed for the walk-in wardrobe at the back of the room. That's when the main door to the room swung open.

"Who is there?!" cried a voice.

The prince, who was relaxing in front of the fire, stood quickly. Duan returned to the room, as well, only to see Loren standing in the doorway with a surprised look on his face.

"Oh, Your Highness! I am so glad you are safe!"

"Thanks, Loren, we just got back. We were thinking of changing before we headed to the library. How's Agnis? Did you find the book?"

"N-no." Loren fell silent a moment but soon spoke up again. "N-no. Princess Agnis is fine and is still looking. It has been quite a difficult task, though. Let me help you change. Come, please. Master Duan, you too."

▭

In their new clothes, Duan and Charles felt refreshed and energized. Their bodies, which had been wet and cold, were warming up quickly.

"I'm so lucky—wearing dry clothes!" Charles exclaimed humbly, causing Duan to smile.

"Oh, Duan!" the prince continued. "Those clothes really suit you!"

Duan reddened at Charles' comment.

Loren had chosen clothes for Duan that were still too big for Charles but very grand all the same. He wore a white lacy shirt and black velvet pants with white tights. The jacket that matched the pants was long and reached down beyond his hips.

The clothes made Duan look every bit a young nobleman.

"True," Loren chimed in. "You look very handsome, Master Duan. Now, what about your armor?"

"Um, never mind," said Duan. "We're looking for a book now; it'll be difficult to move around in armor. I'll just take my short sword."

"I see. Then, let us hurry—Princess Agnis is all alone in the library!"

Charles questioningly tilted his head. "Loren, why did you come back here?"

Loren was taken aback at Charles' question. "Oh dear! I forgot that I came here because Princess Agnis wanted something to eat. You must be hungry, too, Your Highness?"

When he thought about it, Duan realized he hadn't eaten for almost a whole day. His stomach rumbled—and as if they'd somehow communicated in advance, so did Charles'. The boys looked at each other and started to chuckle.

Loren regarded the two of them in wonder.

"We have some food here in this room, although mere snacks, such as chocolate and cookies. Please, wait a moment, and I will prepare a plate."

"Okay. I'd totally forgotten I was hungry. Agnis is so funny like that," said Charles.

Duan laughed and said, "That's true. It's actually the right thing to do, though; if you're starving, you can't think properly, and you can't put your strength into anything. Can't fight when you're hungry—that's one of the most basic rules in adventuring."

"Oh."

"Agnis is really organized when it comes to things like that. She's a strong woman at heart, even though she's a princess. She has spirit, and she doesn't give up. On the other hand, she can be quite fragile, and she wears her heart on her sleeve—but I guess that's what's so endearing about her."

Charles, who was nodding and listening to what Duan was saying, grinned and said, "Duan, you like Agnis, don't you?"

Duan opened his eyes wide. "Huh? What?!"

"It's okay, you don't have to hide it. I like Agnis, too—I have since I was small. I think you suit her better than I do, though. Before, I thought you looked weak and weren't suited to her; now, I'm on your side. I'm rooting for you!"

Charles showed how much he loved this new idea by jovially patting Duan on the shoulder.

Questions filled Duan's head.

Do I really like Agnis? I don't dislike her. I admire her. And she is cute.

Then, inside Duan's head, a vision arose of Agnis, smiling a special smile for him alone.

Her slim waist, her soft and fluffy . . . Aah!

He quickly shook his head.

"When all this is finished, I'll ask Agnis how she feels about you," stated Charles. "Yeah, that's a good idea. You should find out how you feel about each other!"

Charles really was getting excited about his newfound role as Cupid. But Duan frantically waved his hands in protest.

"Please, don't! Um, we're definitely not like that. We just adventure together. And we've gone through a lot of dangerous stuff together, like now. Anyway, she's a princess—we're too different in social status."

"None of that means anything when you're in love! And Agnis is an adventurer now, too—she's just like you."

"Well, I guess that's true. It doesn't mean anything, though. Besides, she's in love with someone else!"

Duan clapped his hand over his mouth, too late realizing he couldn't take back his words.

Charles looked at him, eyes ablaze with curiosity. "Really? Who? Do I know him?"

Duan, who had given up, said, "Y-yes. Please, you can't tell Agnis or the other person!"

Charles' eyes sparkled. "I know! It's Clay Judah, isn't it?"

"Yes, it's him," sighed Duan.

I guess anyone can see it. I was a bit surprised to find out at first, but anyone would fall in love with Clay Judah after spending a little time with him. As a man, I admire him and aspire to be like him. He's just plain cool.

Charles placed a hand on Duan's back, startling him out of his reverie.

"That's too bad," the prince said sincerely. "You can't compete with Clay Judah. Nobody can. Poor you, Duan!"

Duan wasn't all that disappointed; after all, it wasn't as if he were deeply in love with Agnis. He was feeling a little strangely bothered, however.

I guess it's a little unfair to compare me, a Level 3 adventurer, to Clay Judah!

Charles looked at the sad-faced Duan and guessed incorrectly that the expression was one of heartbreak. "Cheer up, Duan. I'll introduce you to a lot of aristocrat girls!"

Duan didn't know how to respond. After all, the thought of aristocrat girls didn't leave him entirely disinterested!

CHAPTER 56:

NO TIME FOR TEA

ow all we need is the book!"

"Right! We have to find it quickly."

"Yes!"

Duan and the prince were getting along splendidly now. Together with Loren, who had packed a basket full of snacks, they headed back to the library.

As they opened the heavy door and went inside, their nostrils were assailed by the musty smell of old books. In the dark room, they could just make out the flickering light that belonged to Agnis. As they were about to call out to her, they could heard her muttering:

"Hmph! Where is that stupid book! Argh—I'm so hungry I want to cry. Hey, Check! Don't fall asleep."

Duan and Charles glanced at each other with knowing smiles.

"Agnis!" cried Charles, and she turned around with a surprised look on her face.

Check, who was beside her, also looked around in surprise, his eyes open wide. The girl and the grinia ran toward them. "It must have been so tough out there! Well, did you find it—the statue of the dog?"

"Yes, we found it," the prince affirmed.

"Where is it now?"

"Duan has it."

"Really! Can I see it? What's it like?"

Agnis was surprised when she saw Duan, who was standing behind Charles. "Oh wow, you changed clothes. I almost didn't recognize you, Duan. You'd totally pass as a nobleman!"

"Do you think so?" Duan asked seriously.

Agnis replied, "Not that it matters. May I see the statue now?"

Not that it matters?

A little disappointed, Duan removed the statue from his rucksack. The ever-curious Check poked in his head to have a look.

"Hm, so this is it," said Agnis. "It *is* a little disturbing. I'm curious as to how you seal the devil with this and the book? That's what I've been wondering the whole time I've been searching!"

"Maybe it's written in the book. It is a book, after all! Say, where's the other book—or rather, the box that looks like a book?"

Agnis held it out to Duan. "Here it is."

Duan took the book, saying, "You haven't checked this shelf yet, have you?" Then, he started to investigate the bookshelf straightaway.

"And you haven't checked this one, right?" In the same way, Charles began investigating a different shelf.

Whereas they'd been at odds with each other before, now they were friends.

Seeing her two friends get down to business, Agnis was impressed.

Loren called out from behind her, "Princess Agnis, I was not able to find much food, but please feel free to enjoy what I could gather." He held out a basket packed full of delicious-looking sacks.

"Yum yum! Can't dream when you're hungry!" She happily extended her hand.

Hearing this, Charles commented, "Agnis, isn't it 'Can't *fight* when you're hungry'?"

Agnis looked back at him blankly. "Oh, really?"

"Yup," answered Duan instead of Charles, and then they looked at each other and laughed.

Agnis widened her eyes farther, and then she shrugged and stuffed her cheeks with snacks. A delicate vanilla flavor spread through her mouth. Check's small hands also held a few snacks, which he started stuffing into his face.

"I have prepared some hot tea with milk, as well." Loren poured tea into three warmed teacups. Apart from Agnis, however, everyone was so wrapped up in searching for the book that they didn't have time for tea.

Duan couldn't stop thinking about the gardener and his granddaughter, who were waiting at home in terror—or about the group of mind-enslaved men he and Charles had passed on the way to the hedge.

We have to save them!

Charles was thinking the same thing.

Agnis, who had been watching the two boys, put down her tea and returned to her search for the book. Loren followed silently behind her.

However, the sheer number of books in the library was staggering. What's more, they were all ancient, and they looked exactly alike. They had to take down every single book, open it, check to see what was written in it, look to see if anything had been hidden on the shelf behind it, and then replace it before moving on to the next. It was a slow, time-consuming process.

At last, after what seemed like hours, they all were so tired and sleepy that they'd sometimes sway from side to side, almost falling to the ground before jolting awake again.

Duan pulled himself together and regarded Agnis, Charles, and Loren. He could see with one glance that they were at their limit, too—especially Charles, who looked to be using all his strength to hold himself upright.

It was then that Charles, holding a book in his hand, sank down to the floor.

"Your Highness!" screamed Duan.

"Your Highness!" screamed Loren.

They rushed toward the prince.

But his face sparkling with surprise and joy, Charles addressed Duan, "I think I found it! Look—this is the one, isn't it?"

The book in his grip was indeed an exact replica of the book that was actually a box.

CHAPTER 57:

THE BEGINNINGS OF A PLAN

hat's written inside?" asked Agnis as she dashed over.

"Look, somebody's left a bookmark," the prince said excitedly, indicating a small slip of paper stuck into the pages about two-thirds of the way through.

"Let's open it," said Duan.

Charles replied with a nod, opening the book to the marked place.

There was a short paragraph in the middle of the page: *Strike him with this book and, in time, the Dog will eat his soul. For a short while, it will be possible to imprison him in the Dog. Then, as quickly as possible, return the Dog to its rightful place.*

"Hm. That means we have to locate Senzrabur as fast as possible, right?" Charles asked Duan.

Duan wrinkled his brow and tilted his head. "Yes, or maybe we can lure him somewhere. . . ."

"Lure him?" asked Agnis. "How?"

Duan turned to look at her. "Agnis, do you remember what the sorcerer in the red robe said when we met him?"

"What?" said Agnis. She fell into silence.

Charles replied in her place. "He said, 'Where is the king?' Right?"

Duan nodded. "Yes. They are looking for the king. It's probably something to do with awakening the devil. If Senzrabur finds out where the king is, he definitely will come!"

After a short period of silence, they all gulped as they realized where Duan's words were leading them.

CHAPTER 58:

CHARLES TAKES CHARGE

 won't do it, and you can't make me!" King Evesrin cried in a voice nearing a shriek. "It's too dangerous. There's no reason to use me as bait!" He forcefully shook his head from side to side and ducked behind his luxurious chair. "Find a substitute!"

"Father, we cannot use a substitute," Prince Charles said calmly. "Senzrabur knows you quite well, and he is a man of Darkness, so he will not be fooled so easily. It will not be as dangerous as you think: All you need to do is to stay here and let the Black Knights protect you. That way, Senzrabur cannot get close to you, but we can get close to him."

However, Charles' persuasive words fell on deaf ears.

The king closed his eyes and stubbornly shook his head.

To make matters worse, the queen began to defend her husband.

"Charles, when have you earned the right to give orders to your father? I will not permit it!" she said angrily.

The king was so grateful that he nearly burst into tears. He'd been sure that the queen would want him to do the right thing, the brave thing, the kingly thing. Now, he thought perhaps she was finally beginning to understand the severity of the situation. And perhaps she also was troubled by the prospect of putting her beloved husband in danger.

Schneider, who had been guarding the king, agreed with the queen.

"Your Highness, let me be the one to face Senzrabur. I also have been subject to his disrespect, and I would like to fight him."

Schneider, confident of his skills, started to stretch in preparation.

Um . . . we don't have time for this right now.

The king's response wasn't surprising; but just as Duan had worried, the prince dropped his shoulders and hung his head when met with resistance from his royal parents. It was a shame, because getting his point of view across in front of his father and mother was a big step forward for the prince.

Suddenly, Agnis' voice sounded. "Charles, you can do it!"

Charles glanced over his shoulder. He saw Agnis, Duan, Loren, and also Check. They all were holding hands and cheering him on.

Squaring his shoulders, Charles stepped in front of the king once more. It was true that Charles had inherited his mother's beautiful features; but at that moment, those features held such fierce determination that his mother gulped nervously.

"If that is how you feel, Father, then you might as well abdicate the throne and hand the kingship over to me right now. I will face Senzrabur myself. Of course, after all this is over, I would hand the throne back to you."

"What?!" King Evesrin leaped out from the shadows behind the throne. "Charles, d-do you mean to go in my place and be the bait? Is that what you're saying?"

Charles nodded sincerely. "Yes."

Everyone in the secret room stirred at once.

"He cannot do it!"

"It is far too dangerous—and anyway, it will not work!"

These were the sorts of comments flying around the room.

Meanwhile, the queen was in hysterics. "No! No!" she screamed. "No, no, no! I will never permit such a dangerous thing!"

"QUIET!"

The shout came from Charles. As soon as he spoke, the room went dead silent.

The prince looked at everyone, and then he looked back at Duan, who was waiting behind him. "Until now, I have been searching with this man for a way to bring this nightmare to an end. You all have been waiting in this room, so I am sure you do not understand how bad things have gotten outside. It is clear that our enemies are not human. Luckily, their leader, Senzrabur, has not had his powers fully restored . . . yet."

"Is he not . . . a devil?" asked the king.

The prince shook his head. "No, we were wrong about that. If his powers return, however, he will be able to summon a devil."

Hearing his words, everyone in the room breathed a sigh of relief . . . and also of despair.

"As I said, I will take him!" yelled Schneider, drawing his sword.

Charles slowly shook his head. "No, I doubt the sword will harm him. I cannot give you any details, as who knows who might be listening, but we have found a way to imprison him. However, in order to do so, we need to lure him out into the open."

Charles turned to the king again. "Please, Father. If we do not succeed, this country—no, the entire *world* is doomed!"

King Evesrin was staring at his feet. He soon raised his head.

"All right," he said simply, approaching Charles.

"You will give me the kingship temporarily? We will have to do away with all the ceremony. Hm. How exactly does one pass the crown?"

Charles asked the aides around him, but nobody seemed to know. As they all looked at one another in bafflement, the King spoke again.

"It's all right. I will go."

This time, the prince was surprised. "What? What do you mean?"

"Well, I don't want to be bait to lure out a monster. You are my son, though, and no fahter in the world would let his son do such a dangerous thing in his stead."

The king's voice as he said this wasn't exactly ringing with bravery. In fact, it was quite pathetic. But he managed a smile as he gently placed a hand on Charles' shoulder.

"All right, son. What do I need to do?"

CHAPTER 59:

SPRINGING THE TRAP

hey decided it was best to lure Senzrabur into the grand hall, where Olba and Land had fought the Red Knights.

It was spacious and also had many pillars that would provide blind spots. But the Black Knight who was sent there as a scout came back shaking his head.

"We can't use it! It's still a battlefield!"

"What? Still?" Duan said unintentionally.

Charles and Agnis looked at each other.

"No, never mind," said Duan. "In fact, it may be better that way. We'll stand on the upper corridor so that we can avoid attacks from arrows. If we cordon off the area, we'll also be able to avoid any off-the-cuff attacks."

Charles nodded and informed everyone else.

Then, they opened the secret door, and King Evesrin and the others exited into the upper corridor, where they could look down on the grand hall.

As they knight had reported, the grand hall was filled with Red and Black Knights in the midst of battle.

"Hey, it's Olba!" screamed Agnis.

Sure enough, in the direction she pointed, they could see Olba propping up Land while he kicked off the Red Knights swarming around him.

Yes. Although Olba and the others had chased the Red Knights inside the riding grounds, they had been forced back into the hall again. And now, there were more Red Knights than before.

Duan began to shout, "It's the king! The king!"

Hearing this, the other Black Knights who were guarding the king also started to yell.

"Look, here's the king!"

"W-wow, how strange—why is the king here?"

"I'm glad you're safe, Your Majesty!"

"Your Majesty, it's dangerous here!"

Duan thought all the chatter sounded fake, but he didn't see any other options.

They're in the middle of battle, and they're all probably tired, so we'll have to make quite a scene for them to notice!

They proceeded to do just that. And while they made a racket on the balcony, shouting and screaming, Olba and the others finally noticed. The Red Knights also stopped what they were doing and looked up. When they saw the king on the landing overlooking the grand hall, silence overcame the room.

"Hm . . ." The king didn't know what to say. Beads of sweat appeared on his forehead as anxiety overwhelmed him.

At that moment, Charles came to stand by him and took his hand. The king was surprised, but he firmly held his son's hand. Although they were king and prince, they also were father and son. And although it was a simple act, they both were overcome with emotion.

The queen couldn't hold back her emotions, either, as she looked at the two of them.

Duan and the others waited nearby. Duan held the book, and Loren held the statue of the dog.

When will he come? Is he really going to come? Maybe his powers are almost full, and he can see through this plan.

Duan was worried but decided to trust their plan and wait.

You shouldn't get scared! You have to protect Prince Charles!

These thoughts filled him with determination. Warmth mounted in his chest, and he felt as though his strength was increasing. The deep emotions and joy he felt when he went searching through the rain for the statue of the dog with the prince came back to him.

After a while, there was a dazzling flash of lightning. Thunder rumbled through the quiet room. Not a moment after, all the windows shattered. Shards of sparkling glass burst and fell to the ground. Rain poured in.

"Aagh!"

"Argh!"

The knights in the hall were beginning to grow restless when, the very next second, the central double doors of the grand hall flew open.

No one was there.

Silence gripped the room.

High above, old men in red robes floated in the air.

It's the sorcerers! And there's one, two, three of them!

The three sorcerers laughed eerily.

King Evesrin groaned and seemed about to crumple down on the spot. If Charles hadn't propped him up, he certainly would have fallen.

Schneider also stood beside the king. With a trembling voice, he addressed the sorcerers. "Where is your master? Where is the coward who used my name?"

The three sorcerers looked at one another and laughed in a strange way, as though air were leaking from their mouths. And then, still laughing, they looked down below at the open door.

Everyone else looked, too. At first, all they could see was the rain and the black space. Then, quite suddenly, a man appeared. For some reason, rain did not fall on him. It bounced off, as if he were wearing some kind of transparent shield. He was dressed in fine nobleman's clothing, and his cape flowed impressively behind him as he strode boldly into the hall.

He looked identical to Schneider.

CHAPTER 60:

SEΠZRABUR MAKES THE SCEΠE

lack, rich hair flowed down to his shoulders, and there was a slight smile on his lips, which were adorned with a well-groomed mustache. He was tall, and his majestic air made him look nobler than any nobleman. He was confident and charming, to boot.

The man who looked like Schneider walked through the spaces between the knights and made his way toward the grand staircase that led to the king.

"Stay away from the king!"

Although all the Black Knights were in a state of paralysis, Sven Giesen managed to break free from the spell and ran toward the man. With a calm composure, the intruder glanced in Sven's direction.

"Argh!"

Sven went flying backward. None of the other Black Knights so much as darted their eyes in his direction due to the strength of the spell they were under.

Olba also had managed to break free, but he had decided to wait a while rather than act impulsively. He could see Duan and Agnis standing near the king. *No doubt they have something planned. I'll wait here until they spring their trap.*

The man walking toward the grand staircase was, of course, Senzrabur, whose powers had returned fully. He slowly climbed the stairs. His overwhelming presence was not that of an average man.

The man who stood at the top of the stairs to face him was the real Schneider.

The two identical men glared at each other.

When Schneider raised his sword and charged at Senzrabur, a MagicArrow hit him on his wrist. It had been released by Ojey, the eldest of the three sorcerers, who continued to make more arrows, flinging them at Schneider.

"Aah! Aargh! AAIEE!"

Schneider couldn't bear it. He dropped his sword to shield his head from the arrows as if from a swarm of angry bees. Senzrabur saw this out of the corner of his eye, but his gaze still remained cool and directed toward the top of the stairs, which he continued to climb. He slowly approached King Evesrin. For some reason, only the Black Knights had been hit with the Paralyze Spell. The king, the prince, the queen, Agnis, Duan, and the others were not affected.

He probably figured we weren't worth casting a spell over, thought Duan. *This works out better for us. I have to hit Senzrabur with this book when he isn't looking.*

Yes, Duan was holding the book that would seal away Senzrabur.

"Eek!"

The pale-faced king kept squeezing Charles' hand. Then, he started to tremble violently.

It was all Charles could do to squeeze back. He desperately tried to stave off his fear by firmly standing his ground and glaring at Senzrabur.

"Ha ha ha. Your Majesty, it seems the young prince has more nerve than you do. What luck, you won't have to worry about a successor. It's your family's final goodbye—why don't you have one last hug? Oh yes, how about you, too, beautiful queen? I will grant you some family time."

Senzrabur confidently regarded the king, the prince, and then the queen.

"F-final goodbye?" The queen's previously rosy cheeks had turned as pale as a sheet of blank white paper. "Darling!"

"Milhene!"

The king and queen embraced deeply.

Senzrabur watched with a sneer. "That's enough. King Evesrin, come this way."

Of course, even a coward like King Evesrin wasn't about to go calmly to a certain death. He furiously shook his head, taking a step back.

"Hmph, so you refuse?" demanded Senzrabur. "Very well, I will make things more painful!"

"N-no, not that," the king managed to gasp out.

"Then, come quickly," Senzrabur invited again. "It'll be over in a second, and it will end without you feeling a thing."

"What's going to end?" asked Charles, and Senzrabur laughed.

"I am going to ask a person of greatness to awaken. And then, darkness will spread over this world, and it will become a very comfortable place."

"Comfortable for monsters and devils!" retorted Charles, but Senzrabur only raised his eyebrows.

"Arrrgh!"

Charles writhed in anguish, clawing at his throat.

"Charles!" cried Agnis, running to his side. She stood in front of him and glared at Senzrabur. "What do you think you're doing? Stop it!"

Senzrabur took no notice of her. He took a step toward the king.

Fortunately, the attack on Charles had ended, but the prince was breathing deeply, his shoulders heaving, and he still held his throat in pain.

"Quickly, now—or do I have to drag you away?" asked Senzrabur.

"H-hey, didn't you hear me? I said 'stop'!"

Agnis clung to Senzrabur's arms and slapped him over and over again.

All of a sudden, he shook her off. "Shush! Go away, child!"

"Oww!" cried Agnis as she fell to the ground on her rear. "Hmph! I am so mad!" Her face reddened as she said this, and she used her staff to get herself up. Then, she closed her eyes and gripped her staff more tightly and started to chant a spell. "Spirits of Fire, I need your help!"

Shoot!

When Duan raised his head in shock, it was already too late. He had been waiting, thinking of the best way to throw the book at Senzrabur without failing. Now, there was no time to stop her.

Agnis gripped her staff with both hands and unleashed her Fire Magic.

It felt like time had stopped. Agnis certainly had chanted her spell correctly and had concentrated her magic power using all her might, thrusting her staff toward Senzrabur in the correct position . . . but no fire emerged. Not a spark.

Senzrabur looked like he didn't know what was happening, either. He had a dumbfounded expression on his face before he blinked and returned to his senses.

"Pah! I don't have time to play magic games with you, child!"

He passed by Agnis, who was now paralyzed, and grabbed hold of the king's wrist. "Come, we're going."

"Eeek!"

King Evesrin desperately tried to break free of Senzrabur's iron grip.

Senzrabur lost his temper and raised a hand to slap the king. Without thinking, the king immediately cowered back.

Now!

Duan silently crept behind them, raised the book high, and brought it down toward Senzrabur's back!

But he was a moment too late.

Senzrabur turned around and avoided Duan's attack.

"Huh, that was close! So, you've found the book, I see."

Although he sounded calm, he clearly was agitated. It was probably a book of bad memories for him. It seemed to Duan that Senzrabur had used a lot of his magic power by now; looking closely, he saw that his adversary appeared tired and weary.

But their plan had failed—there was no going back.

What shall we do?

Charles stared at Duan.

Duan was frantic, doing the best that he could to think about the next step.

How's Agnis . . . ?

The Princess of Fiana was in shock owing to the failure of her magic spell. Her fire abilities had never let her down so badly. She was sitting on the ground and examining her staff as if she'd never seen it before.

CHAPTER 61:

GOING BY THE BOOK

rinning, Senzrabur approached Duan. "Give me the book," he said.

Despite the demon's grin, Duan could sense that he was not quite as confident as he'd been a moment ago. In fact, he definitely was afraid.

Because of this book? Okay, then. I can use that to my advantage.

"Um, Mr. Senzrabur," said Duan.

Senzrabur looked at him with surprise because Duan's tone was so relaxed. "W-what?" he asked suspiciously.

"I'm wearing the clothes of a nobleman; but actually, I'm only an adventurer—and a beginner at that. I'm still only at Level 3!"

Senzrabur couldn't understand what Duan was saying or what he was trying to say, so he tilted his head to one side.

Duan continued. "Do you really think they'd leave such an important book in my possession?"

Senzrabur's expression grew more confused. *I have a bad feeling. It's like the bad feeling I had last time when those priests sealed me.* Senzrabur was drenched in sweat. "I don't know," he said. "I'll find out as soon as I have that book. Give it to me—or I'll crush you like a bug!"

He made to cast a Paralyze Spell on Duan; but before he could complete the spell, Duan dashed forward and threw the book toward Olba.

Olba caught the book with ease. "Got it!"

"You think that will help?" Senzrabur gestured to the countless Red Knights in the grand hall. "Get him! Get that book!"

Some time had passed since the Paralyze Spell was cast, and all the Black Knights finally had broken free of it. They now recommenced their brutal battle with the Red Knights.

Olba managed to deflect the Red Knights' attacks, even while holding the book with one hand and still protecting Land, who was lying down close by.

A red-faced Senzrabur called out to the three sorcerers: "Dammit! Hey, Ojey, Kojey, and Tajey—what are you doing there? Help them!"

The eldest, Ojey, and youngest, Tajey, started to compose themselves to use their magic, but the middle brother, Kojey, stopped them.

"No, Mr. Senzrabur," he said. "I'm sorry, but you're overworking us. Our contract was for helping the disturbance in the castle. This is more than that. Besides, it's almost daylight, and you know we work only at night. Still, if you scratch our backs, we'll scratch yours. If you offer us a bonus . . ." As he spoke, still floating in mid-air, the sorcerer whipped out an abacus and began to figure furiously upon it, mumbling to himself all the while.

Kojey had been hoping to sell the secret location of the king to Senzrabur for a high price, but he'd lost the opportunity when the king had emerged on his own. Now, Kojey wanted seize this latest opportunity to wring a little extra profit out of his employer.

Senzrabur's anger had reached its peak. "Never mind! I don't need you! Go back to the dark hole you came from!"

Kojey just shrugged and made his abacus disappear. "Okay, but things are just getting interesting. It would be a shame to leave now. We'd like to observe things from up here for a little while longer, if you don't mind."

Of course, Senzrabur didn't even feel like responding. He had to get hold of that annoying book as fast as possible! He turned his back on the king and the others as he started to go back down the stairs.

It was at that moment . . .

Clonk!

A pleasant sound reverberated through the grand hall.

An afterimage of Senzrabur clutching his head in disbelief rose up, distorted, and disappeared.

Behind him stood Duan—holding the book he had thrown to Olba.

Duan yelled in a loud voice, "This is the real book!"

CHAPTER 62:

THE PROPHECY REVEALED

Yes, the book Duan had thrown down to Olba was the fake book the prince had discovered first.

Duan had been holding both books, the real one and the fake one, just in case.

When Duan had said confidently, "Do you really think they'd leave such an important book in my possession?" he'd planted the seed of doubt in Senzrabur's mind.

Overcome with fear and doubt, Senzrabur had become a prisoner of suspicion and had lost his cool. And then, he forgot all about Duan and started to descend the stairs—that's when he was hit on the head with the real book.

That book suddenly started to jump around in Duan's hands. He couldn't hold it, and he dropped it on the ground.

A small creature that was at once froglike and buglike leaped out from the pages of the book. Surprised, Duan jumped back.

The thing had sparkly green skin with small yellow dots and protruding eyes that moved around well and seemed to be able to look in two different directions at once. It had six legs, like a grasshopper. It started to leap down the steps.

At the same time, Loren yelped. This was because the statue of the dog had wriggled to life and jumped out of his arms.

The Dog, still with its strange face, made a funny cry that sounded like "Hyon, hyon" and started to chase the strange froglike, grasshopper-like monster.

The monster looked at the Dog, revolved its eyes, and fled with speed. It shot down the stairs almost as if it were tumbling down.

"Ah!"

"Yuck! Gross!"

"Ack!"

The monster ran between the Black Knights in the grand hall, the Dog following right behind, crying "Hyon, hyon" with its strangely divided human face.

Watching them, it was clear to see that the monster was superior in skill; the statue was heavy and lumbering and didn't have very good balance.

"Catch bug, gi-iis!" shouted Check, who was flying around in excitement. "Good Dog!"

Duan wasn't about to leave things to the Dog, though. "Obla!" he cried. "You, Black Knights! Everyone surround that small monster. Don't let it escape, or Senzrabur will get away!"

However, nobody on the ground had seen what happened on the landing, so they couldn't understand what he was screaming about.

Olba's voice resounded through the room. "Hey, just do as the kid says! You can find out why later! It went that way!"

The Black Knights started to chase the monster. Because it was so small and agile, they couldn't catch it very easily.

Duan, Charles, and everyone else from the landing at the top of the stairs came hurrying down to the hall to help.

"C'mon! Hold still, you slimy thing!"

Olba was leading the chase. With a shout, he threw himself onto the monster. He was sure he had it in his hands. He even felt it squirming. Then, the monster appeared from under his hand and hopped away.

"Shoot!"

Olba slammed down his fists on the floor in anger, but he hadn't given up. He jumped at it again.

Hop! Jump! Hop! Jump!

How many times had he missed? Olba tried to steer the monster toward a circle the Black Knights had made. As the monster was looking around, moving its eyeballs in all directions, thinking up an escape plan, the human-faced Dog leaped at it with an astounding speed.

Everyone in the room looked on in shock as the Dog opened its mouth and devoured the monster. The monster struggled violently and gave out a screeching cry.

Amid that cry, they clearly could make out words: "Dammit! Remember me—I'll be back one day, and then you'll be sorr—"

Before Senzrabur could finish, the two-faced Dog swallowed the monster with a gulp.

At that instant, the expression of the Dog changed, hardening. The Dog had transformed back into a statue.

CHAPTER 63:

WASHED CLEAN

At the same time, all the Red Knights vanished into thin air. Watching from above, the three sorcerers, Ojey, Kojey, and Tajey, appeared extremely uncomfortable.

"Hm. Shall we be going?"

"Yes, it seems like our contract is no longer in force."

"I told you we should have been paid in advance!"

So saying, they disappeared, as well.

Cries of great joy spread throughout the grand hall. The Black Knights patted one another on the shoulders in happiness, and the king and queen embraced each other, tears streaming down their faces.

"The monster is gone!"

"It's all over!"

"Three cheers for Prince Charles!"

Duan and Charles held back from the general merriment, however. Their work was not yet done.

"Duan, let's take this statue to the inner garden," said Prince Charles.

"Right!"

The two ran out, holding the statue between them. Everyone else followed in wonder.

It was still dark when they arrived in the inner garden, but the rain had slackened to a light shower. They parted the Bathokiss flowers and looked for the place the statue used to stand. There it was: an empty space inlaid with red stone. They had to pull out some blooming flowers to fit the statue back into place, but that seemed a small price to pay in return for the peace of the world.

In time, it probably would be best to make a proper shrine so that the Dog is never moved again, Duan thought as he looked at Charles, who was holding the dog statue in his hands.

"Duan," Charles said invitingly.

"Go ahead," said Duan with a smile. "You do the honors, Prince Charles. You've earned it!"

Blushing, Charles lowered the strange dog statue with Senzrabur sealed inside and gently placed it on the red stones.

The rain had stopped. Up above, the clouds were getting whiter and lighter as the dawn broke over the horizon. Charles stood and gazed up at the brightening sky. Relief spread through his soul. He turned back to Duan. Laughter swelled up from deep inside. Duan felt it, too. Trying to contain their laughter, the two friends firmly shook hands.

Suddenly, Charles' face turned sour, and he dropped Duan's hand.

Now what? wondered Duan. *Have I offended him somehow?*

Charles spread open his hands and showed him. The tender white palms were covered in cuts, probably a result of climbing the hedge in the pouring rain.

Duan gave the prince a worried look, but Charles nudged him to look to one side.

Agnis was standing there. She gave them a thumbs-up and winked.

At that moment, ex-King Liesbeck and Edward Zamut came running up.

"Oh! Here you are. The Red Knights disappeared! What is happening?"

Charles looked at the ex-king and smiled. "It would take too long to explain right now. And you must be tired. You all must be. I am almost at my limit. Let us rest first, and then I will tell you everything."

Liesbeck raised his eyebrows and looked at Edward Zamut; then, he grinned as he put his hand on Charles' shoulder. "Hmph. So, that means we can rest peacefully? I see. I *am* very tired—staying up all night is a bit much at my age."

Edward smiled silently.

"So, how many injured?" asked Liesbeck.

One of the Black Knights answered, "Ten, including company commander Sven Giesen. None of the injuries are life-threatening, though. Earlier, Lord Shimul and some others were found in a state of total exhaustion, but they seem to be recovering now."

"I see. And I see that many thanks are owed to Princess Agnis and her friends."

Duan and Olba looked at each other. Land stood weakly, holding onto Olba's side, his eyes closed. Agnis still was shocked by the failure of her magic, and she had a terrible feeling.

In fact, everyone had it. Things had gone well, and it seemed that everyone was fine. And yet . . .

Aren't I forgetting something? Something important . . .

Agnis lifted her face. "Where is he?"

Duan and Charles looked at each other and at Check. Land opened his eyes and looked toward Olba.

"Oh, yes! Clay Judah! What's happened to him?" whispered Duan in a small voice.

Clay Judah and K'nock had run off together during the fight with the sorcerer. They hadn't appeared since. Duan remembered Magic Arrows raining down on Clay Judah and blood dripping from his forehead. . . .

"We have to look for him immediately!" Duan shouted.

A Black Knight came running over at that moment. "There's one dead over here!"

The tension immediately rose.

You're joking!? Duan felt his heart beating loud. *I-I wanted to talk to him. There was so much I wanted to ask him!*

"No!" cried Agnis, burying her face in her hands.

Land, still supported by Olba, glared at the Black Knight who had given the dreadful report.

Edward Zamut asked the Black Knight, "Dead? Are you certain?"

Before the man could answer, another voice rang out in the garden, where the birds had just started to chirp. "No, he's not dead yet."

Wrapped in sunlight, an armored soldier came forth, carrying a Black Knight. He walked slowly, a snow leopard at his side. That armored soldier was Clay Judah.

Land squeezed Olba's shoulder. "Huh. You can't kill a man like that so easily. He has the gods looking out for him!"

Shouting joyfully, Duan, Agnis, and Charles ran over to Clay Judah.

Check flew over to K'nock. "Good cat, cha!"

Watching this sight, Olba whispered quietly, almost as if to himself, "Well, that was one long night."

The long night finally was over, though. The rain had stopped. Bright morning sunlight was streaming through the gaps of the clouds and shining down on the castle—a castle featured in many songs and stories, the pride of its nation: the Silver-Gray Castle.

In that dawn light, sanctified by the struggles of the night before, the tower and its ramparts shone sparkling, washed clean.